D0968627

HIDING IN PLAIN SIGHT

A Selection of Recent Titles by Mary Ellis

The Marked for Retribution mysteries

HIDING IN PLAIN SIGHT *

Secrets of the South

MIDNIGHT ON THE MISSISSIPPI
WHAT HAPPENED ON BEALE STREET
MAGNOLIA MOONLIGHT
SUNSET IN OLD SAVANNAH

** available from Severn House*

HIDING IN PLAIN SIGHT

Mary Ellis

This first world edition published 2018
in Great Britain and the USA by
SEVERN HOUSE PUBLISHERS LTD of
Eardley House, 4 Uxbridge Street, London W8 7SY
Trade paperback edition first published
in Great Britain and the USA 2018 by
SEVERN HOUSE PUBLISHERS LTD

British Library Cataloguing in Publication Data
A CIP catalogue record for this title is available from the British Library.

ISBN-13: 978-0-7278-8789-4 (cased)
ISBN-13: 978-1-84751-912-2 (trade paper)
ISBN-13: 978-1-78010-968-8 (e-book)

All Severn House titles are printed on acid-free paper.

Severn House Publishers support the Forest Stewardship Council™ [FSC™],
the leading international forest certification organisation.
All our titles that are printed on FSC certified paper carry the FSC logo.

Typeset by Palimpsest Book Production Ltd.,
Falkirk, Stirlingshire, Scotland.
Printed and bound in Great Britain by
TJ International, Padstow, Cornwall.

This book is dedicated to my mom, Elizabeth Eles, who was one great cook! How I wish I'd paid better attention when you tried to teach me your secrets.

'At the table, no one grows old.'

—Italian proverb

ONE

Savannah, Georgia

It wouldn't have taken much to turn a lousy day into something left of atrocious. First, Kate Weller had argued with her landlord who was suddenly demanding a year-long lease instead of their current month-to-month agreement. Apparently, paying in full and on time can work against a person. The landlord wanted her to stick around forever. Next, the air-conditioning in her old Mustang quit working. Since a person couldn't run surveillance with the top down in a convertible, she was forced to endure an uncomfortable afternoon. Finally, she had to watch a landscaper toil for hours in the hot sun without showing the least bit of interest in his female co-worker. Kate yearned to tell his suspicious wife she was imagining things. But since her newfound career as a PI demanded finesse as well as endurance, she would resist insulting the client and be thankful she had a job, considering the gaps in her résumé.

Kate liked her job and the people she worked with. Beth Kirby, a fellow employee, was given the thankless job of training her during her probationary period. She liked her boss, Nate Price too, despite only meeting the man once. And as the agency's traveling PI, she loved knowing she would soon move on to a new case in a different town. *Where no one knows my name*, she thought, putting a new twist on an eighties sit-com jingle.

Considering how many times she got stuck in traffic, she should have found the answer to world peace, let alone mapped out her future. Because it was definitely time to move on. An occasional hang-up in the middle of the night might not cause concern. But when the same car parked outside her apartment four nights in a row, Kate knew her past had caught up with her.

It wasn't easy to hide in the twenty-first century.

Maybe if I learned how to cook, quilt, and sew my own clothes, then I could hide in an Amish community. Or maybe not.

After parking the Mustang behind the building, Kate climbed the steps to the second floor, turned the key in the lock, and pushed open the door. Silently, she stood listening . . . for what? The cocking of a trigger? The slide of a semi-automatic chambering a bullet? Or maybe the deep breathing of a madman waiting for her to step across the threshold. Kate had no idea exactly who was after her or how deadly were their intentions. But if the past was a good indicator of the future, she didn't want to stick around to find out.

I should've taken Beth Kirby's advice and bought a gun. But tracking down deadbeat dads and making sure those claiming total disability weren't waterskiing on the weekend didn't require firepower. Certainly her current case – checking that a landscaper wasn't stepping out on his wife – required only patience and endurance. Besides, how would her new pastor react to a shoulder holster beneath her Sunday dress and cardigan?

Spotting her two battered suitcases gathering dust in the corner, Kate contemplated emptying her drawers into one and her closet into the other. Except for her toiletries, one picture album, and a folder of important papers – which didn't seem very important any more – she had nothing else to pack. But how could she turn tail and run? Nate had offered her the chance she desperately needed. He'd given her a career she loved and friends that could be trusted. Although her current case could be wrapped up with thirty minutes of paperwork, Kate was still on probation. Hopefully, her new assignment would be far away from these ancient, moss-covered oaks on town squares filled with fountains, locals reading newspapers, and tourists poring over maps. Savannah would be a nice place for Beth and her partner-turned-fiancé to settle down in. But Kate hoped for an assignment someplace obscure. If a place like that still existed.

When the phone rang on her way to the kitchen, she practically jumped out of her skin. Kate picked up on the second ring. 'Hey, Beth, I was just thinkin' about you.'

'Were you wondering why a perfectly sane woman marries a man she's known less than a year?'

'Nah,' Kate teased. 'No way are you sane, not even imperfectly.'

Beth snorted. 'That is the truth, girl. But what I want to know is what are you doing for supper?'

Kate opened the freezer and peered inside. 'Looks like Lean Cuisine chicken with cashews. You know, part of their Asian collection. I'll pair it with a glass of sweet tea and settle down for reruns of *Masterpiece Theater*.'

'As delightful as that sounds, why not drive to Tybee Island instead? My friend Evelyn is throwing an impromptu deck party for Michael and me. Just for a few friends and neighbors and *you*. She wants to meet the agency's newest hire.'

Beth's friend Evelyn Doyle was a well-heeled former client who'd already thrown Beth an engagement luncheon, an early bridal shower, a formal dinner party to honor the couple, and had given Beth a forty-thousand dollar car that had belonged to her late husband.

'Thanks, but I think I'll pass. I'm sweaty and tired. Please give my regrets to Michael and Mrs Doyle.'

'Absolutely not! Hose yourself off, put on a party dress, and climb into that fast Mustang. Evelyn has sold her Tybee beach house to a family from Beaufort. Movers arrive tomorrow to start packing her up. Don't miss your last chance to munch on catered food under the stars, surrounded by priceless artwork, as waves lap the shore in perfect rhythm to the reggae combo she hired for the night.'

'Oh, good grief. Is there no limit to that woman's entertaining budget?' Kate scrubbed her face with one hand. 'If you're not careful, you'll turn into a younger version of Mrs Doyle.'

Beth issued another burst of laughter. 'That would be fine with me. Too bad Michael's and my pockets aren't deep enough. Please say you'll come. I want to show off my protégé. I'm so proud of how quickly you learned the PI trade.'

Praise like that wasn't easy to ignore. 'OK, as long as you promise not to treat me like a trained poodle, I'll come. But

I have no party dress and my *fast* Mustang only fires on three cylinders. Can I wear long shorts and a silk shirt?'

'Absolutely. Put on a studded dog collar and arrive any time after seven.' Beth recited an address she knew by heart and hung up.

Staring out at an alley lined with trash and recycle receptacles, Kate smiled. *I'm going to a party. Just like a normal person in America.* Tonight, she would eat steamed jumbo shrimp caught off the coast of Georgia and chargrilled oysters, along with salads and appetizers without a thought to the cost of the food. No burgers, hot dogs, and macaroni salad for this crowd. Maybe someday her life would be normal like Beth's and Evelyn's. Then she would throw a party for her friends and neighbors and not check over her shoulder one time. Even if it was only burgers and hot dogs.

Kate glanced at her watch and jumped in the shower. Within ninety minutes she had applied makeup to the best of her ability, ironed her blouse, and added curl to her straight hair. Then she assessed her appearance in the mirror: Medium height, medium weight, medium brown hair and eyes – average, in every way. Ordinary, just like hot dogs and macaroni salad. But maybe that would make it easier to disappear.

Kate climbed into her car, programmed her GPS with the address, and headed for the Island Expressway. At least the road could live up to its name since the earlier traffic snarls had combed themselves out. Rolling down the windows, she tuned the radio to a country station. Nothing like country music to get a person in the mood for a party. Either a guest could drown their sorrows at the bar, or in her case, at the dessert table.

With Savannah's city limits behind her and a salty sea breeze wafting through the open window, Kate relaxed for the first time that day. She felt confident she hadn't been followed from her gentrified, Forsythe Park neighborhood. There were only so many times you can check the rearview mirror. Perhaps the gorgeous pink and gold sunset had lulled her into a false sense of security, but Kate's anticipatory good mood didn't last long.

Just as she pulled into a turnout to send a message to her boss, Kate received a text from tonight's guest of honor:

Where are you? You better get here before Michael finishes off the mini chicken kabobs. Just wait until you see the reggae drummer. If ever a man looked like your type . . . Beth ended her message with a series of heart-shaped emojis.

Kate rolled her eyes and slipped the phone into her back pocket. Beth thought every single man was *her type* even though Kate couldn't describe her type if her life depended on it. In order to develop romantic discernment, a person needed to date more than a handful of times in five years.

Perhaps it was her concentration on her lack of romance that caused Kate to pull on to the pavement without thoroughly checking traffic. Luckily, she caused no crashes or near-misses, but a car was approaching at high speed. Stomping on the accelerator, Kate switched on her hazard lights in case the speeder hadn't seen her in the eastbound lane. A long string of oncoming headlights ruled out the other side as an escape route. Yet still the vehicle in her rearview mirror wasn't slowing down one iota.

When the vehicle was only a few yards from her bumper, Kate whispered a short prayer, jerked the wheel to the right, and pulled on to the narrow shoulder. Braking hard, she waited for the crazy driver to go around her. Maybe the idiot would shout a warning or offer a rude hand gesture as he sped by. But instead the driver also rammed on the brakes, squealing his tires to slow down. With the black van matching her speed, Kate couldn't pull back on to the highway. *Was this some sort of lesson for her inattention?*

Kate bumped along on the narrow ribbon of land with one wheel on the pavement, the other on gravel berm. Only inches separated her right tires from the steep drop-off to the marsh below. With her phone in her pocket, she couldn't very well call for help. Kate laid on the horn and flashed her angriest expression toward the van's tinted glass windows. But neither enticed the other driver to speed up or slow down. Gripping the steering wheel with both hands, Kate had no time to argue with someone with a death wish. With the van exactly next to her, it took everything she had to keep her car from careening down the embankment into the bay. And tonight, she was in no mood for a swim.

Ahead, she saw a bridge overpass that would narrow the berm to almost nothing. Closer still was an access road to a fishing pier beneath the bridge, and according to a weather-beaten sign, a nameless road to a marina which may or may not still be in business. Growing up in Florida close to the Gulf, Kate knew both roads would be dead-ends. With daylight fading, neither would provide a getaway route from a road-raged driver out for blood.

Kate sucked in a breath and turned the wheel to the left to gain a firmer hold on the pavement. She came within a hair of the van's right fender. But instead of allowing her back on to the highway, the van driver yanked the wheel to the right and banged the Mustang's door. She rammed on the brakes as her right tire dropped over the embankment in a spray of gravel and dirt. Kate fought to maintain control, and by sheer grace, pulled the wheel back to the berm. The van sped past her, but as it did, Kate saw the passenger window lower. Simultaneously, she heard a blast of gunfire and felt an explosion of shattering glass hit the back of her head.

Any notions that this was simply road rage vanished as warm blood trickled down her neck and her left ear throbbed from the percussion. Her mouth went dry; her stomach tightened, and her vision clouded with tears, but the nightmare was far from over. Fifty feet ahead, the crazy driver rammed on his brakes and swung his vehicle across the right-hand lane. Kate had three choices: a head-on collision with oncoming traffic; the access road to the fishing pier or the dead-end to the marina. *Some choice*. But with a gun barrel protruding from the van's window, Kate accelerated and turned down the marina road in a squeal of tires.

It's funny what a person thinks about in a life-or-death situation. She imagined a speedboat waiting at the end of the dock to whisk her to safety. Perhaps she was remembering an old James Bond movie in which no harm ever comes to the good guys. But as Kate reached the end of the road she saw a steel boathouse, a small office building, and rows upon rows of slips filled with pleasure crafts. Directly in her path lay a concrete ramp where trailers could back up to load and unload boats.

But no speedboat to deliver her to Mrs Doyle's party on the beach.

Kate stopped at the ramp and threw her car into park. Luckily, the black van was nowhere in sight. Jumping out, she ran to the office, but it was locked with the shades drawn. Kate pounded on the door, but her efforts yielded only a flurry of seagulls from the roof. In fact there was no sign of human life in any direction she looked. With few options, Kate sprinted toward the expanse of tall grass behind the boathouse. Their waving, tasseled heads reminded her of pampas grass that grew behind her childhood home in Pensacola.

Too late she realized this wasn't a field of brush on *terra firma*, but acres and acres of sawgrass, whose appearance can deceive anyone who ventures forth without first testing the ground. Immediately, brackish water filled her brand new pair of shoes – the espadrilles with open toes and wedge heel she'd splurged on. When Kate tried lifting her right foot, she heard a horrible sucking sound as her foot pulled free from the shoe. Feeling both foolish and uncomfortable, she bent down to find her shoe just as a pair of headlights turned into the marina. Considering the number of cars she'd seen since leaving the highway, Kate had a good idea who it might be.

With little alternative, she crouched down in eight inches of dark water that smelled like rotting vegetation and dead fish. But at least she wouldn't drown in eight inches of tidal surge. With water soaking her shorts and the hem of her shirt, Kate peeked between the fronds of sawgrass. The black paneled van slowed and then stopped behind her Mustang. When the driver's door opened, a yellow circle of light shone on the pavement. But it closed just as quickly, giving her no chance to identify her adversary.

'Kathryn! Come out so we can chat.' A man's voice called over the marsh. 'I know you can hear me, Kathryn. Or Kate, or Katrina, or whatever you're calling yourself these days. Not very creative. I would have expected better from Liam's little sister.' A malicious laugh punctuated the criticism.

She hunkered down, no longer worried about the fetid smell or her party clothes or her new shoes. If she had to sink up to her nose to keep from meeting the man from the van she would.

Suddenly, a high-powered spotlight illuminated the perimeter of the parking lot and then scanned the marsh on her right. But this cornered animal had no inclination to bolt like a white-tailed deer or a frightened raccoon.

'This is your last chance to come out and talk,' he hollered from behind the white beam. 'I won't be so nice in the future.'

This guy considers shooting at people and forcing cars off the road as being nice? When the beam moved over her area of marsh, Kate didn't twitch a muscle.

Not when the cold water chilled her to the bone.

Not when mosquitos feasted hungrily on the back of her neck.

Not even when something spiny crawled over her bare foot.

'Fine. Have it your way.' The man switched off the spotlight, throwing Kate into darkness except for the weak light of the moon.

As an engine roared to life, Kate lifted her head in time to see the van ram the back of her Mustang. Once, twice, then with the third hit, the van pushed her convertible down the ramp into the waterway. Helplessly, Kate watched her beloved car slide deeper until only the top remained visible. After another moment, even the roof disappeared below the murky surface. Tears filled Kate's eyes as her most valuable possession sank to the bottom.

'Here's a little reminder to make sure your new job doesn't go to your head.' Without warning, her mysterious adversary fired several shots into the marsh. One bullet cut through the tassels a foot above her head, giving Kate more to worry about than a waterlogged car. Then she heard car doors slam and the van sped off without switching on its headlights until well beyond the marina. From her marshy vantage point, she had no better view of a license plate or the van's occupants than on the highway.

TWO

Kate counted to ten and pushed herself stiffly to her feet. A mass of black seaweed dropped from her arm as she waded through the water, fearful of crab-infested holes that could twist an ankle along the bottom. When she reached the parking lot, she waited with dripping clothes and chattering teeth. Surely someone had heard the gunfire and would come to investigate, or at least call the sheriff's department. After five minutes, when no one arrived and she heard no sirens, Kate started walking up the marina road.

Suddenly, she remembered her cell phone in her pocket. *Could it have remained dry during her foray into the Georgia wetlands?* Spending the big bucks for a waterproof cover and impact-resistant case proved worthwhile when the screen lit up with colorful apps. Cold, scared, – and for what it's worth, hungry – Kate punched in Beth's number.

Her co-worker answered with a snarl. '*Where are you, Weller?* The chicken kabobs are gone and the reggae drummer is flirting with a blonde as we speak.'

'Beth, could you come get me or send someone?' Kate tried her best not to sound like a child.

'Why? What's wrong with your car? Don't tell me you ran out of gas between here and Savannah.'

'No, someone forced me off the highway. I had to turn down a dead-end road to a boat ramp. They were shooting at me from a black van.' Kate's chattering teeth made speech almost impossible.

Silence spun out for a few moments. Then Beth asked quietly. '*Who* was shooting at you? Did you call nine-one-one? Are the police there with you now?'

'No, I called you first. I'm here by myself. Whoever was in the van left.' Kate's voice cracked, revealing her emotional state.

'Are you hurt?' Panic etched Beth's words. 'Because if

you're not, jump in your car and get out of there. Those guys could come back.'

'I'm not hurt, but my car is at the bottom of Lazaretto Creek.'

'OK, don't worry about the car. Find somewhere to hide until Michael and I arrive. We'll call the police along the way. Are you at that marina on the left just past the Tybee Bridge?'

'Ye–esss,' she stuttered. 'But what about your party?'

'Never mind the party,' Beth screeched like a parrot. 'Just find a safe place to wait for us. We're on our way.'

After they hung up, Kate glanced around the eerily vacant boatyard. Shadows seemed to leap and grow as she scanned her surroundings. But one thing was for certain, she wouldn't crawl back into the marsh even if the van returned with a grenade launcher. Instead, Kate staggered to the deserted office, unscrewed the sole security light, and plopped down on the steps. At least if she couldn't see anything, no one could see her.

Since the Tybee Island Police Department was closer to the marsh than Mrs Doyle's house, two patrol cars arrived a few minutes later, lights flashing and sirens blaring. One vehicle slammed to a stop with headlights facing east while the other faced west. An ambulance arrived moments later. When several officers jumped out with guns drawn, Kate rose from the steps and approached with her hands raised. She wanted no mistakes made regarding who's the victim and who's the perpetrator.

'I'm Kate Weller, a PI with Price Investigations. My partner, Beth Kirby, is the one who called you.'

The cops lowered their weapons but illuminated her face with their flashlights. 'Are you alone, Miss Weller?' asked a husky voice.

Temporarily blinded, Kate shielded her eyes with one hand. 'To the best of my knowledge. Could you lower that light please? I'm seeing nothing but spots before my eyes.'

With their beams refocused on the ground, the officers closed in and rattled off questions:

'Do you need medical attention?'

'Who was shooting at you, Miss Weller?'

'Did you get a look at the shooter or maybe a plate number? What type of vehicle were they driving?'

The police peppered her with questions faster than Kate could answer. 'I'm not hurt, only cold,' she said. 'I had to hide from them out in the marsh. That's why I didn't get a good look at them or a plate number. The vehicle was a black paneled van. I don't know the make or model.'

The female officer stepped forward. 'You said "they and them." That implies several people were shooting at you. How many, exactly?'

'I have no idea,' Kate snapped. 'Forgive me if I'm not choosing the correct pronoun, but I was just belly-down in the muck while someone emptied their clip over my head,' she screamed with a voice bordering on hysteria. 'After their van ran me off the road,' she added.

'Tompkins,' said the tallest cop. 'Go get that thermos of coffee and a blanket from my trunk. And you two canvas the area,' he said to the others. 'Look for shell casings, tire impressions in soft ground, skid marks, anything we might be able to use.' Then the officer turned his attention back to Kate. 'I'm Lieutenant Myers of Tybee Police. You said you're not hurt, but there's blood in your hair.' He gently turned her chin with one finger.

Kate reached up to pat her blood-matted scalp. 'Superficial cuts from when *he, she, or they* shot out my window. It's nothing.'

'Where is your car now, Miss Weller?'

With the life-saving burst of adrenalin gone, Kate felt overwhelmingly fatigued. As though too tired to speak, she lifted an index finger and pointed at the ramp down to the creek. 'Somewhere out there, underwater, courtesy of an unknown number of perpetrators.'

A hint of a smile softened Myers' face, until a flashy, high-performance Charger squealed to a stop a dozen feet away. Scattered pebbles flew in their direction, hitting the lieutenant's legs. 'What's the matter with you?' he barked at the driver's window. Myers trained his flashlight on the car's occupants.

'Take it easy; those are my friends,' Kate said with tears

streaming down her face. She hadn't cried since the bullets started flying, but seeing her co-workers' expressions put Kate over the edge. Beth Kirby and Michael Preston sprang from the car.

'Good grief, Kate. What happened?' Beth scanned her from head to toe and then wrapped her in a tight embrace.

'Tell us what you want us to do.' Michael crowded in next to his fiancée.

'*I'll* tell you what to do,' said Lieutenant Myers. 'Back up and let me finish interviewing the victim. I'm from Tybee Island Police and y'all can catch up later.'

'With all due respect, Lieutenant, this incident could be connected to a case we're working on.' Beth whipped out her identification and a business card, but stepped back as Officer Tompkins returned to wrap Kate in a blanket and pour her some coffee.

'You'll have time to determine any connection *after* I finish doing my job.' Lieutenant Myers' tone left no room for discussion, but he tucked Beth's card into his pocket and then semi-recounted the sequence of events until her Mustang took the big swim to the bottom. When he finished, Myers jotted down some notes.

Standing side by side with their arms crossed, Beth and Michael exchanged a look. 'How many shots were fired?' asked Beth.

Kate ran her fingers through her tangled hair. 'I don't know – more than five but less than ten.'

Myers looked up from his notebook. 'After the shooting stopped, what happened next? Did they say anything?'

'No,' Kate lied. 'But I heard car doors slam and an engine start up.'

'Did you distinctly hear more than one door slam, as though one after the other?' asked Myers.

Kate squeezed her eyes shut, forcing herself to remember. 'Yes, I distinctly heard two different doors slam.' She exhaled with relief.

'So there was more than one person in the van,' concluded Michael.

'Obviously.' Myers sounded annoyed with her co-workers.

'Otherwise how could someone shoot at Miss Weller from the passenger side while the van was speeding down Route Eighty?'

'We would know that if you'd let Kate tell us the whole story.' Beth sounded as annoyed as Myers.

'You'll get your chance right now.' Myers snapped his notebook shut. 'Take Miss Weller over to the EMTs to have those scalp lacerations looked at. Then take her home so she can warm up and put on dry clothes. I'll notify the harbor-master and owner of the marina about the submerged car. Tomorrow, Miss Weller, you'll have to come to the station to finish giving your statement. At that time we'll arrange to have your car towed from the creek.'

'My Mustang won't be any good any more,' Kate moaned.

'True, but it can't stay where it is. It's a hazard to boats.' Myers softened his voice. 'And your car might contain paint chips from the van so we can identify who tried to kill you.'

With hands on her shoulders, Beth pointed Kate toward the ambulance. 'We'll get her to the station first thing in the morning. And if you'll allow us, Michael and I would like to assist Tybee Police with their investigation. Nobody tries to kill a Price employee and gets away with it.'

'We'll discuss your participation tomorrow, Miss Kirby. Right now, I want Miss Weller to get medical attention.'

After the EMTs poked, prodded, and soaked her entire scalp with antiseptic, they bandaged her up like a mummy. Kate staggered toward Michael's shiny Charger. 'I'm too dirty to ride in your car,' she said.

'Don't be silly.' Michael opened the passenger door. 'Beth can crawl into the pet-sized back seat and you climb in the front.'

Too tired to argue, Kate tried to be as small as possible on the leather seat. Michael followed the ambulance out of the parking lot while the police continued to process the scene. 'I can't thank you enough for coming here so fast.' Kate swallowed hard before continuing. 'But I must make something clear. Price Investigations won't be assisting Tybee Police with their investigation.'

Michael drove slowly up the hill. 'Why is that?'

'Because there will be little to help with. I know who ran me off the road and trashed my car.'

'I thought you couldn't see much from the swamp,' said Beth from the back seat.

'I didn't have to see them to know who was sending me a message.'

Michael braked to a sudden stop. 'And you chose not to share this information with the police?' He stared at her.

'I can't. It would jeopardize someone's life.' Kate looked out the window to avoid his gaze. 'I don't want the cops pursuing this.'

'Is that why you called us and not them? Someone tried to kill you, Kate. The next time they might succeed.' Michael sounded both baffled and disappointed.

'If these people wanted me dead, I would be. That was a warning.'

Michael drove to the stop sign. As he waited for the highway traffic to clear, he glanced at Beth in the rearview mirror. 'I take it by your uncharacteristic silence you know what's going on.'

Beth leaned forward between the seats. 'Not all of it, but enough to know we should trust Kate.'

Michael frowned. 'Does the boss know what's going on? Is this why nothing added up in your résumé but Nate hired you anyway?'

'Yes, but he doesn't know everything, not yet anyway.' Kate dropped her face into her hands.

'Nice to know I'm not someone either of you can confide in.' Michael's disappointment was quickly turning to anger.

Beth started to argue, but Kate interrupted. 'Don't blame Beth. I insisted she not tell anyone, not even you. The less people who know, the safer my brother will be.'

'*Your brother?*' he asked.

'Yes, my brother, but please don't ask me anything more.' Kate swiveled on the seat to face him. 'Believe that I know what's best.'

Seeing a break in traffic, Michael accelerated on to the highway. Ahead the lights of downtown Savannah twinkled in the night sky. 'Fine, I sure can't take both of you on. But if I can help, call me, even if I'm not allowed to ask questions.' Then he stared at the road ahead, while no one spoke for several minutes.

Beth finally broke the silence. 'At least your insurance will replace the car.'

Kate loved how Beth reduced everything to their simplest denominator. She shook her head miserably. 'When I moved to Savannah, I let all coverages lapse except for liability. Since rates are much higher in a city, my agent said I shouldn't bother insuring such an old car.'

'Well, we still have each other.' Beth laid one hand on her shoulder and one on Michael's.

Incapable of a verbal response, Kate merely nodded. She didn't deserve friends like these. Unfortunately, their camaraderie in Savannah was drawing to a close. It was time for her to move on. Or the next bullets might just find their mark.

THREE

Kate's week passed by in a blur. Those friends she thought herself unworthy of rose to sainthood status when they intervened with the boss on her behalf. What business professional in his right mind would permanently hire someone on the run from mysterious assassins, a person who was now without a car? But Nate Price told her to come to the home office in Natchez, Mississippi to discuss matters in person. He wouldn't have done that if he didn't plan to hear her out.

Since Kate was minus a Mustang, Beth and Michael decided to take an impromptu trip back home. While she rode in the back seat of Beth's Lexus, Kate explained to Michael what she had already shared with Beth a while back. In Natchez she repeated the story a second time, after which Nate Price seemed as eager to hire her as a recently paroled Mafia don. And who could blame him, considering how evasive she'd been in the past? Despite assuring Nate she'd done nothing illegal or even unethical, it wasn't until Michael and Beth intervened that Nate agreed to keep her permanently.

Elevated to sainthood status, at the very least.

While Beth and Michael visited their families and booked wedding venues, Kate was able to meet the office secretary for the first time. She filled out insurance and tax forms and completed the registration for her brand-new firearm. The next two days were spent at the firing range, reviewing what she had learned years ago about gun safety and how to properly handle her new Ruger. Then the three of them drove to the Kirby farm in the country where Beth taught Kate how to shoot tin cans off a fence rail. By the time the sun went down, Kate had reached ninety per cent accuracy.

Hopefully, old soup and soda cans would be all she ever had to kill.

That night, while lying in Rita Kirby's guest bed, Kate contemplated staying in the Mississippi backwoods for the rest of her life. How could her brother's cronies find her at a house without a mailbox on a dirt road in a township that appeared on few maps? But her mama didn't raise any cowards and Kate was done hiding.

Today, they were leaving Natchez. Michael would drive the Lexus back to Savannah, while Kate and Beth were on their way to Charleston in Beth's old Toyota. Now Kate's new Toyota.

'Just so we're clear about this car,' she said once they hit the open road. 'You're not *giving* me your Toyota. Now that I'm officially on the payroll, set your price, and I'll pay you in full within three months.'

'You must be joking. This car was ready for the metal recyclers. I'd planned to donate it to charity and take the tax write-off. I only thought of you because the color was right – green, just like your old Mustang.'

Kate smiled. 'Sorry, this particular charity can't issue receipts, but I am grateful. Now set your price.'

'Fine, let's say two hundred but take as much time as you need. The registration has been switched to Price Investigations. Consider this a company car that you will keep. For the foreseeable future, Nate will take care of the insurance, but don't expect a raise any time soon. With your new identity, you should be safe from the Pensacola thugs for a while.'

'I don't know how to thank you all.'

Beth made a squawking sound. 'We'll think of something when you least expect it. For now, forget about it and tell me about your new case.' She switched off the radio. 'I can't believe it's in Charleston!'

Kate nodded. 'I would prefer being more than a hundred miles from where I'd been living, but I guess Nate can't pick where new work comes from. Other than the location, I'm going to love this case. And for all we know, the trail might take me far from the Atlantic coast.' She took a deep gulp of water. 'An adopted woman is trying to track down any of her natural siblings before she dies.'

'Does she have a terminal illness?'

'I suppose so. I'll find out the details once I meet the client.'

'I thought this kind of information was available on the internet.'

'That's what I said to Nate. But the information is only released when *both* parties wish to be found. In this case, one or more have resisted any attempt to be contacted by the adoption agency. And one natural sibling has gone so far as to drop off the grid, for all practical purposes.'

Beth glanced in her direction. 'Sounds like you'll earn your paycheck. Even if you find this person, what makes you think you can convince them to meet the dying woman?'

Kate shrugged. 'My assignment is to find the natural siblings and extend an invitation to meet our client and her family. The rest is out of my hands.'

'Sounds easy enough. What about your safety? Do you think you covered your tracks well enough in Savannah?'

'I sure hope so. I told my landlord I was moving back to Florida. All the utilities at the apartment were in the owner's name. I told my neighbors I hated the south and would look for a job out west. I got rid of my cell phone since the bad guys had the number and bought a couple of pre-paid burners. Plus Nate gave me a phone, but I'm only releasing the number to a select few.'

'Will that include me?'

'Most likely,' she said with a wink. 'And I made no other friends in Georgia other than you and Michael.'

'And Mrs Doyle,' corrected Beth. 'When I told her about

the night of her party, Evelyn said she'd be happy to hide you in Atlanta or down in the Caribbean or inside an igloo in Alaska, her treat.'

Kate shivered at the thought of an igloo. 'That's very kind of her, but I'm done running. I intend to do my job in Charleston without constantly looking over my shoulder.'

'Just don't get sloppy. In the meantime, I'd better start calling you Jill every five minutes so you get used to the name. What made you pick Jill Wyatt?'

'The creep shooting at me said I'd worn out the letter K. Plus I've always liked that name. But other than those connected to the case, I'm only telling a few friends . . . all *five* of you.'

'Are you going to tell your contacts in Florida?' Beth tightened her grip on the steering wheel.

'My brother? Absolutely not, but I will tell my one friend at the Florida Industrial Commission. I trust her with my life.'

'You know what's best, *Jill.* Any idea where you'll live in Charleston? During my one trip there with Michael, I got the feeling that town is even more expensive than Savannah.'

'You are not kidding. The day I was in Nate's office, his secretary helped me narrow my search to places I can afford in the historical district.'

'Thank goodness for Miss Maxine. She's irreplaceable. How many did she come up with?'

The brand new Jill Wyatt stifled a laugh. 'Exactly one, but the location couldn't be better. Right in the heart of the action.'

'One? Look, *Jill*, the historic district is overrated – no free parking, tons of tourists, and all those horse-drawn carriages to maneuver around. Expand your search into the suburbs and you'll have plenty to pick from.'

Like a stubborn mule, she shook her head. 'Nope, I loved those suites you and Michael had on the Savannah River. Just once I want to live someplace charming, even if it's just for a week or two.'

'Tell me about this *charming* place you found. If you can afford it, it must be a flea-infested walk-up as far from Battery or Bay as you can get. Don't blame me when you wake up in the middle of the night scratching.'

Jill giggled. 'Are you forgetting about our expense *per diem*? It might not be much, but it'll pay half the rent for a suite above a restaurant.'

'You're renting a *room* above a restaurant?' Beth looked appalled.

'Yeah, but it has a queen-size bed, a plasma TV with DVR, and a private bathroom. I don't need more than that.'

'Who were the previous tenants – diners too drunk to drive home?'

'No, the owner kept the suite for out-of-town relatives who showed up without an invitation. Those *with* an invitation got to stay at their home in the suburbs.'

'Oh, for goodness sake, Jill. This is a bad idea.' Beth seldom minced words when she voiced her opinion.

'No, it's not. Did I mention the restaurant serves my favorite kind of food – Italian?'

Beth rolled her eyes. 'Does that mean you can raid the refrigerator after they lock up for the night? Hopefully, you didn't commit without seeing it first.' Barely accelerating, she passed two slow-moving trucks.

'I told the manager we'd arrive by eleven tomorrow to check the place out. He said "perfect," because we would beat the noontime rush.'

'At least the manager is a he. I'd pictured a little old granny with a dozen cats and lace doilies on the scratchy sofa.'

'What are doilies?'

'Never mind, you'll find out soon enough. Eleven should work out fine for us. If we reach Macon tonight, we'll have an easy drive tomorrow after breakfast.'

Later the new Jill and Beth checked into a clean Motel 6 on the edge of town. Although the TV wasn't plasma and the free breakfast consisted of cheese Danish, yogurt and fruit cocktail, the coffee was wonderful. That night Jill listened as Beth described her wedding arrangements with increasing animation. She and Michael's plans for a small, tasteful luncheon after the service had ballooned into an after-church brunch, then a riverboat ride for photographs, and finally a barbeque reception at Aunt Rita's farm with overnight guests sleeping in tents in the pasture.

Beth sighed wearily. 'Somehow my mother and aunts interpreted *small and tasteful* as a three-ring circus, culminating with a hoedown, marshmallows and a bonfire.'

Jill popped open another Coke. 'I thought Michael's parents were adding their two-cents.'

'Oh, yeah . . . they're the ones renting the riverboat for an afternoon cruise down the Mississippi.' Beth grabbed two fistfuls of hair and pulled.

'I'm picturing *Maverick* reruns with James Garner. What does your fearless fiancé have to say about this?'

'Michael suggested a chocolate fountain and pony rides at the farm for the kids.' Beth pulled her hoodie over her face.

Jill only smiled. With her limited experience with weddings, she had no advice to offer. 'Please make sure I get an invitation. I've never been tent camping in my life.'

That night she slept soundly with a feeling of utter safety. Maybe it was because they'd paid for the hotel in cash and registered under false names. Or maybe it was because there were two loaded guns in the room. But mostly it was because Kate Weller/Jill Wyatt had a real friend – something she hadn't had in a long time.

The next morning Jill took the wheel on the way to Charleston to familiarize herself with the car and her new town. En route Beth Googled every hotel in the area until Jill stopped in front of Bella Trattoria. 'Look how adorable this is,' she enthused. 'Wrought-iron gate, field stone foundation, walled courtyard, and a red tile roof. Looks like we landed in Tuscany.'

'Somewhere neither of us has been.' Beth popped out of the car and shoved a quarter into the parking meter. 'An hour should be enough time to split a meatball sub and check out granny's attic.'

'Look, if you're not going to be nice, you can wait in the car.' Jill dropped in three more coins and let her gaze travel up to the second floor where the dormer windows had leaded glass. 'Look at that gorgeous English ivy climbing the walls.'

Beth scrunched her nose. 'That stuff attracts bugs and loosens the mortar.'

'Go.' Jill ordered, pointing at the Toyota. 'You were warned. I'll get the meatball sandwich to go.'

'Please, I promise to be good,' Beth begged, steepling her fingers under her chin.

'OK, but I'm holding you to that promise.' She started up the flagstones toward the arched main entrance.

'Where are you going?' asked Beth. 'We should probably inquire at the service entrance.'

Trusting someone with more experience than her, Jill rounded the side of the building with Beth at her heels. When they followed a delivery man through an open door, they suddenly found themselves smack in the middle of a beehive: Pots being stirred on a twelve-burner stove; vegetables being scrubbed at a sink deep enough for a retriever; pans of dough entering the oven with loaves of bread coming out. A young girl was tearing romaine into bite-sized pieces; an elderly woman was polishing silver; and the deliveryman was loading beer and Evian into a cooler. Yet no one seemed to be getting in anyone's way.

'Wow,' murmured Jill. 'Look how many people work here.'

'And almost everyone is smiling.' Beth sounded equally in awe.

'The term *work* implies a regular paycheck,' said the teenaged vegetable scrubber. 'Some of us are indentured servants,' she added with a scowl.

'No talking, missy, or you'll get another forty lashes.' A thirty-ish woman addressed the girl and then turned to them.

'May I help you? I'm afraid guests must enter through the front door, even for courtyard seating.'

'We'd like two meatball sandwiches to go,' said Beth.

Elbowing her in the gut, Jill stepped forward. 'Actually we'd like to talk to Mr Manfredi.'

'Is my father expecting you?' The woman looked curiously from one to the other.

'I believe these ladies are here for me.' A deep male voice came from one of the three commercial stoves. When he turned around, Jill's breath caught in her throat while Beth squeaked like a mouse. In a kitchen filled with people of petite to medium stature, this particular worker had to be six-five at least.

'Mr Manfredi?' asked Jill, regaining her composure.

'I'm Eric Manfredi. If you're Miss Wyatt, I'm the one you spoke to on the phone.' In one seamless move, he pulled off the white tunic and dropped it in a basket. Underneath he wore a sleeveless T-shirt, well-worn jeans, and flip flops. Not only was he tall, he was around 250 pounds of what looked like solid muscle that didn't come from stirring pots.

'That's me.' Jill forced herself to stop staring.

'Follow me and I'll show you the apartment.' He headed toward the staircase along the far wall.

'Careful, Uncle Eric,' called the young salad-maker. 'The short one is packing a gun under her jacket.'

Beth froze in place and threw her hands in the air. 'I'm licensed to carry a firearm in this state. No one here is in any danger.'

'Are you her bodyguard?' asked the salad-maker. 'That is so cool.'

Eric stopped on the first step and pivoted. 'Pay no attention to my niece. She's very observant and, unfortunately, obsessed with crime shows.' When he shifted his focus from the salad-maker to Jill, his dark eyes practically bored holes through her. 'You mentioned on the phone you were a PI.'

'Correct, I'm in Charleston for a case. This is Beth Kirby, who's also a PI.'

He nodded politely. 'Nice to meet you, but the suite is only big enough for one occupant.' Eric unlocked the door with an old-fashioned skeleton key.

'Oh, I wouldn't stay here,' said Beth, a bit too eagerly.

'Why is that, Miss Kirby? Something wrong with the aroma of baking bread or herbs and seasonings simmering in the perfect pasta sauce?'

'Certainly not,' Jill answered, 'but Beth has a fiancé back in Savannah.'

'I'm sure he's one lucky man.' With a wry smile Eric swept open the door and waited for Jill to enter. 'Would you like to wait out here, Beth, to guard against intruders coming up the steps?' He gave Beth a megawatt smile.

'But what if the intruders swing down from the roof?' Beth brushed past him into the room. 'I'd better stay with Jill.'

'Wow,' Jill murmured. 'This is delightful. I love the furnishings and wallpaper.'

'Wow,' echoed Beth. 'I can't believe the ceilings are so low. How do you fit in here, height-wise?'

'I confine myself to the center of the room,' Eric said. 'The architect positioned the bedroom and sitting area under the eaves. I think it adds to the charm.'

'I agree.' Sitting down on the four-poster bed, Jill smoothed her hand over an embroidered quilt. 'This is exactly how I pictured it.' Then she jumped up and ran to the window. 'I can't believe you have honest-to-goodness shutters!'

Ducking his head under the eave, Eric joined her at the window. 'You can open the window but keep the shutters closed. Then you'll hear the foghorns on the bay but still have your privacy.'

'You mean this place doesn't have air-conditioning?' Beth asked indignantly.

'Of course it does. But Miss Wyatt might want to catch the sea breeze some evenings.' Eric and Beth glared at each other like dogs separated by a chain link fence.

'I certainly would. Now let's check out the bathroom.' Jill pushed Beth through the doorway by her shoulders, as though afraid to leave her behind.

'Well, the room sure is big enough,' Beth conceded.

'Marble countertop, lighted mirror, separate shower and whirlpool tub, and that's a heated towel bar.' Eric pointed out the accoutrements one at a time.

'Sold! My mind is made up.' Jill bubbled over with excitement.

'All bed linens and towels are included,' added Eric. 'Along with once a week maid service.'

Beth crossed her arms. 'But there's no kitchen, not even a hotplate.'

Jill shrugged. 'Good, I don't know how to cook anyway.'

'Under the other eave is a small refrigerator and microwave to reheat leftovers or make popcorn for movie night.' Eric's expression showed true pride in his rental unit.

'She's only staying a week or two,' muttered Beth.

Eric straightened to his full height in the center of the room, which was indeed impressive. 'Miss Wyatt can stay as long as she likes.'

Not one to back down, Beth arched up on tiptoes. 'Is this your restaurant or do you just work here?'

'The restaurant is owned and operated by my family. Those were the people you saw down in the kitchen.'

'Speaking of which, how come you're so tall and everyone else . . . isn't?'

Jill gasped with embarrassment. 'I'm so sorry, Mr Manfredi. Beth must have left her manners in Georgia.'

'No problem. I'm asked that a lot. Truth is, Beth, my parents found me in a basket floating down a canal in Venice. When no one claimed me, they raised me as their own, a decision I'm sure they regret every now and then.'

Beth's eyes grew very round. 'It's a miracle that basket didn't sink to the bottom.'

Jill, on the other hand, studied Eric's face with growing skepticism. 'How did your parents know what to call you?'

'My name was written on a piece of papyrus, pinned to my diaper. But Mom thought the name Moses inappropriate for an Italian *bambino*, so they changed it to Enrique. I shortened it to Eric.'

Beth approached Eric until they were nose to chin. 'So, *Moses*, do you live in the house or maybe a crate in the garage?'

'Oh, no crate, I've got a swanky condo down the road.'

'OK, that's enough.' Jill wedged herself between them and pushed them apart. 'Beth, you will wait in the hallway until my business is concluded. No arguments.'

With slumping shoulders, Beth shuffled from the suite.

'I apologize, Eric,' she said, closing the door. 'Honestly, Beth is a really nice person. I have no idea why she's acting like that.'

'I do. She's protecting you from the unknown.' Eric leaned one shoulder against the wall. 'It's rather sweet. Have you two known each other long?'

Jill thought better of revealing too much information. 'Long enough. Getting back to business, the rent is two hundred a week, including breakfast and all utilities?'

'That's correct. And since you have no cooking facilities,

you're welcome to grab dinner downstairs at no charge, sort of catch-as-catch-can.' He smiled, revealing dimples beneath his strong cheekbones.

Suddenly, Eric's persona seemed to loom even larger than his physical body. 'No, thanks,' she said, stepping back. 'I usually work late most nights and eat on the fly.'

'Of course, but I hope you're not too intimidated by my family to grab breakfast downstairs. Don't worry; no one will hold you captive with tales of the old country. Breakfast is causal – cereal, yogurt, fruit, leftover bakery or pizza. Just grab whatever suits you.'

Jill felt her cheeks flush. 'I hope you didn't interpret something Beth said as an ethnic slur. She's not like that at all.'

'Absolutely not, but here's a suggestion: Why not stay here tonight on the house? If anything makes *you* uncomfortable – the mattress, the noise level, aromas drifting up the stairs – you can be on your way in the morning. No charge and no hard feelings.'

His emphasis indicated the invitation was for one. 'You have a deal. I'll get my bag from the car and Beth can call her fiancé to come get her.'

'Come and go as you please, but right now I need to get to work. Saturday lunch patrons usually arrive early.' Eric set the key on the lace-topped dresser, ducked his head through the doorway, and vanished.

How the man passed her cohort on the steps would remain a mystery, because when Beth stepped into the suite Jill spoke first. 'Save your breath, Kirby. I'm staying. I like it here. Now call Michael and ask him to pick you up after work. There's only one queen-size bed and it's mine. Just for the record, you snore.'

'Fine, but don't say I didn't warn you if you're held captive and forced to make salads all day. Oh, and just for the record . . . those lacy things on the dresser are called *doilies*.'

FOUR

The next morning Eric Manfredi let himself in through the front door but left the lights off in the restaurant. It would be hours before Bella Trattoria opened for business. Grabbing his laptop from the office, he decided to work in the kitchen so the overnight guest would see him first when she came downstairs. He had no idea why it was so important that Jill Wyatt like the apartment. It just was. And what would he have done if the pistol-packing girlfriend had needed a place to stay? *Sorry, we don't rent to redheads – they're too unpredictable.* Or maybe: *Sorry, we're holding out for someone with good manners.*

After starting the coffeemaker, he set out a pitcher of milk and plate of blueberry muffins on the sparkling countertop. But he'd barely opened the spreadsheet of this month's receivables when his sister swept into the kitchen like a tornado.

'What on earth are *you* doing here on a Saturday?' Bernie Conrad carried an armload of shopping bags to the sink.

'I could ask you the same question, little sis.' Eric didn't glance up from his computer screen.

'I always do the Saturday baking because Pamela has weekends off.' Bernie began washing peaches and plums. 'Your turn.'

'I thought this would be a good time to catch up on the accounts.' Avoiding his sister's gaze, Eric pulled two mugs from the cupboard as the coffeemaker released a burst of steam.

'Why not the office or at home, for that matter? You're never here on Saturday until the first reservation.' She lifted an eyebrow. 'Maybe you're afraid someone will scare away the new tenant.'

'Obviously, that possibility occurred to you as well.' Eric carried their coffee to the table. 'Speaking of which, where is your juvenile delinquent daughter this morning?'

'She insisted on walking instead of riding with me. Something about wanting to get more exercise.' The two siblings shared a laugh until someone cleared their throat in the stairwell.

'What, exactly, should I be afraid of?' Jill Wyatt strolled down the last few steps into the kitchen.

'Nothing, as long as you wear a rope of garlic around your neck and keep a wooden stake handy.' Eric pulled out another chair at the table.

'Don't pay any attention to him; we're harmless.' Eric's sister jumped to her feet and extended a hand. 'I'm Bernadette Conrad, Eric's sister. Call me Bernie, if you're staying.'

'Jill Wyatt, pleased to meet you.' After the two women shook, Jill turned toward him. 'Last night I slept like a baby. I'll take the suite.' She smiled, a gesture which changed an ordinary face into an extraordinary one.

'Glad to hear it.' Following his four-word reply, Eric stood with his hands in his pockets, befuddled.

Bernie broke the tension after a few uncomfortable moments. 'I think I'll inventory wine in the cellar and bake my fruit cannoli later. Eric, why don't you show Jill where everything is in the kitchen?' she asked and then disappeared.

'First, how 'bout some coffee?' Eric snapped out of his paralysis.

'I would love some,' she said.

He filled a mug and handed it to her. 'This is the non-commercial end of the kitchen. Help yourself to anything on the counter or in this fridge or these cabinets.' He pointed at the bowls of fruit and plate of blueberry muffins. Then he opened the cupboards where they stored an array of cereals, snack foods, and canned soups. 'So no one makes a midnight snack from something meant for tomorrow's daily special.'

Jill added milk to her coffee. 'Got it. I prefer this to a set breakfast time.' She reached for a bowl and the box of Cheerios.

'Did your friend get back to Savannah?'

Jill sat in the chair vacated by Bernie. 'She did, after her husband dragged her to the car. Beth was worried you might chain me to the salad station.'

Eric laughed, his composure restored. 'That punishment is

reserved for my niece, Danielle, who was grounded for breaking curfew on a school night. She might get early parole if she works hard enough. That's up to her parents.'

'I had a feeling it was something like that.' Jill filled her bowl and started to eat.

Suddenly, the subject of their conversation burst into the kitchen. 'Uncle Eric, why are you just standing around?' Danielle Conrad demanded.

'Good morning, Dani. This is Jill Wyatt. She'll be renting the upstairs suite. Your mom is downstairs. Why don't you help her inventory wine?'

The teenager shook her head. 'How did you *not* see the mess when you arrived this morning?'

'*What . . . mess*?' he asked. Before Dani could answer, Eric was out the door with Jill on his heels. But when he reached the courtyard everything looked fine: Tables were upright, chairs in place, candleholders ready to be lit at twilight.

'Not here, Uncle.' Dani ran to the security gate leading to the alley and threw back the bolt.

When Eric stepped into the alley, the reason for his niece's distress became apparent. The restaurant's dumpster, scheduled for pickup that morning, had been overturned. Food scraps from hundreds of unfinished meals lay strewn in a colorful array, along with empty containers, and every other type of trash. Not only had the dumpster been overturned – no easy feat in itself – but the contents had been spread from one end of the Manfredi property to the other. It was as though someone had made a concerted effort to be thorough.

'Whoever did this will pay,' he muttered under his breath.

'It wasn't me. It was like this when I arrived.' Dani looked stricken.

'Of course it wasn't you. I was just blowing off steam.' Eric wrapped an arm around her shoulders and then grew acutely aware of Jill's gaze on him as well.

'Sorry you had to witness this on your first day. Pranks by teenagers happen all too often in this business. But if you'd rather continue looking at rentals, I understand.'

Jill kicked a Styrofoam cup toward the rest of the debris. 'Don't be silly. I'm only sorry I can't stay to help clean up.

I'm supposed to meet my client in a few hours.' She peered up with brown eyes so plaintive, so earnest, his stomach clenched.

'That's nice of you to offer, but I'll call a professional service. The alley must be cleaned and sanitized by strict city codes to reduce the chance of infestation.' Eric stepped on a cockroach as discreetly as possible as Jill pretended not to notice. 'And I better call them fast. We don't need pictures appearing on the internet. That would be a black mark against the restaurant.'

'Sorry, Uncle Eric, but that's why I ran here so fast. Someone already posted this on the internet and tagged me.' Danielle, on the verge of tears, held up her phone, showing a video of the alley taken some time after dawn.

Eric swallowed down the first reply that came to mind. 'It's OK, Dani. I'll take care of this with one phone call. You grab something to eat and then go help your mom.'

Reluctantly, his niece shrugged and ducked through the opening in the wall.

'If you're sure you don't need me,' said Jill, 'I'd better eat breakfast and hit the road.'

'I'm sure, but would you like to join my family for dinner tonight? Then you'll see you haven't fallen in with a bunch of serial killers.'

Jill hesitated. 'Sounds tempting, but I have no idea how long this will take or where I'll end up.'

Eric held up his palms. 'I understand. If you change your mind, we never eat before eight thirty, well after the dinner rush.'

She nodded and ducked through the opening in the wall.

Eric stood alone for a few minutes, pondering, before he called the cleaning service. Despite his assurances to the contrary, he was absolutely certain of one thing: This was no prank by a bored group of teenagers.

Jill's guilt over leaving her landlord ankle deep in garbage vanished the moment she left Bella Trattoria. With a nine thirty appointment in a suburb called Goose Creek, she wanted to be prepared and on time. Luckily, Beth had left her GPS in the Toyota, so finding the white colonial among dozens in the development proved easy. At least the Sugarman family had painted their shutters and front door red to stand out from the rest. Dressed in a tailored jacket and slim skirt, Jill knocked firmly on the bright red panel.

When the door opened, a girl of five or six smiled up at her. 'Hi, my name is Joan, after Joan of Arc. *Stall-wart* and brave, that's me.' The child peered up through impossibly thick lashes.

Jill bent from the waist. 'Are you ready to march fearlessly into battle, Saint Joan?'

She shook her head. 'Oh, no. Daddy said fighting is wrong.'

'O-*kay*.' Apparently, little Joan hadn't heard the full story about her namesake. 'Are your mom and dad home?'

'Miss Wyatt?' A grim-faced man with thick glasses appeared behind his daughter. 'I'm David Sugarman. Please come in and make yourself comfortable.'

Jill followed him into a tidy living room where a young man was watching TV. Plants lined every windowsill and rows of framed photographs decorated the walls. Toys had been piled into an overflowing chest next to the couch, except for one lop-eared rabbit half buried by a cushion.

'That's our son, Robert, and you've already met Joan.' When David released her hand the child ran to retrieve the forgotten rabbit.

'Mr Bugs, you have to stay in here until this lady leaves.' Joan shoved the stuffed toy down in the crate.

Stifling her smile, Jill asked, 'Is Mrs Sugarman home?' She glanced left and right ridiculously as though Mom might be hiding under a cushion too.

'My wife is a patient at UMSC Hospital. We'll go there next, but I wanted to speak to you first. Charlotte thought you should meet us before meeting her.'

'Charlotte is my mom,' Joan explained, hurrying to Jill's side as though she might be having a hard time following the conversation.

David sighed. 'Joan, go watch TV with your brother so I can talk to Miss Wyatt without interruption.'

Jill waited until the child loped off. 'My boss has already accepted the case. I will do everything in my power to find your wife's biological siblings, if any exist.'

'I believe Charlotte has a sister, who's most likely still living in South Carolina. A long time ago, the natural mother responded to my wife's request to meet. She gave Charlotte her original birth certificate and indicated she had given up *two* daughters for adoption, four years apart. The woman didn't let on that she was dying. When Charlotte reached out to her again, she was already dead. Here's a photocopy of that birth certificate, for all the good it'll do.'

Jill tucked the folded paper into her purse. 'I take it the woman doesn't wish to be found.'

'She has refused every request for contact that the agency has made.'

'Then she shouldn't be too hard to find. But I can't guarantee any outcome beyond an address and perhaps a recent photo.'

David dropped his chin. 'I'll get right to the point. My wife has been on a donor waiting list for years. Unfortunately, the likelihood of obtaining a suitable match due to her rare blood type grows slimmer every day.'

'*That's* why I'm tracking down siblings?' Jill blinked. 'You think a complete stranger – someone who's resisted all attempts of contact thus far – will let you remove one of her organs?'

'*Half* of one organ,' David corrected. 'The liver begins to regenerate almost immediately. Without the transplant Charlotte will die, and she doesn't have much time left. We're getting down to the wire.'

Jill could hear Joan crying behind her, along with restrained sniffles from the boy. 'Perhaps it would be better if your children played outside for a while?'

'No, my wife wants them to understand everything happening in their world.' David's point-blank tone of voice matched his erect posture. 'We all die, Miss Wyatt. We would just like to have Charlotte a while longer. Wouldn't we, kids?'

Dutifully, Joan and Robert nodded their blond heads, their faces streaked with tears.

'Now that you know the situation, we can head over to the hospital.' David stood and switched off the TV. 'And it's time you two stopped crying if you want to see Mom.'

'Daddy, can I take Mr Bugs to the hospital?' Joan asked.

'Definitely not. That rabbit is probably covered with germs.'

David Sugarman strode from the room with his children trailing behind like mini-robots. Jill fell in step, too, thinking that alley cleanup was sounding better and better.

Despite David's insistence that they had plenty of room in their van, Jill drove herself to UMSC Hospital. This guy's cavalier attitude about life and death made her nervous. What kind of father frightens his kids about losing their mother? With more people joining the donor registrar, suitable matches turned up every day. Mrs Sugarman could still receive her transplant in plenty of time. And those kids would have been traumatized for nothing.

Inside the medical center's isolation ward, Jill changed her mind in a hurry. Dressed in gowns, masks, and booties, she and David were escorted into Charlotte's private room, while another nurse herded the children down the hall to a play area manned by volunteers. They were ordered not to touch the patient, drink from her cup, or handle anything on the patient's tray. With a weakened immune system, Charlotte must be protected against viral infections. When Jill gazed at the thin, pale woman lying motionless on the raised bed, she no longer doubted David's dire predictions.

'Charlotte?' David bent low and spoke next to her ear. 'Char, honey? Look who came to meet you – Miss Jill Wyatt of Price Investigations. That's the agency John spoke so highly of.'

Jill had no idea who John was, but she wasn't fond of her fame preceding her. Wouldn't that place an unrealistic burden on her, considering the impossible circumstances? 'How do you do, Mrs Sugarman? I'll do my best to track down your siblings.'

Charlotte opened one eyelid. With purple smudges and deep circles under her eyes and the telltale yellowish cast to her skin, she looked older than her husband by decades. 'Thank . . . you . . . for . . . coming,' she rasped through parched lips.

'How 'bout some water?' David placed the straw between her parched lips, tilted the cup, and patiently waited while his wife took tiny sips. Jill's opinion of the man lifted one notch.

After five minutes of difficult swallowing, Charlotte waved the cup away. 'Much better,' she said, struggling to sit up.

Although David hurried to the other side, Jill was afraid to help. The woman weighed so little, she might break with the slightest pressure. Fortunately, David easily moved his wife higher on the pillows.

'Honey, please run along and sit with the children,' said Charlotte. 'I would like to speak to Jill alone.'

'But what if you need—'

She waved away his protest like a mosquito. 'I can survive five minutes without you.'

When he closed the door behind him, Jill felt cut adrift. *Am I allowed to press the call button or just the patient?*

'Mr Price betrayed your confidence, but I have told no one. Soon I'll take your secret to my grave.'

'What secret is that?' Jill grew increasingly uncomfortable.

'Mr Price told me you were adopted. He thought having that in common would create a bond between us. But seeing your face when you walked through the door, it might have had the opposite effect.'

'Forgive me, it's just that I have little familiarity with hospitals.'

Charlotte flourished her hand a second time. 'Please, speak frankly with me.'

Jill met the woman's watery gaze. 'All right, I was hired to track someone down and that's what I plan to do. But I'm not big on approaching someone who doesn't wish to be found. It's an invasion of privacy.'

She nodded sagely. 'Because you wouldn't like someone showing up on *your* doorstep?'

'No, I wouldn't, but I understand in your case. This is a matter of life and death.'

'I don't think you understand at all.' Charlotte reached for her hand, breaking one of the nurse's strict rules. 'I'm not the least bit afraid to die. I'm so sick of needles and hospitals and don't-eat-this, don't-eat-that. I know that when I leave here I'm going to a better place.' She ran out of breath and began to gasp. Jill reached for the water pitcher, but Charlotte shook her head.

'This is about your kids, isn't it?' Jill asked.

Charlotte nodded. 'Joan and Bobby are too young to be without their mother. David loves his children and he's a good father. But he's . . . rigid. He'll want them to stiffen their upper lips and hide their emotions, when they need to cry and stomp their feet. Do you . . . understand?'

'Yes, I think I do.' An unexpected lump rose in Jill's throat.

'I realize the ultimate decision rests with my natural siblings. If, after they hear the facts, they decide not to help me, God bless them. That's their choice. Then I can die knowing I gave it my best shot.' Charlotte's smile revealed her former self before the disease ravaged her outer shell.

Jill laid a hand on her shoulder, careful not to touch bare skin. 'I promise to try my best. If I have to crawl through barbed wire and dodge buckshot, every one of your siblings will hear the full story.'

'Thank you. Sounds like Nate Price picked the right PI for the job. Please ask David to come in. I still have ten minutes before the nurses send everyone home.'

Jill left the room buoyed by the client's confidence. She spotted David sitting in a plastic chair with his head bowed. 'Charlotte wants you to come back.'

He sprang to his feet. 'Are you coming, Miss Wyatt?'

'No, I'm going to sit with your kids for a while.' Jill turned and headed down the hall. Having little experience with munchkins, she had no idea why she chose this option. But maybe it was time to gain some.

'Hi, Miss Jill, we're over here.' Joan called out the moment the door opened. 'Come look at what we made.'

The Sugarman offspring had been industrious at the crafts table. Using purple and yellow Play Doh, animals had been fashioned and positioned inside a plastic barnyard.

'Which ones did you make, Robert?' Jill asked.

The boy blushed. 'I know this is kids' stuff, but I made the chickens because Joanie wanted me to.'

'I thought those were chickens.' Jill perched on a small-sized chair.

'Guess what mine are!' cried Joan, pointing at the purple shapeless critters.

Jill lowered her face to table level to study. 'I believe those are pigs from Mars, because everyone knows South Carolina pigs are pink.'

Robert broke into hoots while Joan jumped to her feet.

'That's right. You're so smart!' She threw her thin arms around Jill's neck and hugged.

A minute later, Jill practically had to pry off her fingers. 'Shouldn't we clean this up and go wash our hands? Daddy will be finished visiting soon.'

Like mini-robots at work, the pair put away the modeling clay and washed up at the sink. It wasn't until they left the playroom neat as a pin that Joan asked, 'Are you going to find Mommy's sister so Mommy can have half her liver?'

Was there no detail they hadn't explained to a six-year-old?

Jill tightened her grip on the child's hand. 'You bet I am, kiddo. And if her sister won't hand it over, I'll give your mommy half of mine.'

That was the world's stupidest thing to say. Once the words left her mouth, she would have given anything to take them back.

Robert took Jill's other hand. 'It doesn't work that way, Miss Jill. You have to have the right blood type, plus certain other factors. But it was nice of you to offer. Could you call me "Bobby" instead of Robert? That's the name my friends use when Dad's not around.'

'I would be honored.'

Jill went from feeling like the world's biggest idiot to an accomplished children's advocate in record time. Something told her this case would involve far more than tracking down a few missing persons.

FIVE

After being scrubbed, gowned and masked, Robert and Joan were permitted a brief visit with their mother with the nurse by their side. Jill and David watched the exchange from the hallway window. Even from this distance, Charlotte looked exhausted by the time her children were hustled out and visitation time declared over.

Upon David's insistence, Jill accompanied the Sugarmans to Applebee's for lunch. It was an invitation she gladly accepted and learned more about family dynamics during a crisis in those sixty minutes than at any point in her life. Hopefully, more than she would ever need. Her own family history was by no means average. As an infant, she was adopted by a nice couple who lived on the outskirts of Pensacola. They had adopted a boy three years earlier and since he'd worked out well, they decided to give a girl a try. Jill got along well with her parents and brother, Liam. She had plenty of friends and earned decent grades in school. But when she was nine and Liam thirteen, her parents were killed in a car accident, ending anything close to normal in her life.

An endless succession of foster homes had turned her brother rebellious. Jill, however, found solace in books and became an exceptional student. When Children's Services could no longer place them together in the same foster home, Liam tried his best to remain in her life. Jill continued to love him even though his body art, multiple piercings, and vulgar language reflected a change in his once sweet personality. Then a string of bad decisions landed Liam in jail and their relationship ended forever.

Until this afternoon, she'd given families little consideration. She had thrived in college on a full scholarship without the need to join a sorority or encircle herself with friends. Sharing coffee with acquaintances, participating in study groups, and sending cards to an aunt sufficed for human companionship. Today as she watched the Sugarmans, sweet memories that had been buried for years rose to the surface, giving her a rare pang of loneliness.

For the return trip to Charleston, Jill opted for Rivers Avenue instead of Interstate 26. With plenty to sort out in her mind, she was in no hurry to get back. Once she reached Calhoun Street – the general demarcation line of the historic district – she rolled down the windows to breathe in the sea air. Millions of tourists couldn't be wrong – the city's unique charm was its vibrancy amidst eighteenth-century architecture. Charleston wasn't static and museum-y, protected to the point of obscurity. This city bustled, night and day. Jill couldn't wait to walk the cobblestone streets and peek into gardens and curtain-less windows. But not tonight. Tonight, she picked up a taco salad, parked next to a shiny Cadillac, and entered through the restaurant's rear entrance.

In the kitchen, the Manfredis and their employees steamed and sautéed, chopped, and flambéed at the top of their game. Jill received only a nod from Eric as she climbed the steps to her room. But that was fine with her. She would eat her dinner, watch a little TV, say her prayers, and fall fast asleep. Safe, blissful sleep, for the second night in a row.

Eric could thrive on six hours of sleep, but less than that left him cranky, clumsy, and easily distracted. Such was the case that Sunday morning, because dozing off in a plastic chair in the ER didn't amount to much of anything. He'd already cut his thumb while slicing eggplant and dropped a pan of bread on the floor. Now if it wasn't for the smoke detector blasting in the stairwell, he might not have known his skillet was on fire.

'*Enrique!*' Nonni yelled for the doorway. Her next phrase in Italian was better off left untranslated.

His grandmother hurried for the bucket of sand in the closet as fast as her arthritis would allow. Eric ran for the fire extinguisher which hung on the opposite wall.

Jill Wyatt, however, was quicker than either of them. She slipped on an oven mitt and covered the skillet with a lid, thereby cutting off the oxygen. Flames went out almost immediately, while the ventilation fan sucked out most of the smoke.

Nonni, her mouth a perfect O, stared at Jill. 'Don't let this one get away, *nipote.* She's a keeper.'

Eric pulled the pan off the burner with the other mitt. 'Jill, this is my grandmother, Donatella Angelica Manfredi, but everyone calls her Nonni, even those not related to her.'

'Pleased to meet you, ma'am.' Jill tucked a lock of hair behind her ear.

'Would you like a job?' asked Nonni. She clutched her pink flowery robe together at the throat.

'No thank you, ma'am. I can't cook.'

She clucked her tongue. 'If I can teach my grandson, I can teach a chimpanzee. Enrique still doesn't know not to walk away from a hot pan of oil.' She shuffled back to the closet to put away her sand.

Eric chose not to explain himself since time was short. 'Nonni, why don't you try to get more sleep? I'll handle things out here.'

'Just don't forget where we keep the bucket of sand,' she said, shuffling from the room.

The moment his grandmother was gone, Eric turned to his tenant. 'Thank you, Jill. My family is in your debt.'

'You're welcome. I couldn't sleep anyway with that loud smoke alarm.' The corners of her mouth turned up in a grin. 'Did your grandmother just call me a chimp?'

'She might have, but don't be offended. Nonni also offered you a job, and that's never happened with a stranger. Sit, I'll pour you a cup of coffee.' Eric switched off all burners and pulled a batch of bread from the oven. But by the time he carried over the coffee, Jill had already gotten out the Cheerios. 'Cold cereal? Why don't I make you an omelet? It's the least I can do for your heroism.'

'Absolutely not. You're already up to your elbows.' Jill's gaze flitted over the commercial kitchen in total disarray. 'Do you open early for brunch on Sunday? Where are your helpers?'

'We're not open at all on Sundays. That's a day to attend Mass and relax. My grandfather always said: "Any restaurateur that can't make a living in six days deserves to go out of business."' Eric slicked a hand through his hair.

'So what happened? The same pranksters from the alley hit the kitchen last night?' Jill took a sip of coffee and grinned over the rim of her mug.

Normally Eric would have fired off a retort since clever banter was his specialty, second only to his *pasta pescatore*. But not today, not after last night. 'No, we had excitement of another kind. My father was robbed on his way to making the night deposit. Some thug conked him on the head and stole his money pouch. Dad hides it in his left inside pocket – never his right side, always his left.'

Jill's smile vanished. 'Oh, my goodness. Is your father OK?'

'He will be. The doctor said his skull is bruised, but not fractured. He has a few cuts from when he fell, but all in all, he's one lucky man. The hospital plans to keep him a few days for observation before sending him home.'

'I hope this isn't too impertinent, but why was your father out alone at night?'

'That's a very legitimate question.' Eric took a long drink of coffee. 'Not only does Dad insist on making a night deposit, he won't let anyone go with him.'

'Sounds like he's set in his ways.'

Eric nodded. 'And we're not talking routines developed in the last decade or two. We're talking habits passed down from generation to generation, carried from one continent to another. The Manfredis are nothing if not *traditionalists*.'

'Nothing wrong with preserving traditions, unless they endanger someone's safety.'

Encouraged by Jill's attitude, Eric continued. 'Not only does Dad insist on walking alone, he takes the same route every evening. He says his evening constitutional settles his stomach and helps him sleep.'

'Perhaps a few Tums would work just as well.' Jill added milk to her cereal and started to eat.

'You're not kidding. My sister and I have talked ourselves blue in the face trying to reason with him. Mom gave up years ago. I suggested an armored car make the pickup at closing time, but Alfonzo wouldn't hear of it. He said *it's not how things are done*.' Finally embarrassed by his outburst, Eric avoided eye contact.

'Aren't most restaurant transactions electronic? I've seen the prices on your menu. Who carries around that kind of cash?' She drained her coffee.

Eric scrambled up to refill their mugs. 'Most people pay with credit or debit cards, except for a few of my parents' friends – those cut from the same bolt of cloth.'

'How much did the thieves get?'

'For less than two hundred dollars they bashed him in the head with a club.'

Jill's spoon paused midway to her mouth. 'Your dad is lucky to be alive. Are your mom and sister still at the hospital?'

He nodded. 'Nonni wasn't comfortable sleeping in a chair so my mom asked me to bring her home this morning.'

He rose to his feet. 'Now I need to cook up a storm for Sunday dinner. When news of my father gets around, we'll have friends and relatives dropping in all day.'

Jill swallowed a mouthful of cereal. 'Under the circumstances, I doubt visitors will have much appetite.'

'Your family must be nothing like mine. At times of joy like graduations, weddings, and new babies, the Manfredis eat! During times of trouble or loss? We eat to drown our sorrows and forget our worries. And of course, we eat on all the run-of-the-mill days too.'

'Yet you don't seem to have an ounce of extra body fat on you.' Jill finished her cereal and lifted her bowl to drink the milk. 'Someday you'll have to share your secret.'

Eric felt his cheeks started to redden. Throughout his adult life, women had commented on his physique. Praise was nice, but he'd never put much stock in it. Today Jill's observation made him blush like a teenager.

'No real secret. I've got a high metabolism, plus I work out an hour a day. It helps me deal with the stress of someone sending back their dinner.' Eric turned the burners on under the pots of water.

'I bet that doesn't happen too often.' Jill followed him to the stove. 'What are you making for the hordes that will soon descend?'

'We're having chicken and eggplant *parmigiana* on *cavatelli* or linguini noodles, Caesar salad, fresh bread, and a Cassata cake. My sister always keeps an extra cake in the freezer for emergencies.'

'What were you doing when you almost burned the place down?' Jill's left eyebrow lifted.

Again, Eric felt a blush creep up his neck. 'Looks like I'll have to prove my culinary worthiness. But to answer your question, my plan was to quick fry the chicken. A very hot skillet will crisp the breading. Then I bake the breasts in a moderate oven to keep the meat moist. Unfortunately, I walked away to stir a pot of boiling-over gravy.'

'Could I be trusted to brown the chicken?' she asked.

The question took Eric by surprise. 'I would never impose on your Sunday. You probably don't get many more days off than me.'

'I've never cooked anything except ramen noodles and heat-and-eats. But if *I* don't burn the place down, the experience will look good on my résumé if my current job doesn't work out.'

'All right, but you must accept free takeout for as long as you're here. No more fast-food taco salads. Sorry, but I couldn't help notice the bag when I took out the trash.'

'Agreed, as long as no one hovers over my shoulder. I can't handle that.'

'I'll give you a crash course.' Eric pulled out another skillet, added some olive oil and turned the burner up to medium. 'Keep careful watch. When a single drop of water bounces around before evaporating, the oil is hot enough to quick fry. Then carefully lay out six breaded chicken cutlets.' He took the timer off the shelf. 'Give them sixty seconds and turn them with tongs. Then sixty seconds more and pull the pan from the heat. Transfer the cutlets one at a time to one of those baking pans. Holler if you need help or have any questions.'

'Got it.' Jill's face glowed with enthusiasm.

'But first you'll have to put your hair up in a ponytail, scrub your hands like a surgeon, and put on a white coat. They're in a wooden cabinet in the employee lounge.' He pointed in the right direction.

'Anything else I can help you with?'

'Nope, that's it. Believe me, you have the time-consuming job. If you distinguish yourself with the chicken, maybe I'll let you work on the eggplant.'

'Are eggplants those odd-shaped, purple vegetables?' she asked.

'Yep.' Eric bit back a grin as Jill left to wash up.

As much as he also hated people hovering over his shoulder, he longed to linger close to Jill while she worked. And it wasn't because he feared a second batch of oil catching fire.

He loved the way Jill smelled. Maybe it was her shampoo or her perfume or the fabric softener she used.

Or maybe he simply spent too much time with rosemary, parsley, oregano, and thyme . . . not to mention garlic. He'd noticed the scent of jasmine in her suite last night and again this morning when she sat down with her box of Cheerios.

But with forty or fifty people expected for Sunday dinner and no help except for a woman who thinks making ramen noodles is *cooking*, Eric forced those thoughts from his mind . . . and went in search of some *odd-shaped purple things.*

SIX

Jill was rather proud of herself. She had browned forty skinless, boneless chicken breasts to utter perfection. Not one of them burned to a crisp. Who said this cooking stuff was difficult? Of course, by the time she finished the last batch of chicken, Eric had already done the eggplant *parmigiana*, baked six loaves of bread and made the biggest Caesar salad she'd even seen. His sister's Cassata cake was defrosting on the counter, waiting to be sliced.

'Those look great, Jill. I can't thank you enough.' Eric picked up her final baking pan lined with chicken and carried it to his work station.

'What comes next?' she asked, following him.

'I'll add seasoning, top with sauce and cheese, and stick them in the oven after the first batch comes out.'

'Should I get out the jars of sauce?' she asked.

'You're pulling my leg, right?'

Her hesitation provided all the answer he needed.

'What do you think that is simmering on the stove?' With his wooden spoon, Eric pointed at a large pot.

'I'm thinkin' you bottled the extra the last time you made it.' Jill shifted her weight between hips.

He winked at her. 'Nice save, but no. I make at least one variety of sauce every day. Restaurants pretty much make everything from scratch, even the pasta. Although we do keep some imported noodles around in case we run out.'

While she hovered on his right, Eric dumped a pot of skinny noodles into a huge colander. A huge cloud of steam rose into the air. 'Are those the linguini?' she asked. 'Would you like me to make the cavadellis?'

Without warning Eric pivoted and placed his hands on her shoulders. 'Yes, those noodles are linguini. The first batch of *cavatelli* is already done. I won't make more until it's needed. What I really want you to do, Miss Wyatt, is relax and enjoy what's left of your Sunday. Your work is officially finished.'

From his touch every muscle in her back and shoulders tensed. She stepped back so fast she practically bowled over his sister.

'Everything OK in here?' Bernie peered from one to the other.

'Yes, we're fine,' said Jill.

'Yeah, other than you sneaking up on people,' said Eric simultaneously.

'Did you expect me to *knock* on the door where I grew up?' His sister picked up the colander, shook out the last drops of moisture, and dumped the pasta into a serving bowl. 'I came back to help, brother dear. What would you like me to do?'

'I've got lunch ready to serve, so why don't you give our tenant a tour of the restaurant?' Eric pulled his soiled apron over his head.

'Sorry, I didn't mean to get in the way,' Jill said, taking off her white coat as well.

'You, in the way? I sincerely doubt that.' Bernie took Jill's hand as though she were a child. 'Come with me. You and I set out plates, napkins, and silverware for the buffet line.'

Jill went willingly, grateful for something to do on her first day off in a new town and for the opportunity to save face. For someone who didn't like people hovering, she sure did enough of it with Eric.

Once they had readied the buffet except for the hot food, Bernie showed her the three dining rooms that comprised Bella Trattoria – each with a different thematic décor. However, they were still in the largest room when the first guests began to arrive. Eric wasn't exaggerating when he used the term *horde* to describe the anticipated crowd.

Speaking of Eric, he suddenly materialized in the main dining room just as Jill decided to make her exit. In that short amount of time, the guy had shed his chef's garb, showered, and donned black slacks and a polo shirt which fit snugly across his chest and shoulders. His damp hair still held tracks from the comb.

'May I keep you a moment longer?' Eric asked as she tried to slip away. 'There are a few people who wanted to meet you.'

'Of course.' When Jill turned on her heel she was face to face with Danielle Conrad. 'Hi, Dani. How's it going? Wow, you look nice today.'

'Thanks, dear ole Dad wouldn't let me take my church dress off.' Grinning, Dani hooked her thumb at the man next to her.

'How do you do? I'm Mike Conrad. You must be the mysterious investigator who moved in upstairs. My daughter tells me you have your own gun-packing bodyguard.'

As Jill tried to make sense out of the ridiculous claim, Eric interrupted. 'She'll get back to you about that, Mike.' Eric took Jill gently by the arm. 'There's one more person who wants to meet you. This is my mother, Irena Manfredi. Mom, this is Jill Wyatt.'

For a moment, Jill stared at his elegant mother. She was tall, at least five-seven, and svelte. Other than her nose and cheekbones, she didn't *fit* with the rest of the family. Irena Manfredi looked like she stepped off an Italian fashion shoot instead of a restaurant's kitchen. And the woman had certainly never eaten a carb in her life.

'How do you do?' Jill asked when Eric nudged her shoulder.

'Nonni tells me if not for you our restaurant might have burned to the ground. Thank you, Miss Wyatt.'

'You're welcome, but I'm afraid your mom exaggerated. All I did was slap a lid on to a skillet. Plus Eric was only a few steps away.'

The woman's smile barely caused a ripple in her perfect skin. 'Nonni is my *husband's* mother. My mother lives in Milan. But accept our heartfelt gratitude regardless. Anything we have at any time is yours.' Irena flourished a well-manicured hand first at the buffet and then at the assortment of imported wines lined up on the bar. 'You'll have to excuse me, but we'll talk again soon.' Her smile revealed perfect teeth to go with her perfect designer suit.

When Irena walked away to greet new arrivals, Jill forgot she wasn't alone. 'Wow,' she murmured under her breath.

'She does have that effect on people,' Eric whispered in her ear. 'In case you're curious, I take after my dad unfortunately.'

'I figured that out on my own.' Jill offered a wry grin, while Eric laughed from the belly.

'If you'll excuse me, it's my job to make sure under-age cousins don't come anywhere near the wine. But don't you dare leave without eating some of the cuisine you helped prepare.'

Jill watched as he strode away, a full head taller than the others in the room. Some men slapped him on the back; one older woman pinched his bicep, and the young girls smiled coyly, perhaps practicing for their dating years. Eric Manfredi was definitely popular among the extended family.

With so much commotion, she could have easily slipped into the kitchen and up the steps to her own room. Then she could have read, or called Beth, or watched the traffic on East Bay Street from her window. But instead she watched the festivities, under the auspices of replenishing the buffet table. Whenever she spotted the linguini getting low or the *cavatelli* bowl almost empty, she sent her new friend, Dani, to tell her uncle. Within fifteen minutes, the pasta bowl was refilled as the crowd ebbed and flowed all afternoon.

From her vantage point, two things struck Jill as odd. First, the guest of honor, the senior Mr Manfredi, wasn't there, yet it seemed to be business as usual. New guests arrived, inquired as to his condition, and then continued to socialize as if nothing were amiss. Secondly, it seemed that everyone older than twenty-five stuck their nose into everyone else's business.

I heard you didn't get accepted at Duke. What was the problem – did your grades slip during your senior year?

I'm sooo glad you're not dating Roger any more. I think I spotted his photo hanging up at the post office.

And in Jill's estimation, the absolute worst: *When are you and Danny going to start a family? You two have been married for two full years.*

What business was it of that woman's? When Jill began

observing the party, she envied all the affection being shown. These Manfredis weren't shy about hugging or cheek-kissing or giving bear hugs that could injure a spine. But when she overheard so many rude questions Jill felt glad she was from a small family with distinct boundaries.

When activity at the buffet table waned and bowls remained full, Jill thanked Danielle and climbed the steps to her room, without fixing a plate of food. Despite having helped all afternoon, she didn't feel entitled to a meal with the Manfredis.

Or maybe she just wasn't that hungry.

Or maybe the fact she hadn't seen Eric in two hours had something to do with it.

Instead Jill popped a bowl of microwave popcorn and had just curled up in front of the TV when someone knocked loudly. When she opened the door, Danielle marched into her room without waiting to be invited.

'Hi, Jill, I can't believe you actually locked the door. Nobody's ever done that before.' Dani reached for the bowl of popcorn and began to eat.

'That's because I'm not a Manfredi, visiting from out of town.' Jill smiled at the girl. 'By all means, help yourself.'

'Plenty of us aren't Manfredis. I'm a Conrad.' She shoved another handful into her mouth. 'By the way, my mom wants to speak to you in the courtyard.'

'What does she want to talk about?' Inexplicably, Jill's stomach tied into a knot.

'I haven't a clue. You'll find out when you get there. She probably wants to thank you for helping out. Grandma was real pleased.'

'I barely saw Nonni today,' Jill said. 'Somebody mentioned she wasn't feeling well.'

Dani looked at her oddly. '*Nonni* is my great-grandmother. My grandma was the one wearing the navy Oscar de la Renta suit.'

'Of course, I forgot. Tell her I'm on my way.'

'OK if I eat the rest of the popcorn? I'll leave the bowl on the steps when I'm done.'

'Sure, I've got plenty.' Jill slipped her bare feet into flip flops and ran a brush through her tangled hair. Then she followed Danielle down the stairs and out the kitchen's back door.

As she crossed the courtyard, a bright full moon reflected off the polished flagstones. Several candles glowed on a bistro table set for dinner under the grape pergola. But it wasn't Bernie Conrad waiting to chat. Sitting at the table was the head chef and her landlord, Eric Manfredi.

'What's going on?' Jill asked, closing the distance with long strides. 'Dani said her mom wanted to talk to me.'

Eric pulled out the opposite chair. 'That was a ploy to get you to eat dinner. If you knew I would be your companion you might not have come.'

'Look, don't take this wrong, but I don't like being manipulated. I rented a suite from you. While I'm in town, I'm not looking for late-night dates under the stars.'

'How could I *possibly* take that wrong?' Eric glanced at his watch. 'It's not even close to being late, and this certainly isn't a date.' He fluffed a linen napkin over his lap and pulled the cover off his dinner plate.

'Then what's with the romantic candlelight?' she demanded.

'It's got nothing to do with romance. Why should I waste electricity by lighting the entire courtyard for two people?' He forked up some *cavatelli* and met her gaze. 'What *this is*, or what I had in mind was two hardworking people sharing a meal. My niece said you didn't eat all day.'

Jill folded her arms. 'What did you give me – eggplant or chicken?'

'A little of both, same with the pasta. I wanted you to sample your handiwork and mine.' He finished chewing and dabbed his mouth. 'But if you're afraid, carry your plate to your room. Fine with me.'

After several moments of watching him eat, Jill lowered herself into the other chair and lifted the cover. 'Sorry if I misjudged you. This looks good, Eric. Thanks.'

'It *looks* the same as it did this afternoon. You better get started since we both have things to do tonight.' He devoted his full attention to his dinner.

'Why didn't you eat earlier?' Jill cut her chicken into small pieces.

'Nonni asked me to take her back to the hospital. She likes visiting her son without a crowd.'

'You're a good grandson.'

Eric sopped up some sauce with a crust of bread. 'And you are the most confusing woman I've ever met. Five minutes ago you were acting like Jack the Ripper had lured you to a deadly rendezvous.' He tossed his napkin down next to his plate.

'Look, I know I was rude and I'm trying to make up for it.' Jill's voice rose in volume to match his. 'Maybe I'm just not good with polite dinner conversation.'

Slowly, Eric's mouth twitched into a smile. 'OK, after meeting your best friend and sometimes partner, I understand. All is forgiven, but I still have a dozen things to do tonight and I'm already bone-tired.'

Jill replaced the cover on her plate and rose to her feet. 'I'll eat this in my room. I couldn't finish it now if my life depended on it.'

Eric blew out the candles and carried his empty plate, while she carried her almost full one inside Bella Trattoria. 'Good night, Jill. Thanks again for helping out today.'

'It was my pleasure,' she said as sincerely as she knew how. 'I truly enjoyed meeting your family.'

'You have a standing invitation to join us any night of the week.' Without giving Jill a backward glance, Eric placed his dirty dishes in the sink and strolled through the swinging doors into the restaurant.

Jill stood alone in the dark, empty kitchen feeling more embarrassed than the time she threw up at her birthday party. *What's wrong with me – a lack of charm school during my formative years?*

She tried to eat dinner while watching TV, but the chicken tasted dry, the salad was soggy, and the pasta stuck in her throat. Only the eggplant parmigiana was delicious. After finishing every bite of Eric's creation, she flushed everything else down the toilet. Hopefully, she wouldn't cause a major sewer crisis in Charleston, but she didn't dare offend her landlord any more than she already had.

* * *

Jill was actually glad to see Monday morning. How many people can say that when they first wake up? It was a work day and work seemed to be the only thing she was good at.

Her next step in the case was to consult the website for the South Carolina Department of Social Services, the government agency overseeing adoptions in this state. After carrying her coffee and bowl of cereal to the courtyard, Jill found pretty much everything she needed to know from their website. All interested parties – adoptee, birth parent, or adoptive parent – must file an affidavit allowing their personal information to be released. If any one of the three refuses consent, it's a no-go. This wasn't the answer Jill had hoped for on behalf of the Sugarmans. For hours, she scanned page after page of organizations that set up private adoptions for a fee, others that provided assistance to expectant mothers, and lists of attorneys that specialized in foreign or domestic adoptions.

Unfortunately, she found no list of attorneys willing to break the law to help a dying woman.

When Bella employees started setting up the courtyard for lunch, Jill moved to her sitting room and called one lawyer after another. After providing a brief overview of what she sought, she couldn't seem to get past the legal assistants. Finally, on Jill's ninth recitation of the pertinent details, an attorney, Jacqueline Devereaux of Kiawah, took her call.

'I'm not sure what help I can be, Miss Wyatt. South Carolina laws are quite specific regarding privacy. If one or more parties refuse contact, our hands are tied.'

'My client was in contact with her natural mother some time ago. The woman indicated she gave birth to two daughters, but she has since passed on. Wouldn't the death of the natural mother make a difference?'

'Not if your client wishes to contact a sibling that doesn't wish to be found.'

'And the fact this is a life-or-death situation makes no difference?'

'Your only hope would be a court order to unseal the records, but frankly, that's very unlikely. As much as I sympathize with your client, I see no legal way to track down this sibling.'

Jill thanked the helpful Miss Devereaux and hung up.

For several minutes she stared into space, while weighing the legal, moral, and ethical ramifications of the situation. After all, wasn't privacy an allusion in this day and age? Bad people hacked into databases all the time to impersonate, to steal, or to create havoc. All she wanted was to ask one woman one question. If after knowing the facts, the woman said no, then so be it. Jill wouldn't have to release any details to the Sugarmans.

Jill knew she was rationalizing, trying to justify a mistake that could cost her a job. But in the end she dug the birth certificate and her cell phone from her purse and dialed Michael Preston, the agency's forensic accountant and computer guru.

'Hey, Michael. It's Jill Wyatt, remember me?'

'Oh, yeah,' he teased. 'Didn't we shoot tin cans from a fence rail not long ago?'

'I need a favor. I want you to track down Baby Girl Allston, born to Gail Allston in North Charleston sometime around 1991. Standard methods of locating this woman have failed. I need you to work your magic.'

Michael hesitated for a second time. 'And you've already run this by the boss?'

'No, but this is solely for my use. The client won't gain access to this information, nor will it become part of my official case report. No one will ask how I came by the information.'

'Oh, boy,' he drawled. 'I hope I don't live to regret this, but I'll see what I can find out.'

'Thanks. Please give Beth my best.' Jill hung up feeling like a heel for putting Michael on the spot – something she had been doing a lot lately.

With little else to do until Michael called her back, Jill put on jogging shoes and slipped out the back door. Usually a long walk cleared her head and allowed her to see a situation more clearly. Was Eric only trying to be nice and not trying to flirt? If that was the case, she had not only offended him but had made a fool of herself. Someone who looked like Eric usually didn't need to stalk their tenants to get a date.

Jill jogged up one cobblestoned street in the historic area and down the next. The closer she got to the water, the larger and more impressive the mansions became. Jill couldn't imagine a modern family living in any of these four-story homes without a dozen full-time workers. Each time she picked out her favorite, along came an even grander home.

In a little shop on Market Street, she drank two cups of coffee and rested her sore feet. But at least in return for her sore feet, Jill had reached a conclusion: The idea of the head chef of Bella Trattoria flirting with her was ludicrous. So it wouldn't kill her to be a little friendlier while she was living there.

SEVEN

Eric plated the last two servings of chicken saltimbocca and signaled for Lilian, the waitress who had placed the order. Checking his watch and squinting at the kitchen monitor, their final reservation had been served. Now any walk-ins would only be allowed to order from a limited menu, plus desserts, cocktails, or any of a dozen types of cappuccinos. Eight thirty, quitting time for the Manfredi family who started work early. Now the paid staff would finish up and close the restaurant.

He wiped down his prep surfaces, loaded his utensils into the dishwasher, and stripped off his hat and chef's coat. Night staff would scrub his pots and pans and clean the entire kitchen. When he finished washing up in the employee lounge, his grandmother and Aunt Estelle, their pastry chef, were already seated at the family table, while his sister carried over napkins, silverware, and a basket of rolls.

'You're dining with us tonight – to what do we owe the pleasure?' Eric nodded at his sister as he took his place at the table.

'Mike went to Columbia on business, so I thought it would be good to spend more time with my family.' Bernie buzzed a kiss across Nonni's silvery head.

'What Mom really means, Uncle Eric, is she doesn't want

to cook for just her and me while Dad's out of town.' Danielle materialized from the back hall where she had shrugged off half her school uniform.

'Why should I dirty *my* kitchen when this one already is?' Bernie carried the bowl of Caprese salad from the fridge. 'Psst, Eric, don't look now, but someone wants to talk to you.' She hooked her thumb toward the far wall.

Eric pivoted in his chair. 'Ah, Miss Wyatt, have you decided to throw caution to the wind and dine with the Manfredis?'

'Yes, I have.' Jill took a few hesitant steps toward the table.

'Hi, Jill!' Dani scrambled to her feet.

'Stay!' Eric commanded his niece.

'Don't be afraid. It's just lasagna with a tomato salad. The roasted eel with seaweed was last night.' He lifted out the casserole, set it in the center of the table, and pulled out a chair. 'Let's put you here.'

'Thanks, after last night I'm glad I'm still welcome.' Jill took the seat next to his niece. 'I'm afraid I jumped to all kinds of silly conclusions.'

'For thinking I set you up with Uncle Eric?' asked Dani.

Jill's mouth dropped open.

'Unfortunately, Jill, there are no secrets under this roof.' Eric held out the casserole. 'How about some lasagna?'

While Jill scooped a small portion, Nonni shook her finger at him. 'Why shouldn't you date someone with a head on her shoulders for a change? That last woman thought Sicily was a suburb of New York,' added Nonni under her breath.

Eric adroitly changed the subject as he offered Jill the bowl of Caprese salad. 'Speaking of geography, how do you like Charleston so far?'

'It's beautiful,' said Jill. 'But so much larger than I thought. I'm never leaving the house without a map again.' She held up a mozzarella ball on her fork to inspect.

'I have a great map you can keep,' said Eric. 'That's fresh mozzarella, by the way.'

'Really? I thought they only put mozzarella on pizza.' Jill popped it in her mouth. 'It's delicious.'

'Caprese is finally starting to catch on in America.' Nonni

shook her piece of garlic bread. 'Europeans have eaten it for years.'

'Speaking of new traditions,' said Dani. 'At what age, Jill, do you think girls should be allowed to pick out their own clothes?'

While his tenant considered, Eric slashed a finger across his throat. Unfortunately, Jill didn't look his way.

'I guess sixteen is old enough, providing the girl earns her own money. Otherwise, her parents should make the decision while she lives under their roof.' Jill smiled at Bernie, as though hoping for approval.

'See, Mom. Even Jill thinks I should choose my junior prom dress.' Danielle's brows knit together. 'I earned every penny for it babysitting.'

Bernie chewed her food thoroughly and swallowed. 'I appreciate Jill's opinion, but unfortunately the Conrad family isn't a democracy. If your dad says the dress is too low-cut, back to the mall it goes. Period.' His sister's expression didn't encourage further discussion.

'Now that *that's* settled, did you make any progress in your case today?' Eric directed his question at Jill.

'None whatsoever,' she said. 'I hope to hear something helpful soon from our office's computer expert.'

'Well, I've got a story to tell.' After scooping another portion of lasagna, Aunt Estelle launched into a convoluted tale about her next-door neighbor, Mrs Brockman, a woman none of them knew. For the next fifteen minutes, Estelle explained in detail the woman's fall in the back garden, subsequent hospitalization, and rehabilitation regimen.

Throughout Estelle's saga, Eric stole glances at Jill, but she was either intrigued by the story or a very good actress.

'I hope Mrs Brockman makes a quick recovery,' Jill said when Estelle finally wrapped up the story.

'Yes,' added Eric. 'Let me know if we can send over meals for her. Now, does anyone want dessert or coffee?' His gaze flitted around the table, landing on Jill.

'Not me, I'm stuffed.' Dani jumped up to start clearing the table.

'Ugh, I've got indigestion.' Nonni stood and moved slowly from the kitchen.

'Not for me either,' said Jill. 'But I want to help you clean up before I head upstairs.'

'We've got this, Jill, but I would like a word with you.' Eric practically dragged Jill away from the table. When they reached the bottom of the steps, he burst out laughing. 'Sorry, that had to be the worst dinner of your life.'

'Not by a long shot. I enjoyed it once we got past the prom-dress crisis.' A smile filled Jill's face. 'The food was wonderful and everyone was so . . . straightforward. There's no beating around the bush in your family.'

'The Manfredis are nothing if not forthright.' Eric picked lint off his sweater so she wouldn't see how happy her comment made him. 'Join us whenever you can, but be prepared for anything.'

'I'll keep that in mind. Thanks.'

Briefly, he considered asking the question on his mind all day: *Would you really say no if I asked you out?*

But suddenly her phone rang and his golden moment was gone. 'That could be our office tech expert. Good night, Eric.' Jill bolted up the steps.

He had lost his chance. But as things turned out at Bella Trattoria, it was for the best.

'Michael?' Jill asked, picking up the phone.

'Just getting ready to leave you a message. I have Baby Girl Allston's new name and address. Got something to write with?'

Jill fumbled in her purse for pen and paper. 'Yep.'

'Baby Girl Allston was adopted by a Steve and Betsy Cross who renamed her Emma. She is now Emma Norris, married to Ralph. The family lives on Chester Road in Orchard, South Carolina.'

'Where's that?'

'I have no clue. You're on your own. Hey, how is life above the restaurant?'

'Great. I just shared an amusing meal with my landlord's family.'

'Beth won't like hearing that.'

Jill remembered Beth's distrust of Eric. 'You're right. So let's keep that tidbit between us. Thanks for your research.'

'You're welcome. I just hope this doesn't come back to bite me.'

'I promise it won't.'

Jill hung up, already regretting the promise she might not be able to keep. That night she tossed and turned for hours. When she finally fell asleep, she slept fitfully until the smoke alarm woke her for the second time in two days. She bolted upright and glanced at the clock. *Four a.m.? No one was cooking at this hour.*

Jill remembered seeing emergency instructions hanging on the wall:

> **In case of fire, do not open your door. Exit through the double window on to the porch roof and approach the edge cautiously. Remove metal ladder from storage box, lower over edge of roof, and cautiously proceed down ladder backwards to the ground.**

Oh, is that all? Jill didn't like heights. She liked ladders even less. And the idea of proceeding down a swinging ladder absolutely terrified her. So instead Jill chose the stairs directly to the kitchen. But when she pressed her ear to the door, she heard the distinct sound of sirens in the distance, along with the blaring smoke alarm at the base of the steps. This was no false alarm.

Jill ran back to the dormer, pushed open the double window, and uttered a short but to-the-point prayer: *Please Lord, don't let me break my neck on this ladder.* It wasn't much of a prayer, but she was a novice and didn't have much time.

Kneeling on the upholstered seat, she stuck one leg out, clutched the frame, ducked her head, and maneuvered her body through the opening. Slowly, she rose to an upright position. But when the smell of acrid smoke hit her nostrils, Jill forced her feet to move toward the dark precipice. Operating fully on adrenaline, Jill reached the storage box, pulled out the ladder, and dropped it over the edge.

Don't think. Don't look down. Just go.

Dropping on to her belly, Jill scuttled like a crab to the

edge. Then she blindly felt around for the first rung as the ladder swung wildly.

'Stay where you are, Miss,' shouted a voice from below.

She froze and released the breath she hadn't realized she'd been holding. 'Thank you, Jesus.' Jill whispered words she'd heard her mother use many times. Frankly, she'd thought her Mom was rude to address him so personally.

'Miss Wyatt, are you on the roof?' called the voice.

'Who are you?' she asked, rather stupidly.

'I'm Captain Lewis of the Charleston Fire Department. Don't come down the ladder. We've fully extinguished the blaze and a firefighter will be with you shortly.'

True to the captain's word, someone soon stuck their head through the open bedroom window. But in full rescue equipment including breathing apparatus, the person looked more like an astronaut than a firefighter. He pushed up his facemask to speak. 'Stay where you are, Miss Wyatt, and I'll help you get back.'

Jill did exactly as she was told. She didn't move a muscle until the fireman reached her side and coaxed her across the roof, step by step. 'Aren't you a sight for sore eyes,' said Jill once safely inside her room, which was surprisingly smoke-free.

'Do you feel lightheaded or faint? Would you like some oxygen?' He offered her his mask.

'No, I'm fine. But if that fire is down there, I want outta here.' Jill spoke a bit louder than necessary.

'Shall I carry you down the stairs and out the door?' he asked, steadying her arm.

'Did the steps burn?'

'Not at all. Fire was contained inside the kitchen.'

'Then let's just go. I'll follow you.' Jill grabbed her purse and briefcase and held on to him until they reached the courtyard.

'You're safe now, Miss Wyatt,' said the fireman. After a few moments, he gently pried Jill's fingers from his arm. 'There is no danger, but *everyone* must remain outdoors. No going back inside *for any reason*.' Once she nodded her comprehension, he returned to the flurry of activity.

'Jill! Thank goodness, you're all right.' Eric Manfredi materialized from the smoke and chaos.

When he tried to embrace her, Jill jumped back as though bit by a snake. 'What's going on here? Are you some kind of pyromaniac?' she spat.

'Of course not, I was asleep at my condo. I'm as confused about this as you.' Eric looked stricken.

'Then how could you get here so fast?' Jill thumped her fist against his chest.

'I only live two blocks away. Whenever the alarm is triggered, I'm automatically called along with the fire department.' Eric's eyes flashed in anger.

Jill stopped thumping his chest and held up her hands. 'OK, but two fires in two days? The coincidence is a bit much for me. I may need to rethink my temporary address.'

'I understand perfectly.' Eric spoke without meeting her eyes. 'I'll see that your deposit is returned and reimburse any losses you suffer from smoke damage. Now if you'll excuse me, I need to check on my grandmother. Captain Lewis will let you know when we can go inside.' Eric stomped across the courtyard to where Nonni sat at a back table.

When Jill saw the elderly woman waiting without a bit of hysteria or overreaction, she was embarrassed. But then again, not everyone is afraid of both heights and ladders.

Jill found an out-of-the-way spot to watch fire personnel come and go from the building with much conversation but little drama. Ninety minutes later, Captain Lewis approached her table under the magnolia.

'You may now return to your suite, Miss. Thanks to the sprinkler system, the fire caused no structural damage to the support beams or floor joists, although the restaurant will remain closed for a while.'

'Thank you, sir. And please thank the brave firefighter who rescued me. I will need to go upstairs to pack. Hopefully, my clothes won't smell too much like smoke.' In light of his department's heroic endeavors, it was a very stupid thing to say.

'I hope so too, Miss Wyatt.'

Not wanting to see Eric, Jill hurried up to her room. Although her room now smelled of smoke, surprisingly the clothes in closets and drawers had barely picked up the scent at all. Wisely, the fireman had pulled the door shut behind them when they left.

She took a long, hot shower to wash off the soot and regain her composure. Then she slinked out of Bella Trattoria to her car. With each passing minute, Jill regretted her harsh words to Eric. She of all people should know bad things often happened to good people. But she had lashed out at a man who'd been nothing but sweet to her. After practically accusing Eric of attempted murder, her packed bags would most likely be waiting by the time she got back.

Jill grabbed breakfast at a drive-thru and punched the town of Orchard into the Toyota's GPS. It was time to get out of town . . . and do her job.

EIGHT

Jill had no trouble finding the town, but that was the extent of her success. Chester Road was unknown to her sophisticated GPS system and it certainly didn't appear on the South Carolina map in her atlas. After driving around aimlessly, she stopped in the Lazy Bear Diner for lunch and remembered sage advice from her mentor: *If you need local information, find a diner, sit at the counter, and for goodness sake, smile . . .*

Jill not only ate the best meatloaf sandwich of her life, the waitress she chatted Atlanta Braves with turned out to be Emma Cross's pal from high school.

'So what brings you to the middle of nowhere and how do you know Emma?' asked the waitress once they exhausted the topic of baseball.

'I don't know her very well, but I got a flat tire on their road a few years ago. I was lost at the time. Ralph changed the tire and pointed me in the right direction. Emma told me to stop back if I'm ever in the area.' Jill hoped her aversion to lying didn't show on her face. 'I'm on my way to Charlotte with a little time on my hands, so I thought I'd take the scenic route. Trouble is I can't seem to find Chester Road to stop in and say "hi."' She produced the slip of paper with the Norrises address.

'Whoa, you're not kidding about a scenic route to Charlotte.' The waitress walked away to refill a few cups, but returned with a faded township map. 'Chester is this dotted line, because the road's not paved.' She tapped with one long nail. 'But you won't find a mailbox with an address. There's no delivery out there. They must be living in her parents' old house. Once you turn down Chester, watch for the first drive past an old sycamore tree. It's a very long driveway so don't get scared. Tell Emma that Frannie Davis sends her regards. I haven't seen her since she got married and changed churches.'

I'm supposed to find a certain tree? Jill wasn't sure if she'd stepped into *The Twilight Zone* or *The Waltons.* 'I will be sure to – and thanks.' She slipped the map into her purse, took a last bite of sandwich, and left a large tip. Unfortunately when she walked out of Lazy Bear the light drizzle had changed to a downpour.

Armed with the local map, Jill successfully found Chester Road, but the rain had changed the hard-packed surface to a sloppy mess. After googling what a sycamore tree looked like, she located their driveway easily. Few trees grew among the acres of cotton for as far as the eye could see. But mustering the courage to drive up another dirt road with no house visible was another matter. She considered texting Beth with her whereabouts, but the lack of cell coverage ended that plan.

Jill paused at the mouth of their driveway. *Surely Emma can't be a serial killer if she attends church and knows nice people like Frannie.* So she took a deep breath and guided her Toyota around deep ruts and puddles of standing water for more than half a mile. When a two-story white farmhouse appeared around the next turn, Jill breathed a sigh of relief. Green shutters framed the windows and red flowers overflowed several pots on the porch. Serial killers never planted marigolds along the walkway.

But some of her confidence waned as Jill climbed the front

steps. Two of the porch boards were rotted, while several cracked windows had been repaired with duct tape. Up close the homestead gave the appearance of poverty or neglect or both. As she contemplated fleeing back to her car, a tiny face peeked through the curtains. When Jill knocked, a young girl not much older than Joan Sugarman opened the door.

'Who are you?' she asked.

'I'm Miss Jill Wyatt. Is your mom home?' She realized too late her real name might not have been a good idea.

'Go upstairs with your brother, daughter. You've got spelling to do.' A tall woman with a baby in her arms appeared in the doorway. The child scampered off without a word of argument. 'May I help you?'

The woman had the strongest accent Jill had ever heard and, without a doubt, bore a strong resemblance to Charlotte Sugarman. 'Hi, are you Emma Norris? I'm a friend of Frannie Davis. She thought you might be able to help me or at least point me in the right direction.'

One of Emma's sparse eyebrows arched. 'Are you lost?'

'No, my husband and I are looking for land to buy.' Jill was amazed how easily the lies rolled off her tongue.

'There's a real estate office in Kingstree. They're your best bet for farms for sale around here.' Emma started to close the door.

Jill reacted quickly. 'Please, I've already talked with an agent. You are my last hope.'

'Why is that?'

'All the farms 'round here are too expensive for us. We're looking for ten or twelve acres of privacy, with no road frontage. A place my husband could build a cabin and small barn – more of a subsistence farm than income producing.'

'Good you don't have false hope.' Emma issued a wry laugh. 'There's no money to be made in cotton these days. Ralph barely clears enough profit to pay our taxes.'

'Frannie thought you might be willing to sell a dozen acres or might know one of your neighbors.' Jill produced her most earnest expression.

As Emma studied her, Jill was glad she wore a skirt and blouse instead of a suit. 'I suppose you could get out of the rain for a spell.' Emma motioned her in. 'Please have a seat.'

Jill walked into a spotless living room straight from the movie *Witness*, complete with oil lamps, rocking chair, and a threadbare braided rug. She perched on a sofa that hadn't been in style for years, guessing the Norris family inherited the farm and had changed nothing since. 'That's one huge fireplace,' said Jill, feeling Emma's gaze on her. 'I bet it keeps the downstairs toasty warm.'

'Actually that fireplace heats the entire house.' Emma pointed to grates in the ceiling. 'Heat rises to the second floor. With plenty of firewood in the back acres we'll always have free heat as long as our chainsaw works.'

'That's what my husband and I want too – no utility bills. You have a well for water?'

Emma nodded. 'Plus a spring-fed pond for crops and livestock.'

'I bet you grow all your own food.'

'No one can provide everything a family needs, but I have a large garden, fruit trees, chickens, pigs, and a few cows.'

'But what about your stove and fridge?' Jill tried her best to sound like a would-be new farmer.

'They run on propane.' Emma shifted her infant as the baby began to whimper.

'Do you mean you live without electricity?'

She shook her head. 'We got an electric pump on the well, plus lights we seldom turn on. Right now our windmill and backup generator provide what we need, but we could tie into the grid if necessary. Plus I bought this electric carving knife at the Goodwill store that comes in handy when Ralph bags a deer.' Emma beamed with pleasure.

'Those truly are wonderful inventions.' Jill glanced around the TV-less room. 'And you sure don't need cable.'

'Nope, me and the kids go to the library once a month for all the entertainment we need.'

'Good idea. What about schools in the area? Does a bus come down Chester Road?' Jill laced her fingers over her belly as though she had a reason to ask. But with the false insinuation, her gut took a queasy turn.

'It does not. I teach my kids at home.' Emma's friendly expression faded. 'Ain't that the reason you want backland in the middle of nowhere – so nobody tells you what to teach your children?'

'That's what my husband says, but I don't know if I'm smart enough to be a teacher.'

'The library has all kinds of stuff that makes the job pretty easy. Don't worry 'bout that. The librarian will help you plan a curriculum.' Emma shifted the fussy baby to her other hip. 'Look, Miss Wyatt. I don't think Ralph wants to sell any land, but I will ask when he gets home. I'll check with my neighbors too. You got an answering machine? If I come across any cheap land for sale, I could leave a message when I go to town for the mail.'

'I do have an answering machine. That would be really nice of you.' As Jill dug in her purse for something to write down her number the queasiness ratcheted up a notch.

'I'll get some paper.' Emma jumped to her feet. 'Say, you want some iced tea? I got oatmeal cookies too unless my son finished them off.'

'No, thanks. I ate lunch at the diner where Frannie works.'

While her hostess was gone, Jill took another perusal of the room. The Norrises seemed to live an austere but wholesome life. The children were being fed, clothed, and educated. *Who says everyone needs Netflix, ballet lessons, and soccer games?* She realized her unsettled stomach stemmed not from the meatloaf, but from her steady stream of lies. Why hadn't Beth prepared her for this aspect of PI work? An investigator often had to be a masterful liar.

'Here we are.' Emma set a tray down with two glasses of tea and two cookies, in addition to the pen and paper. 'Just a bit of dessert after your lunch. Food still good at Lazy Bear? I heard that's where Frannie worked now that her youngest is in school. Is she still as pretty as ever? Frannie had her pick of boyfriends in high school.' Emma picked up one glass and drank deeply. It was as though a floodgate had been opened and she wanted to make up for lost time.

Unable to deceive someone who'd showed her nothing but kindness another minute, Jill gripped the arm of the sofa and struggled to her feet. 'Yes, Frannie *is* still very pretty, but I never laid eyes on the woman before today. I tricked her into telling me where you lived, just like I used false pretenses to gain entry to your home.'

'Why on earth would you do that?' Emma blinked her large blue eyes.

'Because I wanted to talk to you and I knew your family liked privacy.'

'So you're not looking to buy backland?' Emma placed the sleeping infant into the cradle next to her chair.

'I'm not. I am also not married and not expecting a baby. What I am is a big liar. I wasn't raised like this and I'm ashamed of myself.' Apparently, Jill's own floodgate had opened wide. 'I'll leave you in peace if that's what you want.'

'What I want is for you to tell me *why*. Is Jill Wyatt even your name?'

'It is. That's one of the few truthful things I told you.'

'It's time for you to tell me a few more.' Emma crossed her arms over her print dress.

'I'm a private investigator who came up from Savannah to find you. Apparently, I'm a bad PI since telling a bunch of lies gives me a bellyache.'

'Who on earth would pay you to find a cotton farmer's wife with three ordinary kids? Is there a reservoir of oil under our property or maybe a goldmine?'

Jill locked gazes with the woman. She should keep quiet and simply pass the information on to Mr Sugarman. After all, she'd been paid to find Baby Girl Allston, not become a liaison for possible organ donation. But Jill couldn't do that. 'The husband of your natural sister – your birth sister – paid me to find you because your sister wants to meet you.'

Emma dropped heavily into the chair next to the cradle. 'We told the Department of Social Services we didn't want to meet anyone from the past.'

'Yes, and they have honored your wishes all these years. I found you in a rather roundabout way that didn't involve a government agency.'

For a while the ticking of the mantel clock was the only sound in the room. Then Emma said, 'I'm sorry you wasted your time and this husband wasted his money by hiring you. My answer remains the same.'

'Even if your birth sister is very sick?'

Emma's eyes rounded, but before she could utter a syllable, a gruff voice spoke from the doorway. 'I believe my wife made herself very clear.' A man who could only be Ralph Norris stepped into the room.

'How long have you been standing there?' Emma asked.

'Long enough to know it's time for Miss Wyatt to leave before I call the sheriff.'

Interesting how hubby has a cell phone, but his wife can only make phone calls while in town. 'I'm leaving. Again, Emma, I apologize for tricking you into talking to me.'

'Goodbye, Jill. Perhaps you can find a job that doesn't involve so much deception.'

Perhaps, indeed. Jill couldn't get into her car and down the driveway fast enough. She had messed up. Hopefully the Williamsburg County Sheriff wouldn't chase her halfway back to Charleston. Jill was so unnerved by meeting Ralph Norris she forgot her current situation until she reached the historic district. Hadn't she told Eric she would pack her bags and move out? Not tonight she wasn't. All she wanted to do was crawl up the steps and climb into bed, whether it still smelled of smoke or not. Unfortunately, when Jill approached the back entrance she heard several voices raised in anger.

Jill plunked down at a courtyard table to wait. If the Manfredis were arguing, this wouldn't be a good time to walk inside.

Eric had to get out of that kitchen before he said something he'd regret to the people he loved most. His friends had warned him that going into business with family was a big mistake. Too bad he hadn't listened. Considering his grandmother's age and everything she had lived through, he expected Nonni to not want the police involved. But even his mother was being unreasonable, insisting his father wouldn't want this. And his sister's penchant for playing 'Switzerland' during family arguments wasn't helping his cause.

When the cool air of the courtyard hit his face, Eric considered a walk around the block. But after the most exhausting day of his life, instead he slumped into a chair and dropped his head into his hands. For several blissful minutes he simply breathed in and out without thinking about anything, until the clearing of a throat jerked him from his nirvana.

Eric's head swiveled around until he spotted Jill under a tree. 'Jill, what are you doing out here?'

'When I returned after seeing my client, I heard your family . . . discussing something. So I decided to give you some privacy.'

'*Discussing* . . . what a polite word you chose.' Eric thumped his forehead on the metal table.

'Truly, I wasn't eavesdropping. That's why I'm way back here.'

He lifted his focus to the woman he had once planned to ask out. 'It wouldn't have been a problem, since you're moving out.'

'Not tonight I'm not. I just had the worst day of my life.' Surprisingly, Jill got up and sat down at his table.

'We have that in common.' Eric plucked leaves from a drooping magnolia which had been battered by the firefighters.

'How extensive was the damage?'

'Luckily the fire was contained within the kitchen. But since the heat triggered sprinklers in the pantry, hallway, and employee lounge those areas will have to be repaired as well.'

'Has the fire department finished their report? Can restoration work start tomorrow?'

Eric tried to fathom a reason for her interest, but he was too tired. 'No, not until the State Fire Marshal inspects the kitchen for arson.'

'Does Captain Lewis think an arsonist set the fire?'

'It's what *I* think. Of course, this morning you accused me of pyromania.'

Jill wrung her hands. 'I said that because I was upset. I'm scared to death of heights and ladders.'

'So you no longer think I torched the place?' Eric refused to drop the matter.

'The restaurant obviously makes money. Why would you want to put yourself out of business? And you certainly wouldn't call someone who investigates fires for a living. I'm sorry I overreacted.'

'We seem to be trading apologies, Miss Wyatt.'

'It's Jill. Care to tell me what the argument was about? Maybe I can help.'

'Why not? I've got nothing to lose.' With a weary sigh, Eric slicked a hand through his hair. 'My mother and grandmother didn't want the police involved. They say the sooner we get a contractor here to make repairs, the sooner we can reopen. An arson inspection will only slow down the process. The insurance company won't pay if someone else can be held responsible.'

'I see your mother's point,' Jill said. 'A closed business generates no profits.'

'Absolutely, but think about it, Jill. Nonni was in her room down the hall. You were asleep upstairs, so I set the alarm. Danielle, Bernie, and I were home. *No one* was cooking at that hour of night. Today I talked to our night cleaners. They were positive no burners were left on, no candles were burning.'

'But someone would have needed a key to get in, right? It sure wasn't me who started it.'

'That's why I insisted on an arson inspection and the wheels are already in motion.'

'Without talking to your parents first? No wonder I heard all that shouting.'

'Arson is a very serious crime. The fire chief probably would have requested one anyway. There was no logical explanation.'

'Nevertheless, I'm surprised there were no fisticuffs.' Jill leaned forward so he could see her smirk.

'Just wait until my father gets home.' Eric tilted back his head to gaze at the sky. 'But seriously, this is our only chance to find out the truth.'

Jill remained quiet for so long, he thought she might have fallen asleep sitting up. 'Do you think the fire might be related to the other stuff happening around here?'

A spike of apprehension ran up Eric's spine. He would do well to remember his tenant was also a private investigator. 'What other stuff?'

'The overturned dumpster in the alley and your dad getting clubbed in the head and robbed. The level of violence seems to be escalating.'

'Since you've only lived here a short while, it's natural to make a connection.' Eric tried to sound philosophical. 'But the dumpster was a prank by teenagers who find that sort of thing funny. The robbers were thugs, who unfortunately can be found in any city after dark. This . . . .' he hooked his thumb at the building, 'was the work of someone far more calculating than a mugger or a bored kid.'

Jill pushed up from the table. 'That makes sense, especially since your grandmother and I could have died, besides your beautiful trattoria burning to the ground.'

'And for that I'm truly sorry. It's probably a good thing you're moving out. You need someplace safer and quieter than above a construction site.'

'Who says I'm moving out? Now that we're even with the apologies, life is far too interesting here to leave. I might even be able to help at some point in time.' Yawning, Jill stretched her arms above her head.

'But breakfast is out of the question. I'll be lucky to keep coffee flowing during the remodel.'

'No problem, I'll just keep cereal and milk in my suite. I have a small refrigerator. Good night, Eric.'

'Good night.' Eric continued to mull long after Jill disappeared inside. He hoped he hadn't overplayed his hand. Things might go smoother without another outsider nosing around. But that would be a problem for another day. Tonight, he'd be lucky to have enough energy to drive home.

NINE

If Jill had to keep driving back and forth to Orchard, she might have to rethink her charming suite in Charleston after all. Not that the Norris neighborhood had plenty of short-term rental options. At least when she woke up that morning, someone had set a box of Cheerios, a quart of milk, and a tub of berries by her door. And the two-hour drive would give her a chance to strategize. Yesterday she blundered into a situation she wasn't prepared for. She wouldn't make that mistake today. After driving up and down Chester Road, Jill chose a semi-hidden easement within view of the Norrises' driveway. Parked behind a mountain laurel bush, she was able to keep watch in hopes Ralph Norris left the farm. If he decided to work the fields near the house, she would try something different tomorrow. Maybe she would leave her car here, hike up the driveway, and hide in the bushes until Emma came outside. Not a terrific plan, but she needed to speak to Emma alone. Fortuitously, her opportunity arrived three hours later, after Jill had read *The Post and Courier*, two magazines, and seven chapters of a new novel.

Ralph and his son pulled on to Chester Road and accelerated to a speed no sane person would try on such a rutted surface. The moment his battered truck disappeared around the corner, Jill wasted no time getting to the Norrises' front door.

Emma answered her knock, her face registering an expression of shock. 'Miss Wyatt, why have you come back? I gave you my answer yesterday. And I fully expect you to honor my request for privacy.'

'I certainly will, after I finish explaining. I'm afraid your husband cut me short.' Jill stood poker straight with her hands by her sides.

'Ralph might have done so, but the outcome would've been the same. I'm sorry you drove all the way out here.' Emma spoke softly with pity, not annoyance. Jill hoped she'd remember such compassion the next time a solicitor knocked on her door.

'Mr Sugarman – that's your birth sister's husband – paid me to not only find you but to convey a message. Once I do that, I can collect my paycheck without reservations.'

Emma glanced over her shoulder. 'Go on upstairs, honey. This doesn't concern you.' Then Emma turned her attention back to Jill. 'Ralph wouldn't like it if I invited you inside.'

'Maybe we can sit out here and talk a few minutes.' Jill pointed at two lawn chairs on the porch.

'Very well.' Emma walked to one and sat primly, while Jill took the other.

'Wow, you have a great view from here.'

'Say what you came for, Jill. Don't beat around the bush.'

Jill inhaled a deep breath. 'OK, Charlotte Sugarman isn't just sick – she's dying from acute Hepatitis C. Her liver is failing and she desperately needs a transplant.'

Emma focused on a row of crows on the fence. 'I'm sorry to hear it, but there are lists for that sort of thing.'

'Charlotte has been on the list for years, but they haven't found a suitable match yet. Her last hope is a blood relative. The doctor determined her children are too young to donate.'

'This woman has children?'

'Two, a boy of eight and a girl of five.'

'That makes the situation especially tragic. I'll remember . . . Charlotte and her family in my prayers.'

'She's a praying woman too. That's why Mrs Sugarman isn't the least bit afraid to die. She wants the transplant solely for her children's sake.'

'I can understand her feelings, but it doesn't change anything.' Emma rose to her feet.

Jill stayed right where she was. 'Look, all I'm asking is for you to have a blood test. If you're not a suitable match, Charlotte can die knowing she tried her best.'

'I thought *all you wanted* was to convey a message.'

'True, but those kids broke my heart when I met them.'

Emma's patience had reached its limit. 'Playing on my sympathies is pointless. I can't give this woman my liver.'

'She only needs half, and it grows back completely within six weeks.'

'That is immaterial. We are members of the Church of Christ, Scientist. We don't believe in medical intervention. We place our full faith and trust in the Lord. Only He has the power to heal. Please tell . . . Charlotte that I will pray for her complete and total recovery.'

Blindsided, Jill sat motionless. 'Do you give me permission to tell the Sugarmans your reason?' she finally asked.

'Yes, I do. I'm glad Charlotte is a woman of faith. Please tell her miracles happen to those who believe.'

Jill held out her business card in her palm. 'Just in case you wish to reach me, my cell phone number and Charleston address is on the other side.'

Emma walked inside and closed the door. But she had at least stuck the card in her pocket.

Jill ran to her car and high-tailed it out of there, similar to Ralph's style of driving. As much as she liked and respected Emma, she preferred *not* to meet her husband on their narrow lane. Once she was far away from Chester Road, Jill contemplated heading back to Charleston. After all, hadn't she done exactly what her client paid her to do? She could complete her case report for Nate Price and explain the situation to her clients. Once the Sugarmans heard Emma's reason for refusal, they would understand.

And Charlotte would soon be dead.

No matter how hard she tried, Jill couldn't get past that reality – or forget Joan's face at the hospital. She turned the Toyota around in the next drive and headed to Orchard. One more visit to the Lazy Bear Diner wouldn't hurt. Then she would sleep better at night.

'Hey, there. Didn't think I'd see you again.' Frannie Davis greeted her with a warm smile. 'Did you find Chester Road and Emma Norris?'

Jill slipped on to a stool at the counter. 'Yep, that map sure came in handy. Thanks.'

'Well, gimmie the news.' Frannie poured them both a cup of coffee.

Jill swallowed hard, wanting to tell the truth. 'Emma is fine. She has a new baby boy, so that makes two boys and a girl. Ralph still plants cotton and drives an old Ford pickup.'

'Some things never change. Does Emma still home-school her kids?'

'Yes, but there's one thing I forgot to ask her. Do you happen to know which church they attend?'

Frannie thought for a moment. 'I'm pretty sure it's the one in Sumter. Not too many of their denomination around. Why?'

'I might just stop in and check it out. I'm looking for a new church. Are there motels in Sumter?'

'Of course there are, but I thought you were heading to Charlotte.'

Jill flushed at her slipup. 'Eventually, but I'm in no hurry. Except for right now. Could I have this coffee to go?'

Frannie poured her coffee into a Styrofoam cup. 'Lucky you. Someday I'm gonna get out of town and just *drive* with no particular place to go.'

'When you do, I hope our paths cross again.' Jill saluted Frannie with her cup and left a five-dollar bill on the counter. She'd barely reached her car when her phone rang. Caller ID revealed the name of her landlord. 'Hi, Eric. I was just getting ready to call you.'

'What about?'

'Oh, no, you called me first.'

'Since you're not moving out, I'm inviting you to a welcome-home dinner for my father. Against doctor's advice, Alfonzo checked himself out of the hospital. It'll just be immediate family and you.'

'In your restaurant? How are you planning to cook?'

'I'm not. So many people sent food over, we'll be pigging out for days. Please come. I might need your help if there are fisticuffs.'

Jill had planned to spend the night in Sumter, then speak with Emma's pastor tomorrow. Nothing like showing up on someone's front stoop to make a person unavoidable. But considering how she'd treated Eric, she couldn't turn him down. 'I would love to come. I'll be back to Charleston in a couple hours.'

'Great, come to the main dining room at seven. What did you want to talk to me about?'

'Just that I made progress on my case. We can talk about that later.' She hung up, grateful she didn't have to tell any more lies. And rather happy about seeing Eric tonight. Despite her better judgment whispering *this is a bad idea*, spending time with a handsome man who knew how to cook had definite appeal.

Eric paced back and forth between the destroyed kitchen and the front dining room, distracted and out of sorts. He wasn't used to organizing a hodge-podge of food prepared by others into a meal. With their paid staff on unemployment until the restaurant reopened, he only had his niece and sister to help. But it wasn't the menu or the logistics bothering Eric at the moment. His impulsive decision to invite Jill to his father's homecoming might have been a mistake. What if Alfonzo exploded into a fit of rage over how he handled the fire? Jill might get more than she bargained for with Manfredi dinner number two.

For his transport from the hospital, his stubborn father had declined the private ambulance and ridden in Irena's Lincoln. When Alfonzo emerged from the back seat, supported by Mike Conrad, he looked pale and drained. Eric had been ordered to remain at Bella Trattoria instead of coming to the hospital. That didn't bode well for what was to come. When Eric rearranged the platter of fresh vegetables, the bowls of potato and pasta salad, and the basket of biscuits for the third time, his sister poked him in the back.

'It looks fine, little brother. Stop fussing.' Bernie set a stack of plates on the table. 'What's the main course?'

Eric rolled his eyes. 'Tonight's diners have a choice between fried chicken or stuffed cabbage. Sort of like a picnic with an ethnic twist.'

Bernie laughed. 'Sounds like fun, but what's with eight chairs?'

'Jill is joining us. It was an impulsive decision, so let the games begin.'

'Ahhh, *mio figlio e mia figlia*.'

The siblings turned to see his parents and grandmother approach the table. Alfonzo leaned heavily on a cane, but had refused his wife's arm. Danielle and Mike approached from the small dining room where they had been watching TV.

'Open a good bottle of Cabernet, Bernadette,' Alfonzo instructed.

'No, Daddy. You're on meds, so absolutely no wine.'

'Not for me, for the others. I'm glad to be home with my family.' Dad lowered himself into his chair.

'I'll get the wine, Bernie, while everyone starts on salads.' Eric bolted before his sister could argue with him. It was seven o'clock. With Jill expected at any moment, he'd rather not have her wander in alone. Five minutes later, he'd found two decent Cabernets in the cellar and opened one before his guest strolled downstairs.

'At least it's no longer smoky in here,' said Jill. 'What can I help you with?'

'Not a thing.' Eric's gaze traveled from Jill's high heels to the butterfly clip in her hair, with a cool blue sundress in between. 'Wow, you look nice. Did I not mention you were only eating with the Manfredis?'

'When one dines with the patriarch, one should look their best.' Jill held open the door while he carried a tray of glasses and wine bottles.

'Just remember to duck if objects start flying.'

Eric began introductions before they reached the table. 'Dad, this is Jill Wyatt, our new tenant. Jill, Alfonzo Manfredi, my father.'

Alfonzo struggled to his feet. 'A pleasure to meet you, Miss Wyatt.' He extended a leathery palm.

'The pleasure is mine, sir.' Jill shook hands and sat on Eric's left. 'No wine for me,' she whispered in his ear.

'Won't you toast to my son's good health?' asked Nonni, who apparently had a miraculous restoration of her hearing.

Jill replied without hesitation. 'Certainly, but I'll use water.'

'Leave the girl be, Mama, not everyone imbibes.' Alfonzo offered a rare smile in Jill's direction. 'Son, please say grace and let's get started. We can save the toast for another time.'

Eric did as instructed. Soon bowls and platters went flying around the table and an inordinate amount of food was consumed. Conversation was lively, mainly confined to national sports and the effects of the never-ending drought. Just when Eric thought they would make it through the meal without anything embarrassing, his niece asked the question he had hoped to avoid.

'Grandpa, did you hear Uncle Eric insisted on an arson inspection?' Dani popped a grape tomato in her mouth.

As silence fell around the room, five pairs of anxious eyes locked on Alfonzo. 'Yes, your grandmother told me. And I think it's an excellent idea.'

Eric could be mistaken, but he thought he heard the release of a collective breath. 'I'm glad I haven't disappointed you.'

'But when will this inspector come?' Bernie demanded. 'We can't start repairs until he makes his report. The longer we're closed the better the chances people will find a new favorite eatery.'

Mike Conrad chimed in on his wife's side. 'If the inspector concludes it was arson, the police get involved and who knows how long the investigation will take.'

Alfonzo thumped the table with his fist. 'And if nobody inspects, that sly dog will get away with it.'

'What sly dog?' Jill asked.

'Salvatore Borelli, that's who.'

'Why on earth would Sal do such a thing, *mio marito*?' His mother pushed more food around on her plate than she ate.

'Because that sly dog knew I was in the hospital. He'd like nothing better than to put me out of business.' Alfonzo threw down his fork with a clatter. 'I want him arrested.'

Irena clucked her tongue. 'Please don't work yourself up. You know what the doctor said.'

'The police can't arrest someone without proof,' said Eric. 'And any evidence burned up in the fire. Why don't we talk about something else since we have a guest tonight?'

Ignoring his suggestion, Alfonzo turned to Jill. 'What does our resident investigator think?'

Jill was quick to answer. 'I think that inspector needs to get here soon before more evidence is destroyed.'

'Thank you, Miss Wyatt. You are welcome at my table any time. But my son is right. Now is not the time to discuss this, so if you'll all excuse me, I'm tired.' Eric's father struggled to his feet and staggered from the room, with his wife at his side. Nonni followed two paces behind them.

'If you don't mind, Eric, we're going too. Sorry to stick you with clean-up, but Danielle has an early class tomorrow.'

After long goodnight pleasantries, the Conrads finally left and Eric locked eyes with Jill. 'We seem to have both come through unscathed.'

'And no fisticuffs tonight . . . much to my disappointment,' Jill added with a wink. 'Come on, I won't run out on you. Let's clean this mess up.'

'We can wash dishes in the bar sink, but from now on, it'll be paper plates or nothing.'

Never had hand-washing plates and glasses proved so much fun. By the time he and Jill carried the bag of trash to the alley, he didn't want the evening to end.

At the foot of the stairs, Jill poked his chest with her finger. 'I know you're tired, Eric, but soon you *will* tell me all about this Salvatore Borelli. I won't take no for an answer.' Without waiting for his reply, she sprinted up the steps.

'Just when I thought I dodged a bullet.'

For a long while after Jill closed her door, Eric stood on the landing, trying to rein in his emotions. He didn't like Jill and his grandmother alone in the restaurant with an arsonist on the loose, especially with the alarm system ruined. Despite the fact his soft bed in his condo was calling his name, Eric grabbed a pillow and blanket from storage and headed to his office. He'd rather be uncomfortable than worry about either of them.

TEN

Jill awoke to a fragrant breeze coming through the window and birds chirping in nearby trees. Eric had been right about leaving the windows open, but closing the shutters. She had lain awake long after the noisy tourists had gone to bed and the last carriage horse returned to his stall. Then she heard the foghorns from ships on the bay. *Why did sound carry so much better at night?* Lying in bed as a child, Jill remembered hearing train whistles yet had never once heard them during the day.

Now as the city slowly came to life, Jill's thoughts focused on her case. What good would it do if Emma was a match but her religion wouldn't allow her to donate? And Jill was the last person who should debate religious convictions. Her spiritual upbringing ended when she entered the foster care system. Although her Pensacola friend had coaxed her to attend church with her a few times, Jill hadn't stepped inside a church since she left Florida.

Pulling on a T-shirt, sweats, and sneakers, Jill slipped out the back door and hit the streets. Before she drove to Sumter and blundered ill-prepared into a conversation with Emma's pastor, she needed to formulate a plan and learning more about their faith was a good place to start. After jogging past nine churches of different denominations, Jill finally consulted Google. Although Charleston had a Church of Christ, Scientist, it was not in walking distance. However, there was a Reading Room on James Island. That might be a better place to start. Maybe she could find out everything she needed to know by just reading.

Within thirty minutes Jill walked into a small, brightly lit building with racks of books and magazines lining the walls and several tables and chairs. Although there were no other patrons, her plan to learn without confronting another human being wasn't to be. A well-dressed woman stepped out of the back room.

'Welcome. Have you come to learn more about the Church of Christ, Scientist?' she asked with a friendly smile.

'Yes, ma'am, I have. I got a general overview online, but I need more than that.'

Her smile widened. 'Tell me what you learned so far.'

Jill hunched her shoulders. 'Generally you folks don't go to hospitals or see doctors. No blood transfusions or immunizations either. You ask the members of your church to pray so you'll get well.'

'Not a bad start, I suppose. After all, Jesus Christ was the Divine Healer, wasn't He? The Bible is filled with examples of believers healed by faith and faith alone. But we do have trained healers well-versed in Scripture who meet with members individually. They guide the sick through the process.'

'Yes, ma'am, but I have some specific questions. Is your pastor around so I can ask him or her?'

'Why don't you have a seat?' She pointed at one of the chairs.'

'No, thanks, I'm comfortable standing.' Jill shuffled her feet, oddly nervous for no reason.

'We don't have a pastor.'

'A minister or a priest?'

'We have no clergy whatsoever. During worship services, a First Reader reads passages from *Science and Health*. Think of that book as our manual. Then the Second Reader reads passages from the King James Bible. Our weekly Bible lesson is supplied by the Mother Church in Boston.'

'What about all this healing?'

'We have meetings every Wednesday evening where members can give testimony of being healed through prayer. You're welcome to join us sometime. It's wonderfully uplifting. What is your specific question? I'll see if I can help you.'

Jill inhaled a deep breath. 'What if a member desperately needs an organ transplant, or if one of their siblings needed a kidney? What happens then?'

The woman's face filled with compassion. 'To the best of my knowledge the tenets of our church don't specifically prohibit members from being either a donor or recipient. The choice would be up to the individual.'

Jill's mouth dropped open. 'Do you think these Readers in Columbia or Atlanta or Montgomery would agree with you?'

'I believe so, since we share the same Mother Church.'

'Thank you so much.' Jill grabbed the woman's hand and shook vigorously.

'You're welcome, young lady. Don't forget about our Wednesday meetings. They are a sight to behold.'

Jill picked up a *Monitor Weekly* from the rack and ran to her car. Once back to her suite, she showered, packed, and headed toward the freeway. She needed to make sure people in Emma's local church felt the same way as the James Island members. She wouldn't return to Charleston until she got her answers.

It was a good thing she'd packed pajamas and a change of clothes, because Jill wasn't able to track down one of the

Readers until the next afternoon. However, the nice man promised to visit the Norris family and discuss the matter with Emma.

When Jill finally parked her Toyota behind Bella Trattoria late on Friday, she noticed only a Ford SUV under the magnolia tree and no Lincoln. That meant Mrs Manfredi had gone home to the suburbs, but Eric was still at the restaurant. Her good day just got even better.

Eric barely glanced up when the back door opened and closed. Normally he would be happy to see Jill, but right now he was in no shape to make polite conversation with anyone. 'Good evening, Miss Wyatt. Can I interest you in a glass of non-vintage Chianti? We don't serve the good stuff on days like today.'

Jill slid into the chair opposite his. 'You know I don't imbibe. What on earth happened? You look terrible.' She moved the wine bottle beyond his reach.

'You sweet talker. And here I thought I was growing on you.' Eric rubbed a spot between his brows where a headache had begun. 'How was your trip to Reston or was it Weston?'

'It was Orchard, and it went better than I'd hoped. But why don't you share your news first. Did you get a bad report from the State Fire Marshal?'

Eric snorted. 'The inspector is coming tomorrow morning. I still have *that* to look forward to.'

Jill reached out to pat his arm. 'I've only been gone two days. Did something happen to your dad?' Her tender concern touched his heart.

'You could say that. The doctor ordered him to rest in bed, drink lots of fluids, and not stress himself out. So they put an extra bed in Nonni's room so she could keep an eye on him while my mother ran errands. That lasted all of one day – Thursday. This afternoon he told my mother he was going out for some fresh air. Dad refused to let her walk with him.' Eric paused for another sip of bitter wine. 'Instead Alfonzo walked all the way to Tuscan Gardens, a restaurant owned by the Borellis, *half a mile* away.'

'Sal Borelli, the man your dad thinks set the fire?' Jill's voice quivered.

'One and the same. Needless to say, the two men got into a heated argument in front of customers. Sal's wife and sons were furious and tried to kick Alfonzo out. Instead, the two old codgers left and continued their *discussion* on the street.'

'Oh, Eric, the doctor warned him about stress. Is your father back in the hospital?' She filled two glasses of water at the sink and gave him one.

He drank half a glass before replying. 'To the best of my knowledge he and my mother are home in bed in West Ashley.'

'Thank goodness!' Jill exclaimed.

'Unfortunately, the story doesn't end there. According to the evening news, Salvatore Borelli of Tuscan Gardens was found dead in a small park on Meeting Street, two blocks from his restaurant.'

Jill gripped the edge of the table. 'Perhaps the elderly gentleman suffered a heart attack.'

Eric scraped his hands down his face. 'Oh, his heart stopped all right, thanks to a bullet fired at close range.'

'You can't possibly think . . .'

'No, my father might have a hot temper, but he's no killer.'

'Are you going to tell me what's really going on here?' asked Jill after a moment's pause.

'You've heard of the Hatfields and the McCoys? The Manfredis and Borellis have been feuding for years.'

'What started it?'

'Who knows? Maybe one got a better review in the *Charleston Restaurant News*.' Eric rose to his feet. 'We're both tired. Let's get some sleep.'

Jill blocked his path. 'You shouldn't drive. You've had wine to drink.'

'That's why I'm sleeping on the pull-out couch in my office.'

'Good idea.' Jill set their water glasses in the small sink undamaged by the fire. Then she suddenly turned back around. 'Do you fear reprisals from Salvatore's sons?'

Eric stopped in his tracks. 'I don't fear anyone, but I also don't want you and Nonni alone without the security system working. I'm staying here until Sal's killer is caught.'

Jill glanced away the moment their eyes met. 'I'm sure your grandmother will appreciate you around. We'll talk more tomorrow.'

When she headed upstairs, Eric went to his office and pulled out the sofa bed. Exhausted, he fell into a dead sleep without making up the bed or getting out of his clothes. *What had his father done this time?*

The next morning, Eric had a crick in his neck and a sour taste in his mouth. At least he kept an extra shaving kit and change of clothes in the employee lounge. After showering in Nonni's bathroom, he sat down to wait for the inspector with a full pot of coffee. He was down to the last cup when the Fire Marshal arrived, along with two technicians and the crime lab van. Eric wasn't permitted to watch them work, so he caught up with paperwork in the office. Three hours later, the marshal knocked on his office door to take Eric's statement even though he'd already given one to the fire chief. The marshal would issue his conclusion within forty-eight hours.

Eric followed him out the door to the parking area. Jill's car was already gone. Briefly he had considered knocking on her door earlier but changed his mind. Jill rented a suite from him. She hadn't signed on to be part of their family drama.

When Eric reached his parents' home and spotted two cars in the garage, a wave of relief swept over him. But that relief was short lived. Irena Manfredi stepped on to the front stoop when he was halfway up the walk.

'Enrique, I'm so glad you're here.' Her flawless complexion was mottled with tears.

'What's wrong? Where's Dad?'

'He's in his study.' When Eric tried to step around her, his mother grabbed hold of his arm. 'Two Charleston police detectives just left. They asked your father questions . . . about . . . Salvatore's . . . murder.' Her words were a broken staccato.

Eric took his mother gently by the shoulders and led her to the couch. 'That's to be expected. They will talk to *everyone* who saw Sal that day.'

'But the things Al said inside Tuscan Gardens, in front of witnesses . . .' Her face crumpled into tears.

Eric patted her back as though she were a child. 'That only proves they had a fight, nothing more. You know Dad would never hurt anyone.'

Mutely, Irena focused on the porcelain vase holding a dozen yellow roses.

'Why don't you make us some iced tea?' he asked. 'I'll go and to talk to Dad.'

When she nodded and tottered away on high heels, Eric marched down the hall to Alfonzo's office. No one entered his private domain without an invitation, which were few and far between.

Eric pushed open the door without bothering to knock. 'What on *earth* were you thinking?'

Seated behind his massive black walnut desk, Alfonzo peered up with deep creases beneath his red-rimmed eyes. 'By all means, son, come in and make yourself comfortable.'

Eric shut the door and pulled one of the chairs close to his father. 'Good afternoon, sir. Now if you would please answer my question. It's just you and me.'

'I went there to talk sense to Sal, to stop the animosity between our families. There's enough dinner clientele for both of us in this town.'

'And you thought accusing him of trying to burn down your restaurant would be a good start?'

Alfonzo pounded the desk with his fist. 'Who could have done such a thing but a Borelli?'

'Gosh, I don't know. Maybe one of a dozen other competitors or maybe just a sicko who likes starting fires.' Eric couldn't seem to control his sarcasm.

'It wasn't just the fire. What about the robbery and the big mess in my alley? I know Salvatore was behind all of it!'

Eric leaned back in his chair. 'Your hatred has poisoned your judgment. What exactly did you tell the police?'

'That I didn't do it and that they should get out of my house!'

'You and Sal were seen arguing in the restaurant and on the street. What are people supposed to think?'

'People should take my word for it. The Manfredis are law-abiding citizens. It's the Borellis who have bad blood running through their veins.'

Eric sighed as though the weight of the world rested on his shoulders. 'Please, don't talk to the police again without an attorney present. And not that same lawyer who looks over your tax returns. A criminal lawyer. I'll make some calls and we'll talk later.' He jumped up and headed to the door.

'I didn't shoot Salvatore, son.'

Eric glanced back at a man who'd aged a dozen years during the last week. 'I know that, Papa, but plenty of innocent people go to jail every day. I don't want you to be one of them.'

ELEVEN

Jill couldn't wait to get out of her suite that morning. She skipped her morning exercise routine, skipped her Cheerios with berries, and made do with a single cup of coffee. As much as she liked Eric and had even grown fond of his family, the last thing she needed was to get tangled up in a murder investigation. *Of all the bizarre luck*, she thought. She didn't want to be interviewed by the police with the chance of some hot-shot reporter asking her questions. When you're running from your past, you don't want your picture appearing in any newspaper. And you don't get tangled up with a handsome chef whose family history sounded like a Mario Puzo movie script. So she crept silently down the stairs like a thief fleeing a crime and didn't call her client until halfway down the block.

'Good morning, Mr Sugarman. I'd like to give you an update on the case.'

'Excellent, Miss Wyatt. Why don't you stop by the house? The children don't have school today.'

His suggestion sent a cold shiver up Jill's spine. 'No, why don't you and the kids meet me at the University Medical Center? Then I can speak with Mrs Sugarman too.'

'Very well. We'll see you there. We were planning to spend the whole day at the hospital.'

As Jill parked in the visitor lot, the Sugarmans' van pulled in two spots away. What timing! Bobby and Joan spotted her as soon as Jill climbed out of her car.

'Hi, Jill!' cried Joan. The child ran headlong toward her despite her father's admonition.

'That kind of rash act can get you killed, young lady,' David Sugarman admonished. 'You didn't even check for cars.'

'Sorry, Daddy.' Joan tried to hide a stuffed animal behind her back, but she wasn't quick enough.

'And I told you not to bring Mr Bugs to the hospital.' He yanked the toy from her hands and threw it in the van.

When Joan burst into tears, Jill picked the child up in her arms. 'You'll see Mr Bugs later. Right now, let's go visit your mom.' Jill shifted Joan to her hip, took Bobby by the hand, and headed toward to the entrance. *How could a father upset his daughter right before visiting his dying wife?*

David frowned but said nothing as they crossed the lobby and entered the elevator. Then he looked down his nose at Jill. 'Stuffed animals can harbor germs and viruses, Miss Wyatt. Don't you realize how tenuous Charlotte's condition is?'

'I do, but I also know you can throw Mr Bugs into the washer with hot water or into the freezer overnight. Either should take care of any bacteria.'

'Are you speaking from experience?' he asked. 'I didn't know you had children.'

'I don't, but you'd be surprised what you can learn on the internet.' With that, neither spoke until the foursome reached the nurses' station on Charlotte's floor. Then Jill set Joan down and said, 'Bobby, would you please take your sister to the playroom? I'd like to speak to your mom and dad alone.'

David waited until they left and then practically exploded. 'You seem to be taking charge here, Miss Wyatt. I'm not comfortable with you making decisions for my family.'

'Look, with all due respect. You're the one who put me in the middle of not one, but two family crises. I'm doing the best I can, so trust me to do my job.'

'By all means.' David swept his hand in the direction of his wife's room. After scrubbing up, Jill and David donned masks and entered Charlotte's room with big smiles. 'Hello, darling. How are you feeling?'

'I'm better today. I see you brought Miss Wyatt.'

'Hi, Mrs Sugarman,' greeted Jill.

'Actually, she brought me. Jill has news for us.' Crossing his arms, David leaned against the window ledge.

In her pale face Charlotte's eyes sparkled. 'Come sit by me, Jill.'

Jill complied, scooting the chair as close as possible. 'I found your biological sister. She's married and lives on a farm outside the town of Orchard. I suppose the closest city would be Columbia. Her name is Emma and she has three kids, one of which is a baby.' Jill purposely omitted their last name.

'Does she look—' A coughing spasm interrupted Charlotte's question.

'Look like you?' Jill finished for her. 'Yes, I would say so. Quite a bit actually.'

'Is the woman healthy?' David asked. 'Does she smoke or is she grossly overweight? Because either of those could impede a transplant.'

Jill turned to him with a frown. 'Emma looked to be in perfect health. Please save your questions for the end, Mr Sugarman.'

The corners of Charlotte's mouth pulled up into a smile. 'Continue, please.'

'I told her about you and that you needed a new liver. She was very sorry to hear that and said she would pray for your restored health.'

'Is she willing to have her blood tested?' David couldn't seem to help himself.

Jill didn't turn around a second time. 'I asked her that specifically. She said it wouldn't do any good even if she was a match.' Jill took hold of Charlotte's hand. 'Emma belongs to the Christian Science church. They don't go to doctors or hospitals, or receive blood transfusions or immunizations. They pray instead and put their lives in God's hands. They don't have pastors, but the First Reader will ask the whole church to pray for you.'

'Well, there's our answer then.' Charlotte smiled at her

husband with complete composure. 'Thank you, Jill, for finding my sister and pleading my case. You've done everything we asked for and I'm grateful.'

David, however, wasn't quite so obliged. '*That's it?* She won't even have the blood test?'

Since socking the man in the nose would upset Charlotte, Jill rose to her feet. 'Why don't we finish talking outside and let your wife get some rest?'

David stalked from the room and down the hallway ten paces with Jill on his heels. 'Why can't the woman just get tested? If she's worried about money, I'll pay any expenses she incurs.'

'Money isn't the issue. Emma's church normally doesn't allow medical intervention.'

'What do you mean *normally*?' he asked.

'After reading up on this denomination, I tracked down a member of her church. He said the tenets of the Church of Christ, Scientist don't specifically forbid a member from being a transplant donor or a recipient. That decision would be left up to the individual.'

David gasped. 'So her church won't stand in her way?'

'No, but the man who reads Scripture won't encourage Emma either. He will explain the tenets of their religion and then leave the choice up to her. Remember, it's fundamental to their faith that all Christians need is prayer to be healed.'

'Give me their address. Let *me* talk to her husband. Once he hears from another husband and father, he'll help his wife make the right decision.'

'Absolutely not, Mr Sugarman. I promised to respect Emma's privacy.'

'Look, Miss Wyatt, I signed a contract with your agency and paid the advance. If I must, I'll sue Price Investigations. I'm entitled to the information I'm paying for.'

'Calm down. Allow this Reader from her church to talk to her and then give Emma time to think it over.'

'My wife doesn't have time. Without a donor, the hospital wants to move her from intensive care to hospice. People don't come home from hospice.' David's angry eyes filled with moisture.

'Just give it a few days,' Jill said, fighting back her own tears.

'Two days, Miss Wyatt. If I don't hear from you on Tuesday, I'm calling Nate Price and my lawyer.' He stomped down the hallway toward the playroom.

Unable to face the Sugarman children in the elevator or parking lot, Jill hurried to the nearest stairs to exit the hospital. She had no idea what she was doing. Was the client legally entitled to the Norrises' name and address? Would Nate fire her when he heard about this? Nothing in Beth's training had prepared her for this. All she had was gut instinct and a few prayers of her own.

Beth. Sound advice might only be two hours to the south. Beth said to call her if Jill ever needed help. Jill jumped into the Toyota and set the GPS for Savannah, Georgia. How busy could Beth and Michael be on a Saturday to not make time for a friend in need?

Eric knew having the entire Manfredi extended family over for an afternoon potluck was a major mistake. For one thing the restaurant's kitchen remained a disaster. Although the Fire Marshal hadn't officially issued his report, he had released the area as a potential crime site, so there was little doubt as to his conclusion. Restaurant staff began cleaning last night, but it would be days before a contractor could start reconstruction. Why couldn't they skip a few Sundays until Bella Trattoria was fully up and running?

But Alfonzo – the man who had just been in the hospital – wouldn't hear of it. He rebutted every argument Eric gave during their phone conversation. 'I feel fine,' Alfonzo blustered. 'So why shouldn't I be surrounded by friends and family? We don't need the kitchen, since we'll eat their cooking instead of them eating ours for a change. And people can use the office bathroom or the one in Nonni's room.' A hearty belly laugh punctuated his final word on the subject.

Eric stood in what remained of their commercial kitchen inhaling bleach fumes and smoke residue. Even the coffee tasted bitter on his tongue that morning. Hearing the approach of his grandmother, Eric set his mug in the sink. 'Good morning, Nonni. Are you ready to go?'

'Ready as I'll ever be. Were you able to talk sense into your father?' Nonni crossed the kitchen and grabbed hold of his arm. Since the woman insisted on walking to Mass, she used a cane for additional support.

'What do you think? *Your son* won't change his mind and Mom has already left messages for everyone to come at three o'clock and bring food.'

Nonni muttered something in Italian as they made their way out the door. 'When word of this meal gets back to the Borelli family, they'll consider it dancing on poor Salvatore's grave.'

Eric chose not to point out that Sal had yet to be buried.

'It's not right, Enrique. We were all friends, once upon a time,' Nonni pointed out as they crossed the courtyard.

Eric patted her hand and refrained from mentioning that was over thirty years ago.

'Well, you can just tell Alfonzo, I won't have any part of this disrespectful spectacle. After Mass, I'm locking myself in my room until everyone is gone. People can't use my bathroom either. I'll lock the door from the hallway. They can either use the office or find the nearest gas station. I don't care. And that's all I'll say on the subject!'

Actually, Nonni had plenty more to say on the subject. The only time she wasn't pouting or griping was in line to receive communion. Eric didn't mind because he agreed with his grandmother. Unfortunately, he was trapped in the middle with no one else on their side.

After Mass, Eric called a taxi to take them to breakfast. Nonni was worn out when the taxi brought them home. She would doubtlessly sleep through the *disrespectful spectacle*. Just as Eric walked her to her room, he heard his father's blustery voice in the back hall. 'I'll tell Dad your bathroom is off limits,' Eric said. 'And when the last guest leaves, you and I will eat together in the courtyard. How's that?'

'*Molto buono*, Enrique. You're a good boy.'

'The jury's still out on that one.'

Nonni clutched his arm. 'You mark my words, grandson.

God won't like the Manfredis having this big party before Salvatore is laid to rest. Something bad is going to happen.'

Eric waited to roll his eyes until Nonni closed her door.

While his mother, sister, and aunts gossiped and prepared for their weekly get-together, Eric kept busy in the kitchen. He packed up smoke- or water-damaged spices, seasonings, and dry goods from the shelves into crates. They would be inventoried on Monday by an insurance claim adjustor before workers hauled them to the dumpster. Linens, glassware, paper products – almost everything stored in the kitchen or pantry must be replaced. Only items in the freezer and wine cellar had escaped the smoke, flames, or sprinklers.

Soon Mike Conrad tired of the regular Sunday crowd and joined Eric in the kitchen. A few cousins wandered back and forth too, occasionally helping, but usually just chewing the fat while he and Mike worked.

Eric hadn't seen his father since he delivered Nonni's directive about her bathroom. Irena brought him a plate of food – which remained untouched – and invited Eric to meet her cousin's niece who just happened to be 'beautiful, talented, and had a great job in advertising.' Eric told his mother he would be *right there* . . . two hours ago. He vastly preferred emptying spoiled vegetables from the fridge to enduring another Irena Manfredi fix-up with the daughter of a shirttail relative.

'Hello, Eric. Hi, Mike. Can anybody join the fun?'

Eric heard a familiar voice over his shoulder. 'By all means, Jill. Put on rubber gloves, grab a gasmask, and dig in.' He grinned at his tenant. 'How was your trip to Savannah? I got your text about spending the night. I hope your suite isn't still smoky.'

'Not at all. I just needed Beth's advice. After dinner she and Michael talked me into staying.'

Eric labeled his packing box with the contents. 'After hearing about the fire, I'm surprised Beth let you come back.'

'She tied me to a chair, but I slipped the knots and escaped.' Jill winked as her head emerged from the industrial-strength apron.

'I can just picture that. Are you hungry? You could make a plate of food before you jump into work. The weekly buffet is up and running in the dining room.'

'*Today?* After everything that happened to your dad?' Jill sounded incredulous.

'Nothing stands in the way of a Manfredi Sunday dinner,' said Mike while Eric only shook his head.

Jill reached for a crate. 'Thanks, but I ate on the road. How 'bout if I start boxing up these—'

Irena cut her off mid-sentence. 'Eric, you must come quickly.'

The look on his mother's face chilled him to the bone. Eric and Mike pulled off their gloves and followed her out of the kitchen, with Jill close behind. As they fought their way through the crowd in the front dining room, helpful guests filled them in with details:

The police are here, Enrique.

They slapped the cuffs on Uncle Al and you know he has a bad right rotator cuff.

How can the police march in here and arrest Alfonzo – on a Sunday, no less? Have they no respect?

When Eric reached the front of the restaurant, he found his father scowling between two policemen. One officer was reading him his Miranda rights above the din of relatives and his mother's sobs.

'Officer . . . Billings,' he said, reading the badge. 'I'm Eric Manfredi. What is my father being charged with?'

While Officer Billings led Alfonzo out the front door, the second cop whose badge read Lieutenant Schott blocked Eric's path. 'We're arresting him in connection with the murder of Salvatore Borelli.'

'What evidence do you have? You just questioned him yesterday at his home.'

'A handgun registered to Alfonzo was found in a storm drain one block from the body. Looks to me like the same caliber as the bullet that killed Mr Borelli. What do you wanna bet the ballistics will match? Better call your dad a good lawyer.' Lieutenant Schott backed out of the doorway.

Eric's fingers curled into fists just as Jill reached his side.

'Don't argue with him, Eric,' she warned. 'Let's just worry about your father right now.'

Eric met her eye just briefly, but it was long enough to do the trick. He walked calmly out the door. 'I'll get you that lawyer we talked about, Dad,' he called. 'Don't answer any questions until he gets to the station.'

Alfonzo flourished his hand, indicating he had heard. Then he was placed in the back of a squad car. While his relatives chattered like magpies, Eric silently watched the police take the Manfredi patriarch away.

'Thanks, Jill.' He spoke softly so no one else could hear. 'My hot Italian blood was taking exception to the lieutenant's attitude.'

'You're welcome. Now let's go call that hot-shot lawyer.' Jill pulled him back inside.

'I haven't had a chance to find one yet. But thanks to you, my father doesn't know that and won't sit there worrying.' As his aunts opened several more bottles of wine, Eric and his helpers returned to the kitchen.

'What can I do to help, bro?' Mike Conrad slicked a hand through his hair.

'If you don't mind, I'd like you and Jill to continue packing up. That insurance adjustor will show up tomorrow whether this family is coming apart at the seams or not. I'll make some calls from my office. Someone is bound to know a good defense attorney in Charleston.' Jill and Mike agreed and went to work, while Eric faced his next challenge.

'What did I tell you, Enrique?' asked Nonni. 'I knew God would condemn this shameful party and bring wrath down on the family.'

'God would not condemn an innocent man, and that's what Dad is. Please wait for me in your room. We'll eat supper after I hire him a good lawyer.'

Nonni wasn't easily put off. 'Tell that to the Roman wives and children. They were thrown into the lion's den same as those soldiers guarding Daniel.' She clucked her tongue as she shuffled from the room.

Eric turned to Jill and Mike. 'Either of you care to join us for supper? I might need backup.'

His brother-in-law answered first. 'Count me out. When I'm done here, I'm going home to my wife. Your grandmother scares me.'

'Count me *in*,' said Jill. 'Nonni fascinates me. Look how fast she came up with the lion's den story. That woman knows her Bible.' Jill pulled on gloves and started counting linen napkins.

'Let's just hope her analogy doesn't fit the Manfredis. See you later.' Even though Eric had no idea if Jill was even remotely religious, he had just invited her to dine with a woman who believed fire and brimstone would soon rain down on his family.

Ninety minutes later he had finally lined up a defense attorney who agreed to go to the county lockup and talk to Alfonzo. But when Eric went to share his news, the kitchen was empty except for dozens of boxes, labeled with the contents and exact count. He and his grandmother, however, found Jill in the courtyard, seated at a table set with three glasses of tea and fresh flowers.

'What a lovely surprise,' he murmured.

'Hello, Nonni,' greeted Jill. 'I hope you don't mind Eric inviting me along.' To him, Jill said, 'When we finished packing everything we could, Mike sent me out here. He's going to serve our dinner and then head home.'

'Why would I mind?' said Nonni. 'That Mike is always trying to butter me up.'

'Let's just hope this works.' Mike appeared, carrying three plates on a tray. He pulled off the lids one at the time. '*Buon appetito*,' he said to a round of applause. Mike had reheated a little of everything from the buffet but added fresh garnishes.

'Thanks, bro,' called Eric as Mike disappeared into the shadows.

At least Eric needn't have worried about Nonni with Jill. Nonni refused to discuss her son's problems. Instead she asked Jill questions about her investigation and listened carefully to her answers, which wasn't one of her usual habits.

After Nonni had eaten half her dinner, she pushed herself away from the table. 'I'm going to my room and I don't need anyone's help. You two stay and get better acquainted, because this family might need Jill's help.' Nonni chuckled until out of earshot.

'I'm glad your grandmother maintains a sense of humor despite her son being in a jail cell.' Jill took a bite of chicken.

Eric wiped his mouth before answering. 'That wasn't Nonni making a joke. That was her reading my mind. When I got off the phone with the lawyer, I realized my father needs more than someone there during questioning and to post his bail. Lieutenant Schott said they found Dad's gun in a drain a block from Borelli's body. What does that sound like to you?'

Jill put down her piece of chicken. 'Sounds like someone *wanted* that gun to be found.'

'Exactly. And with Dad in custody, the police won't look too hard for other suspects or at the possibility of a frame-up. I get it that city cops are overworked, but I don't want my father going to prison for something he didn't do.'

'Are you thinking of hiring a PI?' Jill sipped her tea.

'Yep, and I've already got one mind – you.'

'I can't, Eric. I'm already on a case.'

'You just told Nonni you'd done all you can and now the ball is in someone else's court.' He tried a forkful of coleslaw.

'I don't work for myself. I go and do whatever the boss tells me.'

'Then give me your boss's number. If your current case wraps up soon, I want to make sure Mr Price doesn't send you somewhere else. You already know the details here.'

Jill set down her fork with a pained expression.

'What is it? You don't believe in his innocence? Have you already made up your mind that Dad offed his arch enemy?' As usual, Eric had trouble controlling his temper.

'No,' she said flatly. 'But working with people you're involved with isn't a good idea.'

That had to be the dead-last reason Eric expected. 'You and I are . . . *involved*? I'm surprised to hear it, but in a pleasant way.'

Jill flushed a shade to match the pasta sauce. 'Not romantically involved, but you've practically made me part of the family while I'm here. How could I be objective? That's how I messed up my adoption case – I got myself emotionally involved, unfortunately with both sides.'

Eric had no desire to pressure her. He liked Jill. He also knew she was still new at her chosen profession. So for once, he wisely kept quiet and waited.

'OK, this is what I'll do,' she said after a few moments. 'Tomorrow I'll go talk to this Lieutenant Schott as one professional to another. No charge. We'll see if the police have any other leads or suspects.'

'Thanks, Jill. And no charge for this week's rent. After all, this isn't exactly the Ritz with no breakfast and the lingering smell of smoke.'

'I accept your terms, but I doubt I'll be here another week.' Jill stood and picked up her plate.

Eric pulled the plate from her fingers. 'Cleanup is mine. You get some rest. Tomorrow is another day as Scarlett O'Hara loved to say.'

When Jill left, Eric leaned back in his chair and considered his turn of fortune. If anyone could find another suspect other than dear old Dad, it was her. And he would make very sure she stayed another week – and then some.

TWELVE

Jill had no idea why she volunteered to help Eric and his father. What Mr Manfredi needed was a competent lawyer. And what Eric needed was a professional PI with contacts inside the Charleston Police Department. She was still fresh off the boat and knew no one in this charming old city. According to her mentor, *cops don't cotton to out-of-towners sticking their noses into local crime.* After Beth's case on Tybee Island, she ought to know.

But Jill liked Eric, and it had been a long while since she'd found any man attractive. Not that her infatuation would go anywhere. Not that she *wanted* it to go anywhere. But when it was time to pack up and move on, it might be nice to take a few pleasant memories with her.

The drive to the Charleston Police Station on Lockwood Boulevard took twenty minutes thanks to the traffic, including plenty of tourists in horse-drawn carriages. But as it turned out, Jill had to sit on a hard chair for over two hours until the busy detective could squeeze her into his schedule. Finally she was shown back to Lieutenant Schott's cubicle.

'Miss Wyatt?' he asked, reading the name off her card. 'Dispatch said you had information on the Borelli homicide.'

'Yes, sir.' Jill produced her brightest smile and took the chair beside his desk. 'I've been hired by the Manfredi family to investigate a connection between Salvatore's murder and the recent acts of violence against Alfonzo Manfredi and Bella Trattoria.' She crossed her legs and waited.

'Wow, that was a mouthful.' Schott peered at her curiously.

'It was.' Jill studied him as well. Yesterday during the arrest, Schott appeared gruff, inpatient, and angry. Maybe he'd had a bad experience the last time he dined on Italian cuisine. Today, the homicide cop seemed professional and dignified, yet normal enough to play football with his kids after work.

'I'm sorry you waited so long to see me, but I can't discuss an ongoing murder investigation with a PI from . . . .' He picked up her card again. 'Mississippi. You're a long way from home. What are you doing in Charleston?'

'I'm here on another case, one that doesn't involve murder. But since I rented the suite above Bella Trattoria, I've witnessed the sequence of events leading up to Saturday's argument between Salvatore Borelli and Alfonzo Manfredi.'

'So Manfredi doesn't deny arguing with the victim shortly long before Borelli was shot?'

'Nope, apparently the two men have a long history of animosity.'

Schott reached for his yellow tablet and a pen. 'I'm all ears, Miss Wyatt.'

'Because they compete with each other professionally, they've had a long history of *verbal* battles which have never gone beyond name-calling, usually in Italian. Saturday's disagreement was no different than any other over the years.'

'Except that we found Manfredi's gun a block from the crime scene.'

'Didn't it strike you oddly that his gun – if it indeed was the murder weapon – was so close to the body? With water surrounding the city on three sides, why not throw the gun off a bridge and let the tide take it out to sea?' Jill flourished her hand above her head. 'Plus, anyone who watches television would never pick a storm drain. Cops always look there first.'

'Actually, trash dumpsters are my first choice.' Schott leaned back in his chair. 'Here's a tip for you, Mississippi: People panic after they commit a crime. They do stupid things. So no, it doesn't surprise me that Manfredi threw it in a sewer. Now, tell me about these *connected* acts of violence. Then I'm afraid you'll have to let me get back to work.' He gestured at the pile of cases on his desk.

'Very well.' Jill pulled out her notes. 'Last week, someone turned over the large trash dumpster that sits behind the restaurant. Then one day later, Mr Manfredi was mugged on his way to the bank. The thieves bashed him in the head and put him in the hospital, besides stealing his money. Have you made any progress on those cases?'

'This is the Homicide Department, ma'am. We don't investigate cases of runaway food scraps and missing recyclables. But since you asked so nicely, I'll see what's in the files. When did this happen?'

'It was two Saturdays ago, in the early morning hours.'

Schott tapped his computer screen several times and squinted. 'Let's see. When officers on patrol responded to a neighbor's complaint, Eric Manfredi said Bella Trattoria wasn't interested in pressing charges against neighborhood kids. He told officers he would personally take care of the cleanup. Case closed.' A fake British accent highlighted his words.

'And the mugging?' Jill asked. 'Did the police take Alfonzo Manfredi's statement at the hospital? It would've been late that same Saturday after the restaurant closed. Somewhere around ten o'clock.' When Schott turned back to his computer, Jill tried to read over his shoulder.

'According to the detective who took the statement, Mr Manfredi described the robbers as "young punks wearing black clothes and ski masks." That description fits one third of the population of Charleston. Manfredi couldn't determine their race or estimate height, weight, or age. And he refused to look at mug shots. He said it wouldn't do any good because they snuck up from behind.' Schott grinned as though amused. 'So Miss PI from Mississippi, if the Manfredis hired you to solve those crimes, you have a better chance of finding the lost city of Atlantis.'

'I appreciate your vote of confidence, but what about the third crime – the suspicious fire at Bella Trattoria? The family is certain it was arson since no one was in the building except for me and an elderly woman. We were both asleep.'

'My, my, this plot keeps getting thicker and thicker. Maybe *you're* the one behind the rash of crime at the restaurant.'

Jill frowned. 'I don't own a ski mask, sir. Nor would I ever bash a man over the head with a pipe. First vandalism, next a mugging, and then arson? Don't you see the level of violence escalating up to Mr Borelli's murder?'

'Hold on. It's not arson until the State Fire Marshal says so, and so far he hasn't. But there might be a connection after all, young lady. If Borelli was behind any of these initial incidents, or if Alfonzo Manfredi believes he was, I now have a good motive for murder.' Smugly, Schott laced his fingers behind his head.

Could I make a bigger mess out of things for Eric and his father? Jill felt her eyes fill with tears. 'I was hoping you'd cut me a little slack here, Lieutenant. I was just hired by the Price Agency. Obviously, this is my first official case.' A few tears dripped on to her slacks. These weren't crocodile tears designed to manipulate the detective with pity. Jill was crying because she was the worst private investigator on earth.

'I have cut you some slack. Do you realize how few citizens get invited to my cubicle? Let alone citizens from Natchez.' Schott spoke like she was his daughter who needed to see the error of her ways. Her embarrassment grew exponentially.

'You have been very patient and for that I'm grateful.' Jill pushed to her feet and stretched out a hand. She would shake hands as a professional, even though her behavior missed the mark by a mile.

But instead of shaking, Schott drummed his fingers on the desk. 'What exactly would you like from me, Miss Wyatt?'

Astonished, Jill looked him in the eye. 'I would love to see the report from the officer who responded to the mess in the alley. Maybe I can find something to connect that crime to the mugging or the suspicious fire.' She dabbed her nose with a tissue.

He cocked his head before pointing at the chair. 'You, sit, while I take another look at the report. Don't talk and don't peek over my shoulder.'

When Schott turned back to his computer, Jill did exactly as instructed. She even held her breath for good measure.

After a few minutes, the detective uttered the first words that gave Jill hope. '*Huh*. Well, I'll be . . .'

'What is it, Lieutenant?' Jill couldn't help herself.

Schott swiveled around. 'Apparently, the shop next to the restaurant has a security camera focused on the alley. This is the same neighbor who complained about the mess. The shop-keeper said he would give the police the tape if they needed it. But when *Junior* Manfredi said he wasn't filing a complaint, there was no need to pick up the video.'

Jill abstained from jumping up and down. 'May I have the name of this shopkeeper so that I can ask to view the tape?'

'I'll do you one better, Mississippi. I'll have the patrolman pick it up, if it hasn't already been erased, bring it to the station, and log it into evidence. Then I'll determine if there's any connection between the prior crimes and the murder of Salvatore Borelli.'

'Someone could have a grudge against Mr Borelli, and Mr Manfredi simply made an easy scapegoat.'

Schott smiled. 'It's possible, but it's also possible this will rule out any connection. Then I'm back to suspect number one. Either way, if you'd like to watch the videotape with me and the patrolman who took the call, come back tomorrow at ten o'clock. Not nine or eleven. Ten o'clock, rookie, or you'll miss your big chance. I won't have you going home to Natchez and disparaging the Charlestown PD.'

This time Schott shook when Jill extended her hand. 'Thanks, Lieutenant. I'm in your debt.'

'Now go bother somebody else. I'm a busy man.' He picked up the top file. 'And in the future, cut out the crying. Tears are a sign of weakness. You just happened to land the last soft-hearted homicide cop in South Carolina.'

Jill must have walked out of the Lockwood Boulevard station, but for the next few minutes she seemed to be floating on air. On the way back to the restaurant, she tried to temper her enthusiasm. The tape could have been erased or could show absolutely nothing. Luckily, Eric was deep in conversation with the insurance investigator when she entered the kitchen of Bella Trattoria.

Bolting up the steps, Jill spent the rest of the day catching up with emails and paperwork. She didn't leave to find a laundromat until Eric's car peeled out of the parking lot. No use getting his hopes up, especially since she still had no reason to take the case – other than an overwhelming desire to spend time with him.

Although someone had mysteriously left a quart of milk and basket of fresh peaches by her door, Eric's car wasn't in the usual place when she slipped downstairs for a run. Hopefully by the time she bumped into Mr Tall, Dark, and Handsome, she would know if she had a lead or not.

And if anyone was listening to her prayers last night, she would hear from Emma Norris before Mr Sugarman called for her decision.

Jill did arrive at one conclusion during her circuit of the waterfront – she was out of her league, both as an investigator and as someone who expected results after a few disjointed prayers. Her reintroduction to church and religion hadn't gotten very far before she had fled Florida in the middle of the night. *Just do your best and it will be enough*. Her mother's tender words almost made Jill laugh. Maybe that was good advice to give a nine year old, but it did nothing for her now.

Jill arrived at the police station at nine forty-five. She waited calmly in the outer office and approached the desk at precisely ten o'clock.

'Good morning, ma'am. I'm Jill Wyatt and I have an appointment with Lieutenant Schott of Homicide.'

Jill was given a quick once-over. 'One moment, please,' said the desk sergeant. Then one moment later, 'If you'd follow me.' She was taken to a conference room with a table, ten chairs, two occupants, and a screen against the wall.

'Good morning, Miss Mississippi.' Lieutenant Schott bobbed his head politely. 'You're right on time.'

'I thought following orders might work better than crying, sir.'

Schott's grin stretched from ear to ear. 'You got that right. This is Officer Sandoval. He took the call about an overturned dumpster blocking the alley. John, this is Jill Wyatt. She's a rookie PI from the booming metropolis of Natchez, Mississippi.'

'Sorry, I've never heard of Natchez,' said Officer Sandoval.

Jill decided nothing would be gained by pointing out she'd only been there once herself. 'It's a lovely town on the Mississippi River, north of Baton Rouge.'

'With our geography lesson done for the day,' said Schott, 'why don't you have a seat? We're about to watch the video supplied by Mr Howard Fulsom who owns the dry cleaner's next to Bella Trattoria.'

Officer Sandoval felt the need to explain. 'I didn't collect it earlier because this Eric Manfredi guy said his restaurant wasn't interested in pressing charges against a bunch of neighborhood kids. Bad for business and all.'

Lieutenant Schott responded before Jill could react. 'Miss Wyatt knows all about that. She indicates the Manfredi family might change their mind in light of other acts of violence against them. Roll the tape, John.'

The police officer hit a key on his laptop and the surveillance tape appeared on the screen. It was grainy, but clearly showed two slimly built people wearing tall fishing boots and black clothes push over the dumpster. Then using a rake along with their feet they spread the trash as far as it would go to maximize the mess. Neither suspect uttered a word as they worked. And with ball caps pulled low on their faces it would be impossible to identify either of them.

'OK, Rookie, watch closely,' said Lieutenant Schott. 'This is where the movie gets good.'

Jill did as instructed, but saw nothing other than the two punks having fun at someone else's expense. Then, just as one litterer wandered out of view, the second suspect stopped kicking garbage. He was listening to the sound of an approaching siren, which could clearly be heard on the audio portion of the tape. The man glanced around at his handiwork and then looked right at the camera mounted on a utility pole. It was impossible to tell if he saw the camera or not, but he took off running, leaving his image indelibly caught forever.

'Gotcha,' said Officer Sandoval.

'What do you think, Rookie? Do you recognize the thug that could propel your career as a private eye?' The lieutenant leaned back with a smug smile.

'I don't, but I know someone who might.' Jill could barely keep herself in the chair. 'Could you print me a copy of the suspect's image?'

'I might be able to,' said Schott. 'After all, this tape will go back into evidence storage since we don't have an official complaint to follow up on.' He nodded at Officer Sandoval who scrambled to his feet and left the conference room.

'Please don't destroy the tape. I have a feeling the Manfredis will change their mind about pressing charges.'

'I thought as much. In the meantime, I'll run facial recognition against the image to see if your thug is in the system. Give me a few days. This won't be high on my priority list until someone files a complaint or you get proof there's some kind of tie-in to the mugging or the Borelli murder.'

'I understand. And thanks for calling me.' Jill laid her business card on the table.

Schott tucked it into a pocket as he guided her from the room. 'Just don't get your hopes up. I'm pretty sure we've got a slam-dunk case against Alfonzo Manfredi. But Charleston is all about keeping its warm and fuzzy image.'

Officer Sandoval handed Jill two grainy photocopies of the young man's image. 'Good luck, Mississippi.'

Again, Jill thought about correcting him but changed her mind. She had nothing to gain and plenty to lose. Instead, she hurried to her car where she studied the image for several minutes. With his Mediterranean complexion, dark eyes, and thick wavy hair, he could be one of Eric's younger cousins, but she doubted that would be the case. What motive would a Manfredi cousin have?

Jill took a circuitous route back to the restaurant. Along the way she picked up lunch at a sandwich shop and followed a carriage tour for several blocks. In between bites of turkey and cheddar cheese, she listened to the guide's narrative of the history of Charleston, unsure why she was postponing her return to Bella Trattoria. If Eric recognized the face from the video, then they would know who overturned the trash bin. But his father would still be the chief suspect in Borelli's murder.

When the tour's customers started giving her dirty looks, she headed to Bay Street and parked in the shade behind the restaurant. However, Jill found Nonni and not Eric in the burned and smoke-damaged room.

'Hi, Nonni, looks like they're gutting the kitchen. What are you doing in here? You might get hurt.' All around the elderly woman, workers were prying off cabinetry, dismantling appliances, and hauling out debris.

'Waiting for you, that's what. I didn't want you sneaking up to your room, sight unseen.' Standing in a cloud of dust, Nonni sneezed.

Jill guided her into the hallway which was relatively chaos-free. 'Here I am. What's up?'

'He's waiting for you in the small dining room.' She bobbed her head in the general direction. 'I couldn't very well make him wait in the courtyard. Not without an umbrella. He couldn't wait in *here* with all these carpenters scurrying around. And I sure wouldn't let him into your suite, since he could be up to no good.' Nonni added a *harrumph* for good measure.

A cold chill ran up Jill's spine at the thought of her past returning to haunt her. '*Who* is waiting for me?'

'I don't remember his name. He said he knew you and wasn't leaving until you two talked. Awfully pushy for a man with mud on his boots.'

'Where's Eric?' Jill demanded.

'Don't know that either. He's been gone all day. Something to do with Alfonzo.' Nonni steadied herself with one hand. 'Go to the front dining room, Jill. Then you'll know.'

Briefly she contemplated running upstairs for her weapon. But the last thing the Manfredis needed was gunplay inside their restaurant. After making sure Nonni got safely back to her quarters, Jill tiptoed through the main dining room. From the doorway, she assessed the man drumming his fingers at a table and breathed a sigh of relief.

'Mr Norris, what a surprise to find you here.' Jill sat in the chair across from the reclusive farmer.

Norris blushed to a shade of crimson. 'Sorry to barge in on you, but you wrote your address on the card you gave my wife. And I'm not good at making myself clear on the phone.' Glancing around, he bunched his ball cap between his hands. 'It weren't easy to find this place or find a place to park.'

'You're not barging in. I'm only sorry you had to wait.' Jill smiled politely.

'I'll get right to the point, Miss Wyatt. I'm asking you to please stop meddling in our life. Emma ain't no kid any more. She don't need no sister, not at her age. No good can come of it.'

'I wouldn't have tracked you down if it were simply one sibling seeking out another. For Charlotte Sugarman, *much* good can come of it. This surgery could save her life. It's the only thing that can save it.'

'Not if you bring the wrath of God down on us all. And if Emma goes against her principles, that's what will happen.'

'I trust your First Reader told you there are no fixed rules in your church against being a transplant donor.'

Norris grew increasingly agitated. 'That's 'cause the rules were written before doctors started cutting out body parts and puttin' them in other folks. That ain't natural.'

'Perhaps God will look upon Emma's actions as an act of kindness, a sacrifice to benefit someone else.'

'And if he doesn't? Charlotte will still die just like he planned and you will have endangered my wife's life for nothing. What about our children? They still need their mother. And what would I do without my Emma?' His rage was almost palpable.

Jill dropped her gaze, ashamed she might have given the wrong impression. 'Please know, Mr Norris, that I value Emma's life every bit as highly as Charlotte's. According to the doctor, there is very little risk to Emma. She will certainly undergo several months of recovery, but her liver will regenerate back to full size. She'll be good as new. Of course, Charlotte has no guarantee the transplant will succeed. But right now we're getting ahead of ourselves. Emma hasn't even had the blood test.'

Ralph stared at his boots. 'She's got her heart set on being tested.'

Jill's breath caught in her throat, but she wisely held her tongue.

'That's why I came today. I tried talking sense to her but got nowhere. Emma's determined to go through with this harebrained idea if she matches. I want you to come with me and tell her you changed your mind. You don't think she should go through with it. Make something up if you have to. Emma will listen to you. Why, I don't know.'

Jill reached for his hand, but Ralph pulled away. 'It has nothing to do with me, Mr Norris. Emma wants to help Charlotte. She wants to save her sister's life. And the decision should be hers, not mine. And with all due respect, not yours. I can't believe God would punish Emma and her family for trying to help a dying woman – her sister, no less.'

'I'd better head for home. She'll be worried what happened to me.' Ralph Norris staggered up from his chair but focused his tired eyes on Jill. 'Let's say the transplant goes smoothly and Charlotte gets her new liver. Then Emma gets one of them infections that are hard to cure. What if my wife refuses the medicine? Charlotte will be fine and dandy, but my wife will be dead.' He shook his finger at Jill. 'We'll call you in the morning with our answer. But in the meantime, I want you thinking about *that* tonight.' Norris stomped out the front door.

Jill remained in the plush, upholstered chair, speechless and more confused than ever. Then her ring tone snapped her out of it.

'Miss Wyatt? David Sugarman. It's Tuesday afternoon. What did you find out?'

'Your timing couldn't have been better, sir. Emma's husband just left. He said Emma was willing to have her blood tested. They will call with their final decision in the morning.'

There was a whoosh of expended air. 'If Emma has made up her mind, why are we waiting?'

Because Ralph wants one last chance to talk her out of it, she thought. But she said, 'Just to be sure, I suppose.'

Sugarman enunciated each word carefully. 'Charlotte is out of time. If her condition deteriorates tonight, the surgery will be off the table.'

'I understand. I'll call the moment I hear from them. It's just one more night.'

'I'm telling the surgeon we're a go for the transplant. If Emma doesn't match, he can turn around and sue me later. I don't care. To save time, have Emma come here to the Medical Center for her blood work.'

'I'll bring her there myself. Try to get some sleep, Mr Sugarman.'

'Sleep? I've forgotten what that is. Goodbye, Jill.'

THIRTEEN

Eric couldn't remember a more stressful Tuesday in all his life. Whoever said the wheels of justice turned slowly wasn't kidding. With so many cases on the court docket it was almost noon before the judge read the charges against Alfonzo Manfredi, accepted his plea of not guilty and set the bail at seven figures. Although the expensive lawyer Eric hired argued for a reduction of bail, citing his dad's record of community service and clean slate of previous crimes, the judge remained firm.

'In light of the seriousness of the charges and considering Mr Manfredi still has friends and family in Europe, bond is set at one million dollars. Plus I demand that Mr Manfredi surrender his passport.'

It took Eric only two hours to obtain the necessary ten per cent to secure the bond. Not for the first time, he was grateful his grandfather had advised against an expensive four-year college with plenty of student debt. Instead Eric had taken two years of classes in restaurant management and invested his inheritance plus every spare dollar since graduation in a mixed portfolio of stocks and bonds. After one quick phone call to his broker, his underperforming assets were liquidated, and Eric had the bail money. However, his mother couldn't seem to find their passports which she'd tucked away 'in a safe place.' It was four o'clock before his father was finally released into his care.

'Good to see you, son.' Alfonzo, looking pale and haggard, staggered toward him.

'Likewise, Dad.' After a clumsy embrace, Eric led his father through a rabbit warren of hallways and out the door to the parking lot.

'Where are your mother and sister?'

'Bernie is overseeing work on the kitchen to the best of her ability. Mom is at home, cooking something special for your dinner tonight. I wouldn't let her come. Waiting in the courtroom would be very hard on her, plus I thought you and I needed time to talk, man to man.'

When Eric opened the passenger door and helped his father inside, he expected some kind of argument. After all, Alfonzo was used to giving orders, not taking them. But his father surprised him.

'That's probably a good idea,' Alfonzo murmured. Eric helped him with the seatbelt and they headed out of Charleston. 'Where are we going?' his father asked, once there was nothing but sky above and the Cooper River beneath their wheels as they crossed the bridge.

'Mount Pleasant. I was thinking about how we used to go fishing on Shem Creek. We would spend the whole day in the sun and barely get a nibble. But we enjoyed ourselves anyway.'

Alfonzo smiled, turning his face into a roadmap of wrinkles. 'Your mother always packed us lunch with a thermos of cold tea. Then at dusk the shrimp boats came in to sell their fresh catch right from the dock.'

Eric jumped into the reminiscence. 'Pelicans walked right up to us, hoping for a handout. My, those were some good steamers, dripping in garlic butter with just a little cayenne pepper.' He kissed his fingertips with the memory. 'We would buy seven or eight pounds, thinking it would be enough.'

'But it never was,' Alfonzo chuckled. 'That skinny little Bernadette ate like a mouse all week. But if we brought home fresh shrimp, she could eat two pounds by herself. Not your mother though,' he added after a pause. 'Irena considered eating peel-and-eats quite uncivilized.' His smile turned bittersweet. 'Poor Irena. Is she very upset with me?'

'I would describe her as very worried and why wouldn't she be? You've been arrested for murder. Right now you're charged with second degree, but if they find any evidence of premeditation, they'll amend the charges.'

'They won't,' he said simply. 'Because I didn't kill anybody.'

They rode in silence until they reached Eric's destination. Then his father straightened in his seat. 'Where are we, son? I don't recognize this place.'

'This is the new park they built since you and I last went fishing. They put up a half-mile-long boardwalk too.' Eric parked and opened the passenger door. 'Let's take a walk. Times have changed this area, but the shrimp boats still come in at dusk.'

With some difficulty Alfonzo climbed out and breathed deeply. 'Smell that sea air. That hasn't changed.' As though revitalized by the salt-tinged breeze, he lengthened his stride toward the boardwalk.

Eric kept pace by his side. 'I want you to explain why you have a registered handgun, and how someone else could get their hands on it.'

Alfonzo didn't answer right away. He seemed to choose his words carefully. 'I bought the gun when you were taking college classes and seldom around. Bernadette had her hands full with little Danielle. I often stayed late at the restaurant doing the books. Your mother was afraid someone might break in while I was alone.'

'I can't imagine you ever shooting anyone or Mom encouraging resistance during a robbery. That usually ends badly for the inexperienced.' Eric tried to sound philosophical on a very emotional topic.

'Thank goodness, I never was tested. You took over the books and I was allowed to create new dishes and greet my beloved patrons. And frankly, I forgot all about the gun in the office.'

Eric shook his head. 'Are you kidding? You forgot about a loaded gun in your drawer with little Danielle virtually growing up in the restaurant?'

'It wasn't loaded. The gun was hidden under some papers and the clip deeper in the drawer. I made sure nothing was chambered.'

Eric rolled his eyes. 'Since we don't keep the office locked, *anyone* could have wandered in and rifled through the desk.'

'But in all these years, no one ever had. Not until now.'

'*Someone* knew the gun was there. I need a list of everyone who knew about that gun. I've hired our tenant to investigate Sal's murder.'

'That's a waste of money.' Alfonzo focused on the setting sun. 'Shouldn't we head back? You said your mother was cooking for me tonight.'

'It's my money to waste. And I'm not taking you home, Dad, until you tell me what started this feud with the Borelli family.' Eric plunked down on a wooden bench.

Alfonzo sighed. 'Salvatore is gone now, so why rehash past history?'

'Because you're charged with his murder, and I don't want you spending the rest of your life in Kirkland Correctional, maximum security. And don't tell me it's *just business*. There are plenty of Italian restaurants in Charleston. Yet only Tuscan Gardens holds such contempt for you.'

Alfonzo looked at him in a way he never had before. It was an expression of anger and regret and . . . resignation. 'It was your mother who didn't want you kids to know. She saw no point in it.'

Eric crossed his arms over his jacket. 'I've got all the time in the world, since we're not going anywhere.'

Slowly Alfonzo lowered himself to the bench and launched

into a tale of young love between family friends. 'You knew your Nonni and Nonno were best friends with the elder Borellis. It was only natural that sparks would fly when their children were no longer children. But those sparks were between your mother and Salvatore Borelli.'

Eric was rendered speechless for a moment. 'Mom fell in love with *Sal*? Oh, good grief! What happened?'

He shrugged. 'We usually went places in a big group – the movies, the pizza shop, the beach. I fell in love with your mother too, and I made up my mind I would have her for my wife.'

Eric felt a twinge in his gut that had nothing to do with hunger. 'Is this some kind of script for bad daytime TV?'

His father's chin snapped up. 'Show some respect, Enrique! This is no script. You wanted to know the story and this is it!'

'I apologize. Please continue.'

Another shrug and then, 'The summer Sal and Irena got engaged, I knew my time was running out. People like us marry for keeps, not like young people these days. So I plotted a strategy to make my feelings known to Irena. Salvatore was already working in his father's restaurant. Plus, he'd shown his temper one time too many to his fiancée. You know how . . . delicate your mother is. Believe me; it didn't take much to woo her away from him.'

Woo? Did he really use the term woo? 'How soon before the wedding did Mom finally come clean with her feelings?' asked Eric.

'Two weeks.'

Eric gasped. '*Two weeks*? Everything is set in motion by that time.'

Alfonzo dropped his face in his hands. 'Bridesmaid dresses bought, tuxedos rented, the hall booked, the catering lined up. All announcements and invitations had gone out. Even a few relatives in Toscana had booked airline flights. Then Irena announced to Salvatore and his family that the wedding was off because she was in love with someone else.'

'I guess that caused quite an uproar.'

Alfonzo pivoted on the bench. 'It did. Salvatore was all ego, all about appearances. I think he was most angry about losing a personal possession while not paying attention. He never once thought Irena should have a say in this.'

'Mom did accept Sal's proposal. She shouldn't have done that if she wasn't in love with him.'

'Our parents were old country. Her mama had been pressuring Irena to make a good match. My father's restaurant wasn't as well established as Tuscan Gardens.'

'You make it sound like a business arrangement,' Eric said with disgust.

'Marriage is a partnership, so it is a business arrangement. But I fell in love with your mother, and she with me. End of sad story. Take me home, son. I'm hungry for some of Irena's cooking.'

Eric helped him to his feet and together they started back to the car. 'It's not really the end of the story, is it? Salvatore is dead, and you're the prime suspect. What you told me only underscores a long-standing feud. The police will eventually find out and use it against you.'

Alfonzo spoke as though he hadn't a care in the world. 'How is this ammunition for the prosecution? Like I said . . . . I won Irena but Salvatore is the one who's dead. He had reason to shoot me. But me . . . I am content with my life.'

Eric couldn't argue with that, even though he knew the prosecutor might see things differently. 'All right, let's go home. I hope Mom made enough for three, because I'm barging in on your romantic reunion.'

His father linked his arm through Eric's elbow. 'That's fine because when you're done eating, I'm sending you on your way.'

Jill punched her pillow and turned on her left side for the third time. After her conversation with Ralph Norris, she couldn't get comfortable in the Manfredi suite, no matter how hard she tried. Padding to the dormer, she opened the window and stuck out her head. But thick foliage prevented her from seeing what she wanted. Grabbing her bathrobe from the hook, Jill crept downstairs as quietly as possible.

Outside a breeze stirred the dead leaves into whorls and

eddies. Yet no moon illuminated the employee parking area to the right of the courtyard.

'You waiting for my grandson to come home?' A voice emanated from the shadows.

'Maybe.' Jill's response couldn't have been more inane. She picked her way through the haphazard arrangement of tables and chairs. 'Good evening, Nonni. Are *you* waiting for your grandson?'

'I am. I want to hear news about my thick-headed son, and I refuse to give Alfonzo the satisfaction of calling him.'

'I understand,' Jill said, even though she didn't. 'I want to know how things went too. Plus, I have an update for Eric.'

'Then join me and we'll wait together.' Nonni patted the seat beside her. 'I won't be able to sleep until he's home.'

Jill considered the offer. After all, the breeze felt good on her overheated skin. 'No, thanks. I don't want Eric to know I'm sitting around, waiting.'

Nonni grinned. 'Ah, yes, never let a man know your heart.'

She shook her head. 'My *heart*? You've got the wrong idea. Eric hired me to investigate the murder of Mr Borelli. That's what I want to discuss.'

'Sure. Everybody talks business at one o'clock in the morning.' Her laugh sounded like a cackle.

'Good night, Nonni.' For some inexplicable reason, Jill brushed a kiss across the woman's silvery head.

'Good night, *il mio piccolo*.'

When Jill crawled beneath the handmade quilt, she fell asleep within minutes. Was it knowing that someone else was watching for Eric? Or maybe it was the realization she had her first ally since leaving Savannah.

The next morning Jill awoke with a start, glanced at the clock, and jumped into the shower. Today she had to be ready for anything. She was on her second cup of coffee when the phone rang.

'Hello?' Jill's heart was beating so fast, you'd think she was the one who needed a transplant.

'Miss Wyatt, Emma Norris here. I've decided to have my blood tested to see if I'm suitable.'

Short, sweet, and to the point. Yet Jill still had questions. 'Have you discussed this with Mr Norris?'

'Of course I have. He told me last night he came to see you, but he said the final decision was mine.'

'And this won't cause marital problems for you?'

'Our marriage has withstood financial ruin, infertility in the early years, several seasons of drought, and off-and-on infestations of carpenter bees. If it's God's will, our marriage will survive one little blood test.'

Jill shook off her trepidation. 'When can you be ready? Are you willing to come to Charleston for the test? That would make things easier.'

'I am. Ralph and I can be ready within the hour. May we bring our children along?'

'Certainly. Mr Sugarman insists on putting your family up in a hotel during the procedure and recovery period *if* the results are what we're hoping for. I'll be there as soon as I can to pick you up.'

'That's very generous of him. I can ride with you, but Ralph will follow in his truck with the children. He'll need to drive back and forth to tend the livestock if we go ahead with the . . . procedure.'

Very generous of him? You're the one giving up half a liver. 'Thank you, Emma, on behalf of Charlotte and from the bottom of my heart.'

'You're welcome, Jill. We'll be ready when you arrive.'

She grabbed her purse and called David Sugarman on her way downstairs. When she told him the news, he became very quiet. Then Jill realized the man was crying. 'I'm on my way to pick Emma up,' she said. 'I'll call you along the way so you can estimate our arrival.'

Sugarman coughed and cleared his throat. 'Everything will be ready on this end. I'll meet you at entrance C.'

Jill pulled up in front of the Norris house in record time. As promised, Emma was in a rocking chair on the porch, looking as serene as can be. A cloth satchel was at her feet along with her purse. Her two older children were playing with a kite in the yard, but their father was nowhere in sight. 'I hope you haven't been waiting long,' she said.

'On a day as beautiful as this? I could sit here all day.' Emma pushed to her feet. 'Let me get little Andrew. Ralph just finished feeding the animals. He will be down after his shower. Would you prefer to wait inside?'

'No, I'd rather stay here and watch your children play,' Jill said. But in reality she wasn't ready to face Ralph Norris.

Fifteen minutes later, Emma walked outside with a baby carrier and sleeping infant. Ralph nodded to Jill, picked up Emma's satchel, and headed down the steps.

'Don't drive too fast, Miss Wyatt,' he said. 'I don't need no speedin' tickets trying to keep up.' His son and daughter left the kite in the grass and followed him mutely to his truck.

As Jill maintained the speed limit on the way to Charleston, she attempted to engage Emma in conversation. Yet all her questions garnered zero reaction.

Do you have any concerns about the surgery?

Are you interested in the arrangements Mr Sugarman has made, in light of the fact your three children are with you?

Are you worried about your farm animals during your absence?

Finally Emma met Jill's gaze and set the matters to rest. 'I'm not worried about anything. My future, along with that of Charlotte, my family, and even the cows and chickens are in capable hands. Instead of talking, could we listen to the radio? I love country music and the radio in Ralph's truck is broken.' And so the two women listened to music and hummed along to several songs.

Jill called David Sugarman midway as promised. Although Emma's spirits remained high, the closer they got to the South Carolina University Medical Center, the more nervous Jill became. Ralph's words circled through her head on a continuous loop. *What will you do if Charlotte is fine, but Emma develops a hard-to-cure infection?*

When her green Toyota and Ralph's battered pickup pulled into parking lot C, Jill was no closer to an answer. But at least she knew who to talk to.

David Sugarman met them inside the door. He stared at Emma Norris, blinked, and stared some more. 'Forgive me,' he said. 'I'm Charlotte's husband. I don't know why I'm surprised by the strong resemblance, but I am.'

'You think I look like your wife?' Emma asked softly.

'Very much so.' He extended his hand toward Ralph. 'You must be Emma's husband.'

'Ralph Norris.' He offered the barest of handshakes. 'Let's get this blood test over with before we waste more time. It could prove these two ain't kin at all.'

Not hardly, Jill thought, considering the resemblance.

A young woman met them halfway down the hall. 'Hello, Emma. I'm Brenda, one of Dr Costa's medical assistants. I'll be with you during the blood test and explain the pre-op procedures in case you're a match. Your husband and children can wait in the family area.' She pointed in the correct direction.

Without hesitation, Emma passed the baby carrier to Ralph. 'Jill, will you be staying with me?' she asked.

'I need to speak with Charlotte but I'll see you later.'

'I'd like to speak to my sister too while I'm here. Could you take me to her after we're done?' Emma asked Brenda.

'I would be happy to.'

'See you after the blood test, wife.' Ralph took his daughter's hand and nudged his son with the baby carrier. Then he walked away as though about to face an executioner, his head down, his shoulders slumped.

When Emma and Brenda disappeared into the lab, Jill and David crossed the parking lot to building B. 'Where are your children, Mr Sugarman?' Jill asked once they reached Charlotte's floor.

'Staying with my sister for a few days. I thought it would be best.'

'Would you mind if I spoke with Charlotte alone for a few minutes?'

Sugarman looked as though he might object but changed his mind. 'I'll get us cups of coffee.'

Jill scrubbed up, donned protective clothes, and slipped into Charlotte's room. 'Charlotte, you and I need to discuss something important.'

By the time David returned with beverages, they had chosen the perfect course of action. Charlotte released Jill from any guilt or culpability with the same poise and assuredness Emma had demonstrated. For the next two hours Charlotte slept, David read, and Jill pondered how two women, separated at birth, could grow up to be emotional carbon copies of each other.

Finally Brenda stepped into Charlotte's room wearing a mask, gloves, and lab coat over her clothes. 'Are you ready to meet your sister?' she asked, sounding like the host on a reality show.

Charlotte's eyes sprang open as she struggled to sit up. Emma Norris, dressed exactly like Brenda, entered the dimly lit room.

Charlotte covered her mouth with her hand and laughed. 'For goodness sake, I've waited all these years! Take off that silly mask and let me see you!'

Emma pulled off the mask and ran to her bedside. 'Nice to meet you, sister.'

'Look how beautiful you are.' Charlotte reached for her hand.

Emma peeled off a glove. 'Is that because I look like you?' While the two siblings giggled, Jill, David, and Brenda dabbed their eyes.

'Those are my two children, Joan and Robert.' Charlotte pointed at the framed photograph on her bedside table.

Emma leaned over but didn't touch the picture. 'They look like good kids. My three are with their dad in the family waiting room. Brenda said I can't bring them to see you until long after the surgery.'

'I look forward to meeting them,' said Charlotte in a thready voice.

Brenda approached the bed. 'We shouldn't tire you. We'll visit more after they issue the test results.' She began herding everyone to the door.

'No, I must speak to Emma now,' Charlotte demanded with all her strength. Brenda, Jill, and David froze in place.

'I'm right here.' Emma pulled the chair to the bedside.

Charlotte rose up on her elbows. 'If the test shows that we match, you must agree to my terms or I won't let you donate half your liver.'

Emma looked confused. 'What terms are those?'

'You must agree to accept blood transfusions, all necessary medication, and anything else the doctor deems essential for survival. Your religious beliefs have been explained to me and I respect them. But if you're not willing to help *yourself* while helping me, I will refuse the transplant. End of discussion.' Charlotte lowered herself to the mattress.

Emma looked at Jill. 'Did you have something to do with this?'

'That doesn't matter,' said Charlotte. 'These are my terms, sister. Take it or leave it.'

'All right, I accept your terms. If it's my time to die, neither blood transfusions nor all the medicine in the world will change the outcome.'

FOURTEEN

Glancing at his watch for the third time, Eric jumped at a noise behind him. But it wasn't Jill as he'd hoped; it was his grandmother.

'Be patient, Enrique. The girl has a job to do, but she'll be home by and by.' Nonni plunked a bottle of wine and two glasses down on the table.

'Exactly how long is "by and by"?' he asked. 'And I told you, Jill doesn't drink.' Eric refocused on the driveway.

'You both need to learn patience. Last night she had been waiting for you until I sent her to bed.' Nonni examined the bottle of vintage Bordeaux. 'What about Welch's grape juice mixed with club soda? Do you think Jill would like that?'

'I have no idea. What are you up to, Nonni?'

The diminutive woman put her hands on her hips. 'Taking charge of your life. For such a big, strong man, you have the courage of a field mouse.' Nonni picked up the bottle and wine glasses and marched back to the kitchen. Although the room was in a state of chaos, she had ordered a new refrigerator to be delivered before anything else.

Eric smiled. As much as it pained him to say, his grandmother was right. Although he dealt with contractors and vendors with professional acumen, and had no trouble standing up to his peers, when it came to certain women, he did have the courage of a rodent.

However, when the object of his affection squealed to a stop in her usual spot, Eric decided to prove the eighty-five-year-old woman wrong. Jill Wyatt bounded out of her car and crossed the courtyard with far too much energy for the late hour.

'Eric, what are you doing out here?' she asked, tucking her long hair behind one ear.

'Waiting for you. Apparently we just missed each other last night.' He leaned back in the wrought-iron chair.

'Where's your grandmother? I'm surprised she's not out here.'

'She just was. And trust me, she'll be back. Join me.' Eric pulled out a chair.

'The courtyard is Nonni's domain.' Jill sat down opposite him. 'I have news on your father's case. That's why I had hoped to catch you last night. Today I was at the University Medical Center.'

'From the expression on your face, I take it your missing person has been found.'

'Not only found, but the biological sister has agreed to be tested to see if she's a match. If she is, Emma is also willing to be an organ donor.' Jill's smile lit her face with a near-angelic radiance.

Eric couldn't stop staring at her. 'I'm impressed. You've more than done your job. When do you get the results?'

'Hopefully tomorrow, so I checked Emma and her family into a hotel only ten minutes away from the hospital and then stayed for pizza with them. My clients are paying for the suite. Emma also had a battery of pre-op tests on the assumption she's compatible. Time-wise, we're down to the wire for Mrs Sugarman. I'm going on and on, but this isn't why you were waiting for me.' Jill blushed in the moonlight.

'Actually, I *was* curious about your case. I know how—'

'My, don't you two look thirsty,' interrupted Nonni. She shuffled across the flagstones carrying a pitcher and two flutes.

'This is no night for iced tea, so I brought grape and pomegranate juice mixed with club soda. It's delicious, if I do say so myself.' She poured two flutes to the rim.

Jill picked up one and drank it down. 'Was I supposed to sip it? I am so parched.'

'We'll sip the second one.' Eric drank his and refilled their glasses. 'Thank you, Nonni, but we don't want to keep you from your rest.'

His grandmother picked up her tray. 'Goodnight, Jill. Goodnight, my favorite mouse.'

To Jill's bemused expression, he explained, 'I used to like Mickey Mouse as a child. Nonni doesn't forget a thing.'

'OK, time for an update on your father.' Jill took a sip of the fresh glass.

'Yesterday the judge released him after I paid a ten per cent bond. I took Alfonzo to our favorite fishing spots when I was a child and finally got some answers. Not about who might have killed Mr Borelli, but something from the past I'd been curious about.' Eric shifted in his chair, reluctant to reveal the details of his parents' tawdry past.

'I might be able to shed light on your father's case.' Jill pulled a photograph from her purse. 'I obtained this from the Charleston PD. It's a still-frame from a security video of the alley, taken the night someone overturned the dumpster. Do you recognize this young man?'

Eric plucked the photo from her fingers and studied it for several moments. 'How very sad.'

'You know him?' Jill's voice brimmed with excitement.

'Unfortunately, I do. How I hoped this had been neighborhood punks.' He handed back the photo. 'That's Dominic Borelli, Salvatore's youngest son. The other man must be one of Dom's cronies. This won't get my father off the hook. It's just additional proof of their escalating feud.'

Jill's enthusiasm drained from her face. 'I see your point. Homicide might think your dad was retaliating after a long string of Borelli assaults. But maybe the DA will reduce the charges to manslaughter if Alfonzo was trying to defend himself.'

Eric shook his head. 'My dad didn't kill Mr Borelli. If he

had, he would simply say so and accept the repercussions. That's just how he is.'

'Sorry, I was trying to put a positive spin on the situation, not imply I doubted his innocence.'

'I know, but if you really want me to feel better, agree to have dinner with me on Friday.'

Color rushed into Jill's cheeks. 'As in a *date*?'

'Not exactly, I want you to come to my sister's house for my father's second homecoming. We can't have it here since the carpenters started working on the kitchen.'

'Your family sure loves to throw parties, no matter what the circumstances.'

Eric arched an eyebrow. 'I must not be explaining myself properly. This won't be a party. Only the immediate family and you – our recently hired private investigator. Believe me. We're taking Dad's arrest very seriously. I want him to know at least *you're* looking at other suspects, even if the police aren't.'

'In that case, I will be there. Jot down Bernie's address and the time she serves dinner. In the meantime I'd better get caught up with emails. I don't want my boss thinking I'm on vacation on his dime.' She drained her flute of juice and offered a lopsided smile.

'Just for the record, what's so ridiculous about me asking you out? That's what single people do – they go out for dinner to see if they have anything in common. No strings attached.'

'Nothing, I suppose. The question just caught me by surprise. Don't get your hackles up, Manfredi.' She pushed in her chair and headed for the door.

Leaning back, Eric closed his eyes. Once again, his reaction was an overreaction. Why did he always assume the worst about women? He was so worried about being prejudged he beat people to the punch.

Last night Jill was so tired after meddling in the Norrises' lives she hadn't spent a single minute trying to figure out her landlord. She seemed to offend him on a regular basis. It didn't help that she found Eric attractive, but her skittish and juvenile behavior had to stop. She had enough on her plate without adding a confusing man with hidden agendas.

At least the text from Dr Costa's medical assistant gave her someplace to go after her breakfast of cereal and milk. *Please meet Mr and Mr Norris at their hotel suite in North Charleston. Ralph wishes to speak to you before he heads home with the children to tend livestock.*

A place to go . . . yes, but if Ralph Norris wanted to speak to her, it couldn't possibly be good. Jill's stress shot up to high-alert. But when she arrived at the Norrises' suite, Emma greeted her as though an old friend. 'Good morning, Jill. I hope you haven't eaten yet. I made sausage biscuits.'

Jill glanced at the array of food on the kitchen counter. 'You cooked an entire meal in a hotel room?'

'I had to buy biscuits since there're no baking pans here, but the gravy is homemade. Grab a plate. We're about ready to eat and there's plenty.'

Despite the fact she'd eaten her requisite three hundred calories of cereal, Jill took a small helping. During breakfast she tried to avoid eye contact with Ralph, but it was all but impossible in the small dining room. Unlike Charlotte's outgoing children, the Norris kids didn't speak until spoken to first. They answered Jill's queries about pets and farm animals with brief, to-the-point answers.

Midway through the meal, Ralph put an end to their chatter altogether. 'You two take your plates to the living room. Find some of those cartoons like you watched yesterday at the hospital. Your mama and I need to speak to Miss Wyatt in private.'

Jill's toes went numb. Then she remembered her adoptive father's advice long ago: *The best defense is a good offense.* 'I've been meaning to talk to you too, Mr Norris. If you don't mind I'd like to go first.' When no one objected, Jill forged ahead. 'I wish to apologize for butting my nose into your life. A PI isn't paid to meddle, only to track down missing persons and let them know the situation. I had no right talking you into something, Emma.' Jill stole a glance at her.

'How could you *not* butt your nose in when a woman's life

was at stake?' Emma asked. 'Don't apologize for wanting to help Charlotte.'

'I agree,' said Ralph. 'That's why I wanted to talk to you. I've been selfish, concerned only with my family. That's not how a Christian is supposed to act. If Emma wants to go ahead with the transplant, I'm proud of her decision.'

Emma placed her hand over Ralph's and squeezed. The woman could be the poster child for the word serenity. 'As I told Charlotte, I'll take the antibiotics afterwards to prevent infection. So please don't worry.'

'Bacteria aren't the only problem. There are plenty of things that could go wrong, even if you accept medical intervention. Either of you or both could die during surgery, no matter how your church prays or how strong your faith.' Jill felt her palms begin to sweat.

'And if it's God's will that we die, then so be it.' Emma's tone matched Jill's in intensity. 'This life is simply a dress rehearsal for the one to come. You should concern yourself more with your *lack* of faith than my over-abundance.'

Jill blinked. 'You know nothing about my personal religious convictions.'

'That's true,' Emma agreed. 'But whatever your beliefs, you sit on the fence, afraid to jump in. Get your feet wet. Faith is the only thing that can take that fear away.'

Jill wanted to argue, to insist she didn't walk around being afraid. But when she opened her mouth, she couldn't utter a single word.

Emma patted her hand. 'Since Ralph needs to tend critters for a couple hours, could you drive me to the hospital? Brenda wants me there in thirty minutes.'

Jill jumped to her feet. 'Of course I can. But I thought they finished your pre-op tests yesterday.'

'They did, but Dr Costa wants me prepped for surgery. The lab called and I'm a perfect match to Charlotte.' Emma started stacking the plates. 'It's time to get this show on the road and I want you with me until Ralph gets back.'

Jill carried the stack of plates to the sink. 'You go get ready. Dishes I can handle.'

FIFTEEN

Eric had forgotten how satisfying it was to work with your hands. When one of the laborers from the construction crew called in sick, Eric volunteered to carry lumber, hold sheets of drywall in place, and tote the endless scraps of wood. This had been his most productive day since the restaurant caught fire and put them out of business. Some might describe cooking as physical labor, but not him. His job was more of a fine-tuned juggling act – making each dish specifically to the customer's wishes and then seeing that every meal for a table was done at the same time. Some diners couldn't have shellfish, while another was allergic to dairy products. A chef had to be not only creative, but patient when someone requested such travesties as fat-free cheese, low-cal Alfredo sauce, or *cioppino* made without fish.

Today while the experienced carpenters measured and cut, planed and sanded, stained and sealed to specific blueprints, Eric was able to lose himself in mindless work. It gave him a chance to consider the wisdom of hiring Jill Wyatt. Hopefully her inexperience wouldn't put his father in jail for the rest of his life. But just like he knew his father could never kill anyone, he needed to have the same faith in Jill. And he also needed a better way to make his feelings known.

When the electricians began rolling up their power cords and the carpenters dropped their electric hammers into the job box, Eric approached the general contractor. 'Same time, same place tomorrow?' he asked.

'Sorry, Mr Manfredi. You did great today, but my laborer texted that he'll be back tomorrow. Besides, this is a union job and my guess is you don't have a card.'

'I suppose my membership in the International Association of Culinary Professionals won't cut any slack here.'

The man laughed. 'Nope, but I do plan to bring my wife here for dinner once we finish the project.'

'Finish on schedule and your meal will be on the house.'

'You've got yourself a deal.'

As Eric walked the contractor to his car, a middle-aged man in a suit and tie stepped out of a sedan. 'Eric Manfredi?' he asked.

'Yes, sir, what can I help you with?'

'I'm Lieutenant Schott of the Charleston Homicide Department. Could we talk for a minute, somewhere out of the sun?' The cop fanned himself with a folder of papers.

'Sure, but there's no air-conditioning on inside. Why don't we sit in the shade?' Eric pointed to a table by the back door. 'Would you like a cup of coffee? I just switched off the pot but it's still warm.'

'No thanks. I drank enough today to float an armada.' Schott mopped his face with a handkerchief. Then he peered at the building permit stapled to a post. 'I see repairs are underway after the fire. The State Marshal found no evidence of arson?'

Eric lifted an eyebrow. 'Since the inspector found no evidence of an accelerant being used, he ruled the fire "accidental from undetermined origin."'

'And the insurance company will be forced to foot the bill.' Schott smiled as though pleased about something.

'Isn't that why people pay insurance premiums? Believe me, I would have vastly preferred not having the fire at all. Although the building was insured, I carried no protection against loss of income while we're closed.' Unsure of what the detective was implying, Eric maintained a neutral expression.

'Lesson learned, eh? But I'm not here about the fire.' From the folder of papers Lieutenant Schott pulled the same photo Jill had shown him last night. 'How well do you know this guy?'

'Not very well. Dominic Borelli is quite a bit younger than me. Our grandparents were the best of friends. I believe the two grandmothers are still pals. Our parents were also friends, once upon a time.'

'Then business got in the way, right?'

'Something like that.'

'I'm sure your Mississippi gumshoe told you he's the punk

who created havoc behind your restaurant.' He pointed toward the privacy fence separating the courtyard from the alley.

'She did. Apparently, the third Borelli son didn't turn out well. I hope he's not mixed up with drugs like so many young people today.'

Lieutenant Schott frowned, as though unhappy with Eric's cavalier attitude. 'Hard to believe competition over who makes the best spaghetti would cause someone to do this.' The detective pulled out a second photo, this one taken at the hospital emergency room of Alfonzo Manfredi.

The battered, bloody sight of his father curled Eric's hands into fists. 'Did you find evidence that these are the same men who robbed my father? Other than a fondness for black clothing?'

'The height and general build of them matches Mr Manfredi's description.'

'My father suffered a mild concussion. His description might not be reliable.' Eric nudged the photo back into the folder.

'I'm surprised you would defend Dominic. That young punk cost you several hundred dollars plus plenty of bad publicity. He might also be the one who broke in and set the fire.'

Eric steeled his gaze at the cop. 'Not jumping to conclusions isn't the same as defending him. I had better never see Dominic in my back alley again, or I'll teach that boy a lesson. As for the fire? My "Mississippi gumshoe" pointed out there was no forced entry. If the fire wasn't accidental, it was set by someone who knew the security code. That rules out Dominic Manfredi.'

'It's amazing how information gets around these days.' Schott crossed one leg over his knee. 'Want to know my theory?'

'Sure, then I'll tell you mine.'

'I think Alfonzo recognized Dominic the night he was mugged, but he didn't say anything to the officer who took his statement. He was itching to even the score on his own. Then after a fire almost destroys his life's work – whether started by this kid or a careless cigarette from the night cleaner – your father went to see Salvatore Borelli. They argued inside the restaurant. It carried over into the street and then your father settled the matter once and for all.'

'You've made a big leap from malicious mischief to second-degree murder.' Eric picked up the photo of Dominic. 'Here's my theory: It was all Dominic – the dumpster, the robbery, the fire, and then the shooting of Salvatore at close range. Thanks to their ongoing feud, my father became the perfect scapegoat for an angry son.'

The detective smirked. 'You come up with that just now? How did the kid get your dad's gun?'

'He found it in the office drawer the night he came to start the fire. You know how information like security codes gets around these days.' Eric glanced at his watch and pushed to his feet. 'I don't mean to be rude, but I have a ton of paperwork and change orders to review before the construction crew returns tomorrow.'

Picking up the folder, Schott lumbered to his feet. 'Where is your father?'

'I have no idea, probably at home in West Ashley. Somewhere still in the United States certainly. You made him surrender his passport.'

'Just make sure you don't drive him to the airport. If his bail is rescinded, I'd hate to arrest a funny guy like you for aiding and abetting a fugitive.'

Eric waited for the detective to drive away before heading to his office, but he didn't get far.

'Hold up there, Enrique. We need to talk.' Nonni stepped from behind the huge bougainvillea and hobbled across the flagstones with her cane.

'How long have you been eavesdropping behind that potted plant?' he demanded.

'From the moment that cop turned into the driveway I sniffed trouble. I knew he wasn't with the construction crew – those men all drive pickups,' she added with a grin.

'Well, don't worry about Dad. I already knew about the photo of Dominic. The detective was just fishing and hoping I would bite.'

'That's not why I'm coming to talk to you. I have new information, but I prefer to wait until your secret agent gets home from the hospital. I don't want to chew my food twice.'

'How did you know Jill was— never mind, I know how. And she's a private investigator, not a secret agent.'

'What's the difference?' His grandmother lowered herself into a chair.

Eric held up his palms. 'Nothing, but I need to work in my office. Why don't you wait for Jill and have her come get me later?'

'Hold up there, *nipote*.' Nonni bobbed her head toward the employee parking area. Jill's Toyota just pulled into its usual spot. 'Speak of the angel now,' Nonni added once Jill was close enough to hear.

'Hi, Eric.' Jill smiled at him. 'Were you referring to me as an angel, Nonni? Wait until you know me better.'

'No need to. I'm a good judge of character. Sit down, young lady.'

'First, let's ask what happened with Emma Norris today,' Eric said.

'She was a perfect match!' Jill clapped her hands. 'Surgeons are actually harvesting part of her liver now. I just came home to grab a quick shower and change clothes before going back. I was so nervous this morning, I'm afraid to stand too close to anyone.'

'*Ach*, you smell fine. It's Enrique who needs a shower.'

Jill studied his appearance and burst out laughing. 'Hard day at the construction site?'

'You could say that.' Eric rolled his eyes. 'OK, Nonni. Why don't you tell Jill your news so she can return to the hospital? We don't want to hold her up.'

'Does your news have something to do with why you're wearing a hat and Sunday dress on a Thursday?' Jill grinned at his grandmother.

'It does. You are one observant secret agent!' Nonni slapped her palm on the table. 'Men never notice that kind of thing.'

'You do look very nice,' Eric said, mildly chastised.

'After what I overheard in the garden last night, I asked my best friend to have lunch with me. We usually go to Magnolias. You know, sort of neutral ground halfway between Bella

Trattoria and Tuscan Gardens. And we always dress to the nines, like all women used to.'

Jill patted her hand. 'That's because you and your best friend have class.'

His grandmother's face glowed. 'I knew you and Enrique would have trouble finding anything out about Dominic. The Borellis have an expensive lawyer on retainer to keep bad publicity out of the newspaper. And none of them would start blabbing to a Mississippi investigator, no matter how pretty she was. Although Renaldo would still probably ask you out.' Nonni shook her finger at Eric. 'That Renny is a gutsy guy.'

Jill's gaze rotated between Eric and his grandmother. 'Thanks for the compliment, but there's so much going on under the surface, someone had better hand me a paddle. *Who* is your best friend, Nonni?'

Eric supplied the explanation. 'That would be Francesca Borelli, mother of Salvatore and grandmother of Dominic. Things getting a bit clearer?'

'Somewhat. Go on, Nonni. What did you find out?'

'Salvatore had reached the end of his rope with two of his three sons. Dominic refuses to do his fair share of work around the restaurant, yet still expects to get paid twice a month. He stays out all night with his friends and then sleeps half the day away. And he's had too many run-ins with the law to suit Papa Borelli.'

'And Salvatore didn't even know about Dom's handiwork in the alley.' Eric noticed light reflecting off Jill's hair. For someone in need of a shower, her hair still looked shiny.

'What about the third son? What did he do?' Jill asked.

'John turned out to be the biggest heartbreak of all. He promised to come home when he finished college. But after John graduated from USC, he stuck around to get his Master's Degree and then stayed in Columbia *permanently.* He's an executive at some big advertising agency.' Nonni sighed as though she shared her friend's sorrows.

Jill's forehead furrowed with confusion. 'Sounds like John is doing well for himself. What's the problem – did he shame the family by marrying a Yankee?' She giggled.

'This is no laughing matter, Jill. John promised to

join the family business in Charleston. With Dominic a wastrel, the Borellis need John to come home. Salvatore wants to retire and Renaldo can't do all the work alone. So far, none of the sons have married. Francesca is broken-hearted over no grandchildren. Of course, all I have is *one*!' Again, Nonni sent Eric a peeved look.

Eric crossed his arms. 'You must forgive our family, Jill. The Manfredis never tell a story without peppering it liberally with personal asides. Soon you'll need a shovel, not a paddle.'

'Shush, grandson, I'm just getting to the good part.' Nonni smacked Eric's arm with her Chinese fan. 'Everything that I've explained is old news, Jill. I just wanted you to understand the Borellis. Now, should we wait until tonight to hear the rest, after Mrs Norris gets out of surgery and Eric changes his disrespectful attitude?'

Jill impulsively threw her arms around the older woman. 'Oh, no, I can't wait that long. I'll make sure Eric behaves.'

'I beg your pardon, ma'am.' He bowed from the waist. 'Please continue.'

Nonni sniffed. 'Very well. During dessert, I asked Francesca for the latest news. She said that Salvatore was so angry he told the family he was changing his will and leaving the restaurant to Renny, his oldest and *favorite* son. Salvatore said this in front of Dominic.'

Eric straightened in his chair. 'That should cause some trouble.'

'Of course it did. Dominic argued with his brother and said some ugly things to his father. Then he stormed out of the house.'

'Who would have inherited the restaurant before the change?' Jill asked. 'Salvatore's wife?'

'*Sofia?*' Nonni cackled. 'Over Francesca's dead body! Her daughter-in-law doesn't do much more around Tuscan Gardens than Dominic. Sofia spends her days at the mall, or the nail salon, or getting spa treatments. Although nothing seems to improve her sour disposition.'

Eric shifted in his chair but forced himself to keep quiet.

'All three sons were supposed to own the restaurant together after Salvatore passed. You can see why he wanted John home from Columbia and Dom to finally grow up. What a disaster that would have been.'

Pulling a pen and notebook from her purse, Jill jotted notes furiously. 'Do you believe Mr Borelli was serious about leaving everything to Renaldo?'

'You bet I do. Francesca said Salvatore had an appointment with his lawyer the next day *after he died*.' Nonni's grin was nothing but smug. 'Since he hadn't made a new will, the old one will be sent to probate court. And all three boys will get equal shares. Dominic has already said he wants to sell the place. It might not take too much convincing to get John to go along with him. Francesca is in for more heartache.' Nonni clucked her tongue.

Eric and Jill locked eyes. 'And we have another murder suspect,' she said.

'Thank you, Nonni. Jill and I are in your debt.'

'You're welcome, Enrique. Does this make me a secret agent too?'

Jill nodded. 'We'll get you an official membership card, along with a pen with disappearing ink. But right now I need to jump in the shower.'

'I'd rather have an umbrella that shoots poisoned darts,' said Nonni.

'I'll check the internet.' Eric kissed his grandmother's papery cheek. 'Jill,' he hollered after her, 'should I pick you up here to go to my sister's tomorrow, say around seven? After all, this will be very close to an official date.'

'Seven would be perfect. I'll be tied up at the hospital until then.' Jill vanished into the restaurant.

'You're taking Jill to Bernadette's?'

'I am. Do you approve? Are you happy now?' Eric helped Nonni to her feet.

She shifted her weight from his arm on to her cane. 'I approve, but it's only a start. I won't be *happy* until Danielle has a few first cousins and I have more grandchildren than one.'

SIXTEEN

Jill returned to the hospital and spent most of Thursday night with Ralph Norris and his children while surgeons harvested part of Emma's liver. Finally, Brenda and Dr Costa joined them in the family area with the news that Emma had come through the surgery splendidly.

'Praise the Lord,' murmured several women. They had come from their Sumter church to sit with Ralph.

'Outstanding!' said Jill, unable to sit there and say *nothing* after such news.

Ralph wiped his brow with his sleeve. 'Can I see her?'

Dr Costa placed a hand on his shoulder. 'Not quite yet. Your wife will remain under close observation for the next several hours. You can see her once she's moved to a room. She will remain in the hospital for a few days. At this point, Emma's vital signs are strong and every indicator points to a successful organ donation.'

'What happens next?' Jill asked.

'A second team of surgeons and assistants will transplant the liver into Mrs Sugarman. She's being prepped right now. We have no time to lose.'

'What should me and the kids do now?' Bewildered, Ralph Norris twisted the brim of his ball cap.

Dr Costa placed a comforting hand on his shoulder. 'Go to your hotel and rest for say . . . five or six hours. Then come back. If your wife wakes up before that, Brenda will call you. The hard part is behind us, Mr Norris. Try not to worry.'

When the tired-looking doctor walked away, Jill turned to Mr Norris. 'Would you like me to come back to the hotel with you and the kids? Maybe I can fix them something to eat?'

'No, thanks, Miss Wyatt. I promised them McDonald's when we left here. So that's what we'll have.'

'All right, I'll see you later.'

Jill returned to Bella Trattoria in the middle of the night, stripped off her clothes and fell into bed. She slept soundly for seven dreamless hours and awoke to the sound of hammers, saws, and a radio tuned to a rap music station. It was a good thing Eric's construction crew was at work early or she might have slept through her client's surgery and broken a promise. Jill had given her word to little Joan Sugarman that she would keep her daddy company today. Jill stepped over several extension cords and around a pile of 2x4s on her way out, but there was a bigger distraction waiting in the courtyard.

Eric Manfredi, dressed in jeans and a torn sleeveless T-shirt, was pulling new cabinets from their shipping crates. As fate would have it, Eric turned around just as Jill stopped in her tracks to gape. It's not like she'd never seen bulging biceps or tight stomach muscles before. Jill just never saw them on a man she had a date with that night.

'Good morning, Jill. I'll be right with you.' Eric reached for a flannel shirt hanging on a sawhorse.

'Oh, no, don't bother with that. I need to get to the hospital.'

'All right then, see you tonight.' Eric dropped the shirt and continued unpacking cabinets, while Jill fled to her car feeling foolish.

Every construction worker inside the kitchen had been dressed the same way. Yet she'd paid no attention to them. *Is that what attraction did – made a person feel like a teenager with a crush?*

Jill found David Sugarman in the waiting room with dark smudges under his eyes and in a shirt with more wrinkles than a Shar-Pei. Although his children were staying with their aunt during the procedure, David hadn't left the hospital in twenty-four hours. 'I'm back, Mr Sugarman, if you would like to go home for a while. Dr Costa said the surgery can take up to twelve hours.'

He shook his head. 'No, thank you. I want to stay right here until Charlotte's condition is stable.'

According to the medical assistant, it could be days before Charlotte was fully out of the woods, considering her weakened state. 'Would you like me to get you something to eat?' she asked.

'No, I ate a couple donuts and almost threw up.' He leaned his head back and closed his eyes. 'I'm fine, Miss Wyatt. Don't worry about me.'

Since her client wasn't interested in small talk, Jill read her book, walked the halls, drank two cups of coffee, and repeated the entire sequence a second time. Finally Dr Costa joined them in the waiting room, looking even more fatigued than before.

'I thought you had gone home, Doc,' Jill blurted as David flashed a look of annoyance.

'After the second team of doctors took over, I've been observing in the gallery. So far so good, Mr Sugarman. They removed Charlotte's diseased liver and the surgical team transplanted the donor liver into your wife. Now all the blood vessels and bile ducts must be reconnected, which is a painstakingly slow process. I'm on my way home, but Dr Ajuga will answer any of your questions once he finishes surgery.'

David stepped in his path. 'Any idea how long before I can take Charlotte home? She's been in the hospital so long already.'

Costa swept the white cap from his head. 'Hard to say; ten to twelve days at a minimum. Even with immunosuppressant drugs, rejection remains a possibility. But we'll do all we can for your wife.' The doctor strode away with far less spring in his step than he had yesterday.

David glanced at his watch. 'It'll probably be a couple more hours yet, Jill, but there's no reason for you to hang around.'

'Oh, I don't mind, sir. Maybe we can get a cup of coffee or go to that chapel and say a few prayers.'

'Frankly, I hate coffee and my wife prays enough for both of us. Don't take this wrong, but your pacing back and forth makes me nervous.'

How could anyone take that wrong? 'Sure, just make sure you call me when Charlotte reaches the recovery room.'

All the way home Jill tried to figure out what Charlotte could have seen in David to want to marry him. It certainly wasn't his boyish good looks or his aloof, cold-as-a-dead-fish personality. At least thinking about the Sugarmans kept her mind off the dinner with Eric Manfredi.

After another shower, Jill dressed in a pale green sheath with high-heeled sandals. She coiled her hair at the nape of her neck and let a few tendrils frame her face. Makeup had always been a challenge. Growing up in Florida, heat and humidity melted most face paint away if you planned anything outdoors. So Jill dabbed some bronze shadow on her lids, more bronzer on her cheeks to make up for the fact she'd had little sun-time, and added a deep coral lipstick. Tonight she wanted to look special – or at least like she'd made an effort.

Eric was waiting downstairs in the courtyard. Apparently it had become his domain too since the kitchen was in disarray. This time the man was fully dressed, yet Jill still found herself unnerved by his appearance. Black slacks, white silky shirt open at the neck, and a soft grey sport coat. Maybe it was the Italian leather loafers, or the expensive cut to his longish, wavy hair. But more likely Jill was unnerved by his cool, collected demeanor, as though whether on vacation at Lake Como or dinner at his sister's, Eric Manfredi was the man of the hour.

'Wow, I thought we were just going to supper at Bernie's,' she said.

'We are. Do you think I'm overdressed?' Eric closed the distance between them.

'No, it's just that tall people always look so good in clothes,' she muttered, saying the first thing that came to mind.

'I'm not sure how to respond other than I think you look spectacular and you're not tall.' Eric took hold of her arm. 'We'd better get going. Alfonzo likes to eat on time.'

'Sorry, I'm a little rusty at social conversation. Where is your grandmother? I truly need someone to take the pressure off me.'

Eric's chuckle set Jill somewhat at ease. 'Nonni would only make things worse. Trust me. She took an Uber to Bernie's so you and I would have time alone. Those were her exact words. You'd better run, Jill Wyatt, or Nonni will have us married by Christmas. Change your name, dye your hair, and get lost. Wasn't that William Faulkner's famous advice?'

'Something to that effect.' Jill forced herself to laugh. *If only Eric knew how close to the truth he was.* 'Does your sister live far from downtown?' she asked.

'Not at all. We're turning on to Calhoun, which becomes the James Island Expressway when it crosses the Ashley River. Bernie lives on James Island. We'll be there within twenty minutes, depending on traffic. Tell me what happened today at the hospital. I wanted to drop by to sit with you, but I wasn't sure how your client would feel about that.'

'Mr Sugarman isn't particularly friendly, but I would have appreciated the company. Walking the hall is more interesting with a partner.'

'I'll keep that in mind for the future,' he said.

By the time she brought him up to speed with the Sugarmans, Eric turned into a circular drive leading to a rambling Spanish colonial on a suburban lot. 'We are here,' he announced.

Jill climbed out and let her gaze travel up to the clay tile roof. 'What a lovely house.'

The door swung open when they were still halfway up the walk. 'Hi, Uncle Eric,' Dani greeted. 'Jill, I can't wait for you to try the dessert I made after school.'

'*You* made it, Danielle?' Eric asked. 'Hopefully, there's syrup of ipecac in the house.'

'With a little help from Mom.' Danielle stuck her tongue out at her uncle.

'We're so glad you could join us, Jill.' Bernie gave her a quick hug when they reached the huge country kitchen. 'I'm in charge of pasta. As soon as everyone finishes their task, we'll be ready to eat. Would you like iced tea to drink?'

'Yes, please. What can I do to help?' Jill asked.

Jill was given the task of slicing cucumbers and radishes for the salad. Mrs Manfredi, dressed in a tasteful silk dress, sprinkled parmesan cheese on the garlic bread. Dani set the table in the screened-in porch. And Alfonzo lifted perfectly round meatballs from a skillet with a slotted spoon.

Nonni, who had been watching everyone work, climbed off the kitchen stool. 'I'll pour the tea,' she said. 'Eric, you open a bottle of Cabernet for those who want it.'

Jill would describe dinner with the Manfredis as 'organized

chaos' since everyone was some sort of chef, except for Mike Conrad.

'Dump the pasta, Bernadette,' ordered Alfonzo five minutes later. 'Everyone else, sit!'

The chaos ratcheted into high gear as everyone rushed final preparations. Jill carried her bowl of salad out to the porch, hoping her slices were sufficiently uniform.

After everyone had taken their places at the table, Alfonzo said, 'Since this is your house, Mike, say grace and let's start on the antipasto.'

After the host's short prayer, Bernie passed around a platter of marinated artichokes, zucchini, eggplant, and mushrooms, along with fresh baked bread and butter. The first course was so good Jill had to remember not to fill up. However, the pasta course opened a can of worms at the table.

Alfonzo set down his fork. 'What kind of tomatoes did you use to make the sauce, Bernadette?'

'Campari, Papa. They're juicier than Roma and I like a thinner sauce.' Bernie swirled some noodles using her fork and spoon.

'The Manfredis use Roma tomatoes in the gravy, always.' Alfonzo thumped the table with his fist.

'I know that's your first choice, but Roma can be a bit bitter.' Bernie offered her dad an agreeable smile.

'That's why I add a few tablespoons of sugar to my gravy, to cut the bitterness.'

'With everyone so health and calorie conscious these days, why not use Campari in the sauce so sugar wouldn't be necessary? More garlic bread, Jill?' Bernie offered her the basket.

Jill took another piece and handed the basket to Eric, barely lifting her focus from Alfonzo.

The patriarch's glare remained on his daughter. 'Because in Bella Trattoria, we use the marinara recipe my grandfather brought from Italy. It's tradition.'

'And in *Casa Conrad*, we stick to my tradition, Campari tomatoes for a lighter sauce.' Bernie raised her wine glass.

'Hear, hear.' Eric toasted his sister with iced tea.

'Don't they realize they're arguing about two different

things?' Jill whispered in Eric's ear. 'Gravy and spaghetti sauce?'

Eric stifled his laughter behind his linen napkin. 'No, gravy is the old-world word for pasta sauce. Have no fear of projectiles, Jill. These discussions go on all the time but are harmless.'

Irena shot her son a look of displeasure. 'Do *you* prefer one type of tomato for your sauce, Jill? With so many heirlooms being planted, there are now dozens of varieties.'

Jill swallowed her mouthful and dabbed her mouth. 'No, ma'am. I usually buy whatever jar is on sale that week.'

'Good one, Jill,' said Mike Conrad.

'Worst. Answer. Ever.' Dani mouthed across the table and then giggled.

Mrs Manfredi wasn't to be put off. 'Surely, your family has certain ethnic recipes they hold in high esteem.'

Jill pondered this. 'No, not really. Perhaps because I don't have much family.'

'That could be an advantage at times.' Mike Conrad raised his wine glass, which promptly warranted the evil eye from Nonni.

Confusion furrowed Irena's forehead. 'What ethnic nationality are you?'

Jill straightened taller in her chair. 'I'm American, same as you.'

'Good ole USA,' said Eric. 'Could someone pass me the meatballs?'

His mother handed him the bowl, but kept her focus on Jill. 'I'm not making myself clear. Forgive me. I'm asking what country are your ancestors from?'

Jill gulped some water. 'My adoptive parents were Scottish, I believe.'

'Wow, you were adopted?' Dani exclaimed. 'That is so cool.'

'But what about your natural parents, your bloodlines? They would be your ancestors.' Mrs Manfredi, along with almost everyone else at the table, had stopped eating. Everyone was looking at Jill, except for Alfonzo, who seemed a bit confused.

Jill didn't like the attention one bit. 'I haven't the slightest idea, other than my blood is red and the type is O-positive.'

'You never tracked down your *real* parents?' asked Dani. 'I've seen several shows on TV like that. It seems to be the current thing to do.'

'My parents are in a tiny cemetery on the Panhandle of Florida. They were about as *real* as it gets until someone went left of center, hit their car, and killed them instantly.'

'OK, that's enough!' Eric said in a tone that didn't encourage argument. 'Let's go back to discussing garden vegetables.'

Everyone resumed eating, except from his wasp-waisted, perfectly coifed, over-dressed mother. Irena took a sip of wine. 'I'm sorry, son, if I offended your friend. I merely was interested in cultural traditions, such as stuffed cabbage, fried pierogis, bratwurst and sauerkraut, borscht soup.' Her smile was deceptively placid, like a snake waiting to strike in the grass.

'Don't the Scots have an interesting dish called *haggis*?' asked Mike Conrad.

This time the evil eye came from Bernie, aimed at her spouse.

But Irena wasn't finished. 'I'm curious why you haven't investigated your ancestry. After all, your adoptive parents have passed on and won't get hurt feelings.'

Silently Jill counted to five. Then she drained her glass of iced tea. 'I'll make this simple enough to understand: Because I'm not the . . . least . . . bit . . . interested.' With that, she threw down her napkin and rose to her feet. 'Thanks, Bernie and Mike, for a delicious dinner. Your home is gorgeous and your sauce was perfect, by the way. Eric, I'll wait for you out by the car.'

Jill fled the house as though a pack of ghouls was hot on her heels. Never before had she been in such an uncomfortable situation. Never before had she wanted to make a good impression on people and failed so miserably. All because she really liked Eric. Once outside, instead of climbing into the SUV, Jill wandered into the backyard. A metal swing set sat forlorn, waiting for a little girl to come back and play. Surrounded by rabbit fencing, a garden with a bounty of goodness waited to be picked and savored. Flowers bloomed, grass glistened with dew, and peepers peeped from the hedgerow. All so ordinary, yet so lovely.

All something Jill could never be a part of in a million years.

SEVENTEEN

'There you are. Thank goodness!' Eric was panting when he finally reached Jill's side. 'When you weren't in the car, I jogged halfway to the Ashley River before I realized you weren't walking back to Charleston.'

Jill stepped into a circle of moonlight. 'I'm so sorry, Eric, for embarrassing you like that in front of your family.'

'*You're* sorry? Are you joking? My mother acted like a Gestapo guard on Ellis Island.'

'To my knowledge Ellis Island never used Gestapo to check immigration papers.' Jill seemed to be biting the inside of her cheek.

'I know, but I couldn't think of a better analogy. Bernie and Mike were mortified by my mother. And Danielle? She's in tears because you didn't try her tiramisu dessert.'

'What about your grandmother? Didn't she throw in her two cents?' Jill asked.

'Nonni spoke in Italian to her daughter-in-law so only my father understood. And Dad practically turned purple.'

'Still, I behaved badly and I'm ashamed. I should know how to express myself without storming out like a child. After all, Irena is your mother and deserves respect.'

Eric tipped up her chin. 'My family tends to make *normal* people run away screaming, so please don't be hard on yourself.'

'Are you saying I'm not normal?' She looked him in the eye.

'Not by a long shot. You, Jill Wyatt, are extraordinary.'

Jill's cheeks flushed with color. 'Thanks. You're pretty neat too.'

'Families can either be a blessing or a curse. Most of the time mine is the former. When they're not, I put on jogging shoes and run along the waterfront. The exercise along with the view works wonders. If a person wasn't born with much family, they usually create their own from neighbors or club members or people at work. I got the feeling Beth Kirby is very dear to you.'

'She is – both her and Michael. I only wish I'd known them longer.'

'And we shouldn't forget the people we happen to fall in love with.'

Jill's smile faded, so Eric changed the subject. 'What do you want to do now? I could take you home and maybe stop for dessert along the way.'

Jill gazed up at the stars as though they might hold an answer. 'What I really want is to go back inside. Is that even possible? I hate to pass up Dani's tiramisu. And I don't want to leave things like this with your family,' she added softly.

Eric put an arm around her shoulder. 'It's not only possible, it's the Manfredi way of doing things. We stomp our feet, storm out in a huff, then come back and pick up where we left off.'

'And no one holds a grudge?'

'Nope, just business as usual.'

'Will that work for a Scottish Wyatt?'

'In a heartbeat.' Offering his elbow, Eric felt a surge of joy when Jill took hold.

Alfonzo was first to notice Jill's return. 'Miss Wyatt, you missed the entrée, but I saved you a piece of grilled salmon.'

'Jill, you're back.' Dani ran to them and hugged Jill around the waist.

'I couldn't miss your tiramisu.' Jill tugged on the girl's ponytail. 'Bernie, Mike, Mr and Mrs Manfredi, I apologize for my childish display of temper.'

Eric locked eyes with his mother as they sat down at the table.

'You call that a display of temper?' Alfonzo clucked his tongue. 'You truly must be a Scotswoman.'

'No, Miss Wyatt,' said his mother. 'I owe you the apology. I was very rude to pry into your personal life. Please forgive me.'

'Of course,' Jill murmured.

'Good, everyone is happy again. That means it's time for you to try the fish.' Alfonzo handed Jill and Eric plates with hearty portions. 'My secret is the sauce with tomato butter, fennel, and cannellini beans.'

Jill's eyes grew very round. 'I thought the pasta and meatballs were the main course. May I just taste the fish and take the rest home for lunch tomorrow?'

'She must save room for my dessert, Grandpa,' Dani explained.

Alfonzo nodded. 'Sure, sure, take it home. You eat like a bird, just like my Irena.'

'With that settled, shouldn't we make our plans for tomorrow?' Bernie's gaze drifted around the table. Unfortunately, it was met with six blank stares, all but Nonni. 'Tomorrow is Salvatore Borelli's funeral at St Mary's.'

'And why would that concern a Manfredi?' Alfonzo demanded.

Bernie pushed away her plate. 'You can't possibly skip that funeral. If for no other reason, you will look guilty if you stay away.'

'What do I care what I look like to a Borelli?' he asked.

'Papa, half of Charleston will be there, not just Sal's family.'

'You exaggerate, Bernadette. I will not be a hypocrite by mourning a man who stabbed me in the back every chance he got.'

Irena brushed a crumb from her silk dress. 'Sounds like a rather judgmental attitude, *marito*.'

Alfonzo softened his expression toward his wife. 'I will pray for Sal's eternal soul and light a candle in private. But I will not participate in the honoring of that man. I am head of this family and I say the Manfredis will go about their business tomorrow as usual.'

Eric decided it was time to hear from his grandmother. 'What do you think, Nonni? You've been awfully quiet.'

'My opinion is my own, Enrique. Don't stir the pot.' Nonni shook her finger at him.

'The matter is settled,' said Alfonzo. 'Danielle, aren't you ever going to serve your special dessert? And let's have cappuccinos, Bernadette.'

Eric waited until his sister and niece left the room. 'I'm afraid I will be forced to attend, Papa. I'm the one who hired Jill to investigate Salvatore's murder. Since everyone knows murderers often attend their victim's funeral, I can't let Jill walk into that den of thieves alone.'

Alfonzo considered his son's logic. 'You're right. You must protect Jill, especially from that Renaldo. Even if it is his papa's funeral, that man won't miss an opportunity to turn on the charm.'

Jill had been following the conversation like a tennis match. 'May I remind you both that I'm licensed to carry a firearm in this state?'

Alfonzo chuckled. 'There'll be plenty of Borellis packing heat at Salvatore's funeral. You won't be the only one.'

'Enough, please!' cried Nonni. 'Don't you remember what happened the last time you disrespected the dead?'

Alfonzo looked genuinely confused. 'No, Mama, I don't. Please remind me.'

'The police hauled you away in handcuffs.'

'And with that cheery memory, coffee and dessert are served,' Bernie announced as she and Dani carried trays out to the porch.

Eric waited until the topic changed to Danielle's upcoming basketball game before squeezing Jill's hand under the table. 'Are you apprehensive about tomorrow's funeral?'

Jill pivoted in her chair so only he could hear her response. 'Are you kidding? I'm not afraid of a little gunplay. And I can't *wait* to get a look at Renaldo Manfredi. I just hope I can find something proper to wear.'

Eric picked up his spoon and began eating the Italian specialty. He had no idea whether Jill was joking or not, but Renny wasn't the Borelli brother he was worried about.

'Looks like you found something appropriate to wear after all.' Eric did a double-take when Jill came downstairs in a sleeveless black dress and black pumps. She looked gorgeous with her hair in a long braid down her back.

Jill tugged on the hem of the dress with both hands. 'While you were talking sports with Mike last night, I asked your sister what folks wore to funerals these days.'

'You've never been to a funeral?' he asked.

'Not since I was very young, and nobody cares what kids wear.' Jill gave the hem another tug. 'Bernie said that in Charleston, most women will wear a black or gray dress, neither of which do I own. She said I might be able to get away with navy, but my only navy dress has big yellow flowers.'

'I take it that's my sister's dress?' Eric tried not to stare at her tanned legs.

'It is, but I didn't realize how much shorter Bernie was until I put this on.' Jill frowned.

'Really? I barely noticed that the dress stops and your legs start.' He tried to hide his smirk.

'That's it! I'm going back up to change. I'll cover the flowers with a long cardigan.' As Jill pivoted on the bottom step, Eric grabbed her arm.

'I'm teasing, Jill. The dress isn't too short. You look fine and the funeral starts in twenty minutes.'

Jill gave him a head-to-toe perusal on their way to the parking lot. 'I take it you didn't have to *borrow* a black suit?'

'Nope, I wear this to every wedding, funeral, and charity event. It gets lots of mileage.'

'Aren't you the man about town?'

Eric was about to refute her assertion when he noticed exhaust fumes coming from his tailpipe and someone sitting in the back seat of his SUV. He yanked open the door. 'Nonni, what are you doing in here?'

'Waiting for you two to finish getting ready. And I couldn't very well wait without air-conditioning.'

'How did you get my car keys?' he asked, opening the passenger door for Jill.

'Off your desk while you were taking a shower.' Nonni dabbed powder on her nose.

Jill swiveled around toward the back seat. 'But Alfonzo said the Manfredis wouldn't be attending the Borelli funeral.'

Nonni rapped Jill's knuckles with her fan. 'I don't take orders from my son. Francesca Borelli is my best friend and Salvatore was her son. I must pay my respects. Besides, you two might need my help later.'

'Help with what?' Jill asked, pulling her hand out of Nonni's reach.

'You'll see.'

Eric caught Jill's worried expression as she turned around. 'Don't worry, everything will be fine.'

Nonni rapped the back of Eric's head. 'Your mother wanted to come today too. I heard her and Alfonzo arguing after you two left. I know your papa finally told you the whole story.'

'Care to share that story with me?' Jill asked.

'I will, but not today.' Eric glared at his grandmother in the rearview mirror. 'Let's just get through today with a minimum of drama.'

'As you wish, Enrique.'

However, drama kicked into overdrive the moment they reached the steps of St Mary's Cathedral. All three Borelli sons, including the prodigal John, were greeting mourners by the carved double doors. At the sight of two Manfredis, Renaldo's face registered surprise; John's conveyed ambivalence, while Dominic's expression was pure hatred. Renny and Dom left their brother to man the door and approached the threesome.

Renny spoke first. 'Thank you, Mrs Manfredi, for coming today. Your friendship means a lot to my grandmother. I'll take you to where she's sitting. But first, who is this lovely young woman with you?' Renny completely ignored Eric as though he didn't see him.

'This is Miss Jill Wyatt from Mississippi. She lives above our restaurant now. Jill, this is Renaldo Borelli, Salvatore's eldest son.' Nonni cast a sideways glance at Eric that he couldn't interpret if his life depended on it.

'My sympathy for the loss of your father, Renaldo,' Jill said primly.

'Thank you, Miss Wyatt, for coming to pay your respects.' Renny took hold of Jill's hand and kissed the back of her fingers like some B-movie Casanova. 'And please, call me Renny.'

'OK, and you're welcome,' said Jill, wide-eyed and open-mouthed.

For a long moment, Renny smiled at Jill in his smarmy Borelli style before he turned back to Nonni. 'Are you ready to get out of the sun, Mrs Manfredi? Would you like to sit up front with my grandmother?'

'No, I'll talk to Francesca later. Please find me a seat in the back, close to the door.' Accepting Renny's arm, Nonni was escorted inside as though a guest of honor.

'I'll see you later, Miss Wyatt,' Renny said over his shoulder.

Before Eric could react to Renny's outrageousness, Dominic stepped up to take his brother's place.

'You've got your nerve showing up today, Manfredi.' Dominic kept his voice low, but there was no mistaking the hostility.

Eric stepped in front of Jill in an effort to shield her. 'I brought my grandmother out of respect for your father. Let's not cause a scene on the steps of St Mary's.'

'If you were so worried 'bout a scene, you wudda put your grandma in a cab and stayed away.' Dom loomed close enough for Eric to smell his breath. From the fumes Dom exhaled, along with his glassy dark eyes, the man was obviously drunk.

Eric stepped back and held up his hands. 'Look, let's just go into Mass and give your father a proper send off. It doesn't have to be like this between us.'

Dominic refused to be placated. 'You think I'm stupid, Manfredi? You bring your new girlfriend to the funeral of the man *your* father put in the ground? Is that your idea of impressing a woman?'

'My father didn't put anybody into the ground. Back off, Dominic. If you prefer I leave, I will. But don't go throwing around unsubstantiated accusations.'

Dominic lunged toward Eric and lost his balance. He might have tumbled headlong down the steps if John Borelli hadn't grabbed him. 'Take it easy, brother.' John snaked an arm around Dominic. 'Let's go inside and cool off.' John took hold of Eric's sleeve with his other hand. 'Please, Eric, take the young lady inside and sit down. Our grandmothers will be furious if we can't show my father due respect. Please.'

'Let's do as he says.' Jill practically pulled him up the steps.

'I would just as soon have waited for Nonni across the street in the shade,' he muttered as they slipped into the same pew as Nonni.

'I know, but I have a job to do.' Jill winked at him.

It was a small gesture, but it was enough to control Eric's anger at Dominic's behavior. Instead he concentrated on the people in attendance. Most he didn't know, but some he recognized as regular customers of Bella Trattoria. Apparently, the Charlestonians who enjoyed Italian cuisine patronized both establishments. Next he spotted the mayor and several councilmen in the pews, along with an assortment of vendors and local restaurant critics in the culinary world.

Finally, after a sharp elbow to the ribs from Nonni, Eric started paying attention to the funeral. After all, it was the reason they were there.

It didn't take him long to realize many people actually mourned the loss of Salvatore. When Renny and John stood in the pulpit and described how their father had taught them to hit a baseball, catch a fish, and say their prayers at night, Eric felt ashamed. It was so easy to despise someone based on your own limited perspective. Apparently Mr Borelli had been a good father, just like his own dad. He was also a major benefactor to the church, supported local homeless initiatives, and was a patron of the theater arts.

But what especially touched Eric's heart was the priest's message. As Christians, this life was but mere preparation for the next – the one that lasts forever. A training ground for the hereafter. Those who believe will have their sins forgiven and spend eternity with the saints and angels if their hearts are true. *Would it be that easy?* Eric didn't think so, at least not for him. While he was busy judging Salvatore Borelli, he should examine his own thoughts and actions. When was the last time he expressed gratitude, other than 'thanks for the food, let's eat.' Or bowed his head in prayer, other than for a win for his beloved Carolina Panthers? Sure, he took his grandmother to Mass each Sunday, but how often did he pay attention to the priest's message? Simply showing up might fool some people, especially those whose minds were also wandering, but it didn't fool the one who mattered. As the mourners stood for the pre-communion prayer, Eric choked back a lump in his throat. The emotion wasn't for Salvatore Borelli. It was because he was nothing but a shameful hypocrite.

At the conclusion of the service, the priest invited everyone to Holy Cross Cemetery for Salvatore's interment, and then back to the church social hall for lunch. People rose to their feet as the coffin was wheeled down the center aisle, flanked by eight pall bearers. Sofia Borelli, wife of the deceased, sobbed piteously as John and Dominic supported her on both sides. Francesca Borelli, clinging to both Renaldo and Nonni, came next in the procession, followed by an assortment of sisters, brothers, nephews and nieces in various states of distress.

Eric noticed Jill slip a small tablet and pen into her purse as they joined the throng exiting the sanctuary. 'Taking notes?' he asked next to her ear.

'You'd be surprised what an objective bystander can learn at a funeral,' she whispered.

Eric waited until they were alone in the vestibule before asking, 'OK, what did you find out?'

Jill checked to make sure no one was in earshot. 'Dominic wasn't the only one with something to lose if Salvatore executed a new will before he died. John Borelli would have been disinherited too. And that man didn't shed a single tear throughout the entire service. Even I cried during "Amazing Grace," and I had never met Mr Borelli.'

Eric scanned the crowd for Nonni and found her holding up Francesca while they loaded the coffin into the hearse. 'That's because you have a big heart,' he said. 'I told you that John has been estranged from his family for years. He even legally changed his name from Borelli to Borell to sound more American. Of course, no one in his family acknowledges the name change.'

Jill pursed her lips. 'OK, but losing one's father usually softens the hardest of hearts. I'm checking into what Mr *Borell* was doing that day.'

'As you wish, but my money's on Dominic. That guy is bad

news.' Eric glanced up to see Nonni climb into the limo with Francesca. 'Looks like my grandmother will remain with her friend. Let's get out of here. I can check with Nonni later to make sure she has a way home.'

Jill shook her head. 'Absolutely not! I want to keep my eye on Dominic and John. If you refuse to go to the cemetery, maybe I can ride with that charming Renaldo.' She fluttered her eyelashes in parody.

'Over my dead body.' Eric took hold of her hand. 'Come on, I need to pull my car into queue.'

Approximately half of the mourners from church attended the graveside final prayers. Eric managed to stay out of sight in the back, while Jill surreptitiously spied on the brothers from behind a tree. As Jill had concluded earlier, only Renny seemed genuinely saddened by his father's passing. He mopped his face several times with a handkerchief. Just when Eric thought they would escape unscathed, the funeral director circulated through the crowd passing out long-stemmed yellow roses.

'What am I supposed to do with this?' Jill asked, rejoining his side.

'Guests place the rose atop the casket just before it's lowered into the ground. But we can give ours away and leave after the last prayer.'

'Oh, Eric, this is my first funeral. Can't we stay until the end?'

Looking into Jill's honey-brown eyes, Eric realized this was the first of many times he wouldn't be able to say no to her. 'Fine, but don't make eye contact with any of the brothers.'

'Will do.' She plucked the rose from Eric's fingers. 'I'll take yours up too when the time is right.'

Jill waited until most mourners had placed their flower and headed for their cars. Then she picked a way between the graves up to the dais and small circle of family members. Whether it was because Jill was unaccustomed to walking in high heels, or due to her short dress, or maybe she simply tripped on the green carpet, she went flying toward the rose-covered casket.

If not for Renny's quick reaction, Jill might have fallen into the gaping hole, providing a memory no one would forget. Renny caught Jill in his arms and lifted her safely back from harm's way.

Eric wasted no time reaching Jill's side. 'Are you all right?'

'I'm fine, just a little embarrassed.' Her cheeks blushed brightly. 'Thank you, Renny.'

'You're welcome. I'll take care of those flowers.' Renny made sure Eric had taken hold of Jill before placing the two roses on the coffin.

But Renny's civilized behavior didn't sit well with the youngest brother. 'Why are you still here, Manfredi?' Without warning, Dominic wound up his arm and socked Eric on the jaw.

Eric stumbled back and tumbled over a grave marker. Jill gasped. One of the Borelli aunts shrieked. And someone in the back started to cry. Unfortunately, the spectacle was by no means over. John intervened and received a left cut to the nose from Dominic, which didn't sit well with the peacemaker, Renny. Soon a mini brawl ensued as several cousins joined the fray. With so many mourners already in their vehicles it took several minutes before a few level-headed uncles and one cop restored order to the sacred ground.

'Detective Schott, what are you doing here?' Jill asked once the combatants had been separated.

'What are *you* doing here, Miss Wyatt?' Schott took Jill by the arm and dragged her away from the gravesite. Eric had no choice but to follow them.

'I'm trying to figure out who killed Mr Borelli,' she said in a hushed voice.

'That's not how it looked to me.' The cop's glare landed on the hem of Jill's dress.

'She had to borrow an outfit from my sister.' Eric felt compelled to defend her.

'Fine, but you need to learn subtle, *unobtrusive* surveillance.'

'You're right.' Jill covered her face with her hands. 'I'm sorry, Eric. But at least Dominic Borelli showed his hot temper. With so much to lose with the new will, Dom must be one of your suspects now.' Jill peered up at the detective.

Schott sighed. 'He might be if he wasn't at alcohol rehab during the time someone shot Salvatore. When Dominic found out his dad was dead, he signed himself out. So he's been ruled out as a suspect. Trust me to do my job, Miss Wyatt. And I suggest you *both* stay away from the funeral luncheon. For some reason Dominic hates Eric, and thanks to the brawl, Dominic now knows you've been helping me, Jill. Or whatever it is you're doing.'

After the cop stomped off, Jill and Eric took their time getting back to their car. They had run into enough Borelli relatives for one day. When they climbed into his SUV, Nonni was sitting where she had been this morning.

'You two done causing trouble?' she asked.

'Yes, ma'am.' Jill turned the key to start the air-conditioning.

Eric locked gazes with Nonni in the rearview mirror. 'I'm surprised you didn't stay with Francesca for the rest of the day.'

'Nope, I had planned to but changed my mind. I need a nap after all that excitement. What did you think about Renaldo Borelli?' Nonni asked, tapping Jill on the shoulder.

'He seems like a nice enough man, why?' Jill cast a curious glance into the back seat.

'I was wondering if you noticed those sea-blue eyes – rather striking against his olive complexion. The Borellis are from Florence, thus the high cheekbones and rather straight hair. Women are always throwing themselves at him.'

'What are you up to, Granny?' Eric chose a term he knew Nonni despised.

'Nothing, my little field mouse. Just checking to see if Jill was paying attention.'

'Actually, I was paying attention to potential murderers to get your son off the hook,' said Jill. 'Unfortunately my favorite suspect, Dominic, has been crossed off my list.'

'Bad apple, that one,' Nonni concluded. 'Renny got the good looks, the smarts, and the charm in that family.'

Tightening his grip on the wheel, Eric trounced down on the gas pedal. None of them spoke for the rest of the drive. Once inside Bella Trattoria, Nonni shuffled off to her bedroom, but Jill remained in the kitchen.

'I really am sorry, Eric. I made things worse.'

'No, you didn't. Dominic did. It's not your fault you tripped on uneven ground.'

Jill closed her eyes, as though trying to force away the mental image of her inglorious near-fall. 'I promise to make this up to you by finding the real killer.'

'I know you will, but as long as you haven't fallen in love with that blue-eyed Lothario, I'm happy.'

'Only an idiot kisses someone's fingers. Renaldo had no clue when I last washed my hands.' Jill headed for the steps but hesitated. 'You've got nothing to worry about, Manfredi.'

'You know, my *pappardelle Bolognese* runs circles around Renny's.'

'I have no clue what that is, but someday I hope to find out. Right now I need to call my client, David Sugarman, and then my boss. Nate Price sent me a text that you called the office and discussed terms with him. I'm officially on the case.'

'Will I see you later?' Eric tried not to sound too hopeful.

'Probably not. If I don't drive to the hospital to visit Charlotte and Emma, I'll need to catch up with emails and paperwork. I also need to wash this dress and give it back to your sister. See you *domani*.'

'Look at you – learning Italian during your free time.'

Eric watched Jill disappear around the corner, feeling he might have a chance with her after all. *Tomorrow couldn't come soon enough.*

EIGHTEEN

Jill had an entire day stretching before her without a clue what to do. Both David Sugarman and Ralph Norris told her their wives were in a stable condition, but no visitors would be permitted other than immediate family. It would be several days before either woman was out of the woods, and for Charlotte, a disastrous setback could happen at any time.

But they had survived the long, intense surgery and for that Jill was grateful.

Nate had mixed feelings about her lining up another case on her own. Apparently Beth, her mentor-turned-mother-hen didn't trust the tall, dark, and dangerous landlord. At least that's how Beth had described him to Nate. However, since Nate had no other immediate cases lined up, and Eric Manfredi wired Price Investigations a healthy advance, Jill could stay on his father's case for now.

'Just don't get too personally involved with the client,' had been her boss's parting words on the subject. Jill wasn't sure if that stemmed from office policy, or from Beth's overly suspicious intuition.

When Eric and his grandmother left for Mass, Jill searched Google for Protestant churches close to the restaurant and chose First Scots Presbyterian on Meeting Street. Perhaps it was to honor her adopted ancestry. Or maybe it was simply because she still would be able to make the eleven fifteen service after breakfast and a hot shower. The long walk there and back felt good after being cooped up, except for their brief time in the cemetery. The cemetery . . . the less she thought about yesterday's brawl the better. Jill had just finished heating her lunch when Eric and Nonni returned from church.

'Hi, Jill, ready to eat?' Eric greeted. 'I left a pot of *pasta e fagioli* simmering on the stove. It should be done by now.'

'I'm having the leftover fish from Friday's dinner.' She held up Bernie's plastic container. Eric looked at her in disdain. 'All right, I'll have a small bowl,' she said.

Just as Jill sat down at the family table with her fish, a man pushing a handcart walked into the kitchen. With wine cases stacked to his chin, there was no doubt as to what he sold.

'Hi, Mr Manfredi. Shall I take these down to the cellar?'

Eric stopped stirring his soup. 'Hi, John. Why on earth are you delivering on a Sunday?'

'My office said you called about restocking the cellar. I brought four cases of your best-sellers.' The wine salesman carefully set his load upright. 'Your remodeling is coming along nicely.'

'Yes, but we're not reopening for another two weeks. There wasn't any hurry.'

'Sorry, I've been out sick for a while, so I'm trying to get my route caught up. Should I come back another day?' John's expression revealed he hoped he wouldn't have to.

'No, no, you're here now, but I won't be able to inventory until tomorrow.' Eric glanced over at her. 'John, this is Miss Wyatt. Jill, this is John Russo. Why don't you sit down and have some soup while I write your check?' Eric ladled up two bowls, delivered them to the table, and headed off with the salesman's invoice.

'Thanks, Mr Manfredi, don't mind if I do.' John immediately plopped down on Jill's left. 'Hi, I'm from R & H Distributors,' he said, inhaling the pungent aroma. 'Ahh, *pasta e fagioli*, one of my favorites!'

'Jill Wyatt,' she said. 'What exactly is in this? It looks like chili.'

John held a spoonful to his lips and blew on it with near reverence. 'So much better than chili. It's ground beef, diced tomatoes, white beans, red beans, small elbow macaroni, and of course plenty of garlic.'

'Of course.' Jill contentedly ate her salmon while the soup cooled.

'*Delizioso!*' he declared after swallowing the first spoonful. 'You're a new face. What do you sell? Boy, if only all restaurant owners were as good to vendors as the Manfredis, eh?'

Jill wiped her mouth, while considering how much to reveal. 'I'm a guest of the Manfredis, not a salesperson.'

'Is that right?' John arched an eyebrow. 'Good for you. I tried fixing my daughter up with Eric, but it didn't work out. I was so disappointed.'

'I'm not dating Eric. I'm working here . . . on a special project.'

Much to Jill's surprise, John went to the refrigerator for the pitcher of iced tea. He poured two glasses, handed her one, and then clinked glasses. 'Take it from me, a gal can do far worse than snagging that boy,' he whispered. 'Rumor has it he's loaded. When everybody else got burned in the '08 market correction, Eric emptied his bank account and bought stocks.

Buy low, sell high – that's the ticket. The son of Alfonzo Manfredi is one smart cookie!'

Jill could only stare at the man with her fork midway to her mouth. *Why do middle-aged people think everyone is out to make the perfect match . . . or should be?*

'Thanks for the tip, but I think I'll leave this fish for a woman angling for such a good catch.' Jill stabbed her last piece of salmon with the fork.

'Ha, ha, you're a quick one, Jill Wyatt. Do you enjoy your present career? Because you'd be a natural at sales. The wine business could use a few funny women.' John pulled a business card from his wallet and laid it on the table. Then he began devouring his soup now that it was sufficiently cool.

Jill recognized an opportunity. 'I'm curious. What did you mean by "if only every restaurant owner was like the Manfredis"?'

John glanced around to make sure they were still alone. 'Did you notice how Eric took my invoice and immediately went to write the check for the delivery? He wasn't even expecting me today.'

Jill spooned up some soup, which tasted wonderful. 'So you're saying most customers *don't* pay their bills promptly?'

John laughed. 'You're pulling my leg, right? It's easier to squeeze blood from a turnip than to get money from some restaurant owners. They'll charge thirty bucks for an entrée, yet make vendors crawl on their knees to get paid. The Manfredis – they're the exception!'

Jill was about to ask who wasn't an exception when Eric strolled into the room. 'What's so exceptional about us?' he asked.

'Your *pasta e fagioli*, for one thing.' John tipped up his bowl to savor the last drops.

'*Grazie*, John. How about you, Jill? Are you reserving your opinion until you taste the competitor's?' Slipping into the opposite chair, Eric slicked a hand through his thick hair.

If the wine vendor hadn't been there, Jill might have cracked a joke about Renaldo Borelli. But with a sneaky plan percolating, she smacked her lips instead. 'This is the best *fagioli* I ever tasted.'

'It's the only *fagioli* you've ever tasted,' said Nonni, pulling Jill's braid on her way to the table. She had changed out of her Sunday dress into a cotton skirt and blouse.

'Would you like another bowl, John?' Eric carried a bowl of soup for Nonni and one for himself.

'No, thanks. I'd better take those cases down and mosey on to my next customer. My wife's expecting me home by four for dinner.'

'I'll check inventory on the computer against what's on the shelves and send in my order tomorrow or Tuesday.'

'Sounds great, Mr Manfredi. Nice meeting you, Miss Wyatt. Call me if you'd like to change careers.'

The moment the vendor disappeared down the steps, Jill turned toward Eric. 'Mr Russo gave me an idea. What do you want to bet Salvatore Borelli owed plenty of people money around town?'

Nonni readily agreed. 'Very likely. According to Francesca, half of Sofia's credit cards were confiscated by the store because Sal wasn't making minimum payments. Never seemed to slow down Sofia's spending though.'

'Are there no family secrets you and Francesca don't gossip about?' Eric asked his grandmother.

Nonni tapped her lips with a finger. 'I can't think of any, but you don't have to worry, Enrique. I say only good things about you and Bernadette.'

Eric met Jill's gaze. 'See what I'm up against?'

'I'm starting to, but getting back to my theory, what if someone Sal owed money to got tired of waiting? He might have followed Sal and your father from Tuscan Gardens. Then after your dad left, the man lost his temper when Sal refused to pay him.'

Eric stretched out his long legs. 'You could be on to something, but I doubt it's one of our suppliers. If a restaurant gets too far behind, the purveyor stops supplying them. A chef can't cook and serve food he doesn't have.'

Jill leaned across the table. 'But the owner could buy the food elsewhere and end up owing money all over Charleston.'

Eric's smile turned his handsome face into something irresistible. 'High-end cuisine isn't the same as buying burgers and bagged salad at Kroger's,' he explained patiently. 'Imported seafood, specialty meats, and vintage wine usually have only one source in town. A restaurant can't remain in business if they don't satisfy the foodies.'

'Hmm, I see your point.' Jill slung her purse over her shoulder and set her bowl in the sink. 'Thanks for the soup, Eric.'

'How about a run along the waterfront or maybe a bike ride out to Sullivan's Island? Today is supposed to be a day off, remember?'

'Maybe later, but right now I need to follow up on this. Call it feminine intuition.' Jill picked up Russo's business card and bolted for the door.

Or call it listening to her better judgment for a change. Unlike Beth or her boss, Jill didn't believe Eric Manfredi was the least bit dangerous. But a person on the run couldn't afford to get involved with anyone. It was too bad really, because jogging along the waterfront with an attractive man who cooked soup this good definitely had appeal.

Jill punched in the wine vendor's number the moment she reached her car. 'Hi, Mr Russo. It's Jill Wyatt. Bet you didn't think you'd hear from me so soon.'

He hesitated only briefly. 'No, but what a pleasant surprise. What's on your mind?'

'I'd like to continue our earlier discussion, but not in earshot of my present employer.'

'Gotcha. Why don't you call my office and set up an appointment for next week?'

Jill needed to come up with something fast. As much as she hated lying, she knew the truth wouldn't go far with Russo. 'Unfortunately, I'm about to accept an offer elsewhere. That's why I was hoping to talk to you later today.' She held her breath as she waited.

'*Today?* I still have three more deliveries to make.' Russo didn't sound quite as eager for a humorous saleswoman as he did before.

'Could we have coffee after your next call? I'll come wherever you are. I'll even buy the coffee.' Jill added a friendly chuckle.

'You sure are as persistent as a salesperson needs to be. OK, write down this address. It's where I'm headed next. Find us a coffee shop nearby and text me the location. I'll get there as soon as I can.'

Jill did as requested, and true to his word, John Russo arrived at the Java Stop sixty minutes later.

'Just so you know, Miss Wyatt, I texted my wife our location. So if you slip something into my latte and attempt to kidnap me, she'll track you down like a dog. She's very fond of me.'

Utter silence spun out since Jill had no idea how to react.

'Ha ha, you should see your face.' Russo slapped his knee. 'Get me a double espresso and we can talk shop.'

Jill thought the last thing Russo needed was more caffeine but filled his request anyway. Once she returned with his espresso and her regular coffee, she pulled out her notebook. 'The idea of wine sales intrigues me, but I'm concerned about a few things.'

'Ask whatever you want.' He took a sip of the strong brew.

'I'm nervous about those restaurants that place big orders and then don't pay you. You said not everyone is responsible like Bella Trattoria.'

'It's a headache, to be sure, but it's not your worry. You're not personally responsible for collections. The company has people in the office who deal with that sort of thing. If necessary, we turn it over to an agency or take the deadbeats to court.'

Jill whooshed out her breath. 'Whew, that's a relief. But I'm still shocked that top-end restaurants would behave like this.'

Russo shrugged. 'Most top-end establishments are still family owned, instead of corporate controlled. The chefs might have reached the zenith of their careers, but many still let their wives handle the books. Some just hate turning over their books to a professional accountant.'

She sipped her drink. 'I overheard the Manfredis talking and it seems their biggest competitor is Tuscan Gardens. I was curious if the Borellis could be one of those late payers.'

Russo studied her curiously. 'This will stay just between us?'

'Absolutely,' she said.

'Sal was the absolute worst. Now that he's passed on – may God rest his soul – I hope Renaldo Borelli will handle day-to-day operations more professionally.'

'We can only hope.' Remembering how Nonni tried to make Eric jealous by touting Renny made Jill smile. But the amusing memory led to her undoing.

Russo's expression changed. 'You're not really thinking about changing careers, are you, Miss Wyatt?'

Since she wasn't a good liar, Jill looked the vendor in the eye. 'No, sir, I am not. I love my job, plus I don't know the first thing about wine.'

'Then why buy me a six-dollar cup of coffee?'

'I've been hired by the Manfredis to find out who's been targeting them maliciously. And lately, I've expanded my scope to figure out who killed Salvatore Borelli.' Jill laid her business card on the table.

Unexpectedly, Russo broke into peals of laughter. 'You're pulling my leg again, right? The Manfredis and Borellis are certainly not friends. No way would Alfonzo Manfredi hire you to find Sal's killer. He would just raise an expensive glass of Cabernet in toast.'

'Not Alfonzo – Eric Manfredi. Finding the real killer is the only way to clear his father's name.'

Russo sobered. 'You think it might have been someone Sal owed money to?'

'It crossed my mind after talking to you.' Jill gripped her coffee with both hands.

'Then your list of suspects will be longer than the US Tax Code.' He took another hearty swallow of espresso. 'Just for the record, on the Friday Sal Borelli died I went straight from work to my daughter's school. She was in a play and my wife has plenty of video of the event, in case I need to prove my whereabouts.'

'I'll cross you off my list of suspects, but what I really need is someone to narrow the field.'

Russo scrubbed his hands down his face. 'Sal probably owed plenty of people money, but Colin MacFaren, the seafood purveyor, comes to mind. Colin has quite a temper on him when someone's account is more than two months overdue. Colin doesn't have a large enough operation to give restaurants much leeway.'

Jill jotted down the seafood salesman's name. 'Can you think of anyone else that might not like getting paid?'

Russo finished his espresso and crumpled the cup in his large hand. 'Not offhand. Nobody likes not getting paid, but it's a huge leap from that to shooting someone in the head. After all, vendors will simply stop delivering the products the restaurant needs to survive.'

'That's what Eric said.' With a sigh, Jill closed her tablet. 'This could be another dead end.'

'OK, Miss Wyatt, since you spent six bucks on me I'll give you one more tip. When people don't pay their bills, they've usually had that bad habit their entire life. Six years ago, Salvatore Borelli built a huge fancy house on Kiawah Island. I've never been to one of his parties, but I heard the house described as palatial. Dollars-to-donuts I'd bet Sal still owes plenty of people money from construction.'

Jill's exuberance waned. '*Six years?* Wouldn't they have done something by now? And how would this be any different than owing money to a product vendor?'

'Pay attention, young lady.' Russo shook his finger at her. 'A vendor would cut off your supply if you get too far behind, but if you owe money to a marble importer, a plumbing contractor, or the guy who installed your Olympic-size swimming pool, they're not allowed to take back the countertops or chrome faucets. Their only recourse is to file a lien against the house, which the owner isn't forced to pay off until the property is sold.'

'And if the owner doesn't sell the house for twenty years?' Jill asked.

'Now you're catching on. That poor plumber just has to wait for his money.' Lumbering to his feet, Russo picked up Jill's business card. 'You came all the way to Charleston from Natchez, Mississippi?' He hooted with laughter. 'Don't tell me you didn't get a look at Eric Manfredi on the restaurant's website before taking the case.'

Jill shook her head. 'John, you are impossible, but I appreciate your help.'

'You're welcome. Just don't call me again unless you're serious about getting into the wine business. You know what will happen to you.'

'Your wife will hunt me down like a dog?'

'Exactly right.' With a final wave, Russo headed for the door.

Jill added one more item to her to-do list after Colin MacFaren's name and headed back to Bella Trattoria.

NINETEEN

'Eleven, twelve, thirteen.' Eric jotted down the figure next to Chardonnay Chateau Ste. Michelle, and moved on to sparkling wines and Proseccos. He usually never inventoried on Sundays, but with his parents visiting out-of-town relatives and Nonni napping, he had little else to do. Actually, it was the fact that he'd planned to spend the day with Jill that had him cranky. Hot and cold, over and over. Every bit of encouragement she threw his way was quickly dashed by her actions. Why on earth did she run after the wine salesman? Jill couldn't possibly consider him a murder suspect. John Russo was an all-round nice guy, who couldn't hurt a fly. Jill must have needed an excuse to get away from him. Maybe his grandmother was right. Maybe he was a field mouse, lurking in the tall grass, waiting for a crumb to fall.

Seven, eight, nine bottles of Gaston Chiquet – a French champagne purchased by those celebrating an anniversary or special occasion.

Fifteen, sixteen, seventeen bottles of Bellavista Franciacorta Brut – an Italian sparkling from the Brescia valley.

'Eric, are you down there?' Jill's voice floated down the stone steps.

'Nope, I'm the Ghost of Christmas Past,' he answered.

Jill tramped downstairs and wound her way through the maze of aisles. 'I looked everywhere for you. I thought you weren't going to inventory stock today.'

'I hadn't planned to. I had *planned* to jog or ride bikes and just sit and get better acquainted with someone. But as Steinbeck once said, the best laid plans of mice and men . . .'

She pressed her fist to her mouth. 'I believe that was Robert Burns, but no matter. I caught your meaning and I'm sorry.'

'No need to apologize, Miss Wyatt. You made it clear from the start you were merely my tenant.' Eric tried to count bottles of Spanish cava, but his mind refused to cooperate.

'Eric, stop. Please.' Jill laid her hand on his arm. 'Give me a chance to explain.'

He tucked his clipboard of order sheets under his arm, feeling suddenly like a rejected adolescent. 'Did you catch up with John Russo?'

'Yes. And as much as I would've loved a day off, last night when I realized how much money you're paying for my *investigation* I felt like a flimflam man in a traveling sideshow.'

'Those were outlawed years ago in South Carolina.' Eric felt his back muscles start to relax. 'Was Russo able to shed light on the case?'

'Yes, and he completely agreed with you – a vendor wouldn't remain unpaid for long without cutting off the supply, something no restaurant can afford. But Russo did drop the name of Colin MacFaren, a seafood seller who Borelli owed plenty to. He also said the guy has a hot temper.'

'I can easily check into Colin MacFaren tomorrow. I'm acquainted with him.'

'Good. Then Russo pointed me in another direction. He said that Salvatore had a very expensive house built on Kiawah. If he still owed money to any of the sub-contractors, they have no recourse but to file a lien.'

'And a lien doesn't get paid off as long as the Borellis own the house.'

'Exactly. While you look into MacFaren, I'll look into liens on their property as soon as the Charleston County Courthouse opens in the morning.'

'And your plans until then?' Eric dusted off a bottle of vintage Krug. 'It's too late to ride bikes to Sullivan's Island.'

'I thought we could drive out to this Kiawah Island. It's on my short list of places to see anyway.'

'Because you hope a shirtless Renaldo might be out trimming the hedges?'

Jill punched him squarely in the solar plexus. 'Get this straight, Eric. Renny is Nonni's fantasy, not mine. I'm interested in seeing Salvatore's palace. Then I hope to pry a non-Italian meal out of you. No offense.'

'None taken. What a load off my mind.' Eric patted his abdomen. 'I have but two questions: What kind of food did you have in mind?'

'Cheeseburgers – fully loaded with grilled mushrooms and onions, lettuce, tomatoes, pickles.' Jill ticked off condiments on her fingers. 'And the cheese must be American, not gorgonzola or something I can't pronounce. Plus French fries with Cajun seasoning and lots of Coke. Can we find this somewhere on Kiawah, hopefully not too far from the water?'

'I'm sure we can and I will admit American cheese melts well on burgers.'

Jill's eyes sparkled with animation. 'Now we're getting somewhere. What's your second question?'

'What will we do after we spy on the Borelli house and dine non-gourmet under the stars?'

'Maybe we can get to know each other better. I've always wanted to walk the beach on an island.' Jill curled her fingers into a fist a second time. 'But no funny stuff, Manfredi. This will be our first *official* date. Dinner at Bernadette's didn't count.'

'I wouldn't dream of funny stuff. Are you wearing that?' Eric gestured to the dress she had on this morning when they returned from church.

'Goodness, no. I'll go change and meet you outside.' Jill strode toward the steps. 'Just don't let anyone hiding behind the bougainvillea climb into your back seat.'

'If we have to, we'll jump into your car for a clean getaway.'

Eric turned off the cellar lights and followed her upstairs. After glancing down at his chinos and white shirt, he dug through his office closet until he found an old pair of cut-offs and T-shirt.

'Is this too casual?' he asked when she joined him in the courtyard.

'You look just fine,' she said, slipping a tiny purse over her head.

She, on the other hand, looked better than fine. In her black Capri pants and long white tank top, Jill looked heartbreakingly pretty.

During the one-hour drive from downtown Charleston to Kiawah Island, Eric talked about his life as the head chef of Bella Trattoria. Not that he thought balancing accounts and making shopping lists for the week's daily specials and regular items was that interesting. But this way Jill would have no excuse not to open up to him later.

Once they turned on to the Kiawah Island Parkway, Jill started talking without prodding. 'Gosh, it's been so long since I've been anywhere like this. The best days of my childhood took place at the beach. Body-surfing, building sand castles, playing sand volleyball, I absolutely never wanted to go home.'

'How close to water did you live?'

'My adoptive parents lived about an hour from Panama City, so we went to the public beach every Saturday in the summer. After my parents died and I stayed with various foster families, I only got to the beach once in a while.'

'But a passion for water never dies.' Eric turned into the parking lot for the East Beach Town Center.

'No, if anything absence only makes the heart grow fonder.' Jill pointed to a sign for The Market. 'Is that where we're headed?'

'It is – the best burgers on the island. I promised you nothing unpronounceable on the menu and plenty of American cheese.'

'As long as we don't have to cook the food ourselves, let's go.' Jill slipped her hand into his.

Eric savored the touch of her fingers on their way into the restaurant, but he waited until they were seated with menus before he asked another question. 'You said you grew up in Panama City, but I thought you were from Mississippi?'

Jill shrugged. 'Natchez is what's on my business card, but I've only been to the home office once for some paperwork. I have such a convoluted history, I usually let people believe what they want until it becomes an issue.'

'If you would prefer that I respect your privacy—'

'No, this is our first official date, so it's time the traveling queen tells all.' Jill gave the waitress her order, which was exactly as she'd described in the cellar.

Eric duplicated the order for himself. 'How did you manage to get hired by a Mississippi agency?'

'At the time I was on a temporary job in Savannah. Beth and Michael were working a case on assignment. Thanks to referrals, they suddenly had more work than they could handle and started interviewing for another investigator. I was the lucky applicant.'

Eric could almost see wheels turning in Jill's head, but he knew better than to push too hard.

'When Beth and Michael finished their assignment, they decided to stay in Savannah. I became the roving agent and thus landed in Charleston.' Jill took a gulp of Coke.

Eric couldn't bring himself to ask the next question, since he didn't want to hear her answer. 'So that clears up the "where you're from" mystery,' he said instead.

'There is something else I wanted to come clean about – something I wasn't truthful about.' Jill looked up with eyes full of regret. 'When we were at your sister's house, I told your mother I had no family. That was a lie.'

For a brief moment, Eric feared Jill was running from an abusive spouse. He'd been pinning his hopes on a woman who would one day reconcile and return home. 'Are you married?' he asked.

'No, no, nothing like that, but I do have a brother I don't like to talk about.'

Eric almost choked on his joy. 'Is he a natural brother?'

'No, Liam was adopted, same as me. But we were very close. Even after the county separated us into different foster homes, we stayed in touch.'

'I'm surprised they didn't place you together.'

Jill shook her head. 'The county only tries to keep natural siblings together. In our case they didn't bother, even though we were just as important to each other as blood relatives.'

'Maybe more so. He was all you had and vice versa.

Want to tell me why you're not close any more?' Eric asked after a short silence. 'You don't have to if you don't want to.'

Another shrug. 'Liam's new friends were bad influences. They started breaking into cars for spare change and GPS units and stealing stuff from backyards to resell. All petty crimes. Then one day he wasn't a juvenile any more and landed in county lockup where he met some very bad men. After his release he looked them up and together they robbed a bank. Unfortunately Liam was the only one caught. Now he's in prison and will be for a long time.' Jill lifted her teary gaze. 'I'm so ashamed of him.'

'Jill, you're not your brother's keeper. No one judges you based on his actions.'

Eric was thankful the waitress chose that moment to deliver their meals. He didn't want to minimize her pain by saying the wrong thing. For several minutes they dipped fries in catsup and piled the toppings high on their burgers. After a few bites, he was ready to venture forth. 'As sad as your brother's story is, many families have a member who have fallen far short of expectations. Someday I'll tell you about my Uncle Guido who's doing time for selling moonshine from a hotdog pushcart. And this wasn't his first bust for bootlegging.'

Jill smiled. 'Is his name really *Guido*?'

Eric returned the smile. 'Yes, it is. He's incarcerated in upstate New York.'

'Not to make light of poor Uncle Guido, but it's not the same thing. You're *surrounded* by loving family. I saw them at your dad's homecoming party. Liam was all I had.'

'No aunts, uncles, or cousins?'

'None that I'm close with. I think they felt bad about not taking us in after my parents died.'

'As they should.'

'Everybody has their own problems. I don't harbor any bad feelings.'

'Maybe someday I can change your lack of family.' When Eric reached for her hand, Jill immediately yanked back.

'Maybe, but this is our first date, remember? Let's focus on the food and not get ahead of ourselves.' Jill picked up her burger.

So while they finished eating, Eric described snorkeling among hundreds of jellyfish and Jill shared being buried in sand infested with sand fleas. By the time he paid the check and they strolled back to the car, the evening had cooled off. 'What's next?' he asked. 'You're in charge.'

'Do you know where the Borellis live?' Jill asked. 'Is it close enough to walk?'

'Definitely not. We'll have to drive. And in order to get a good look we'll also have a long walk ahead of us.' Fifteen minutes later, Eric slowed down in front of a three-story house surrounded by a tall fence with an electronic gate. There was so much shrubbery and dense foliage the home was barely visible. '*Voila*, the Borellis.'

'Hmmm, I see what you mean. Certainly is private.'

'Let's find a place to park and take one of the boardwalks over to the beach. Then we'll walk along the water.'

Once on the boardwalk, they meandered along at a leisurely pace. But once they reached the sand, Jill pulled off her sandals and ran pell-mell toward the surf. With her long hair streaming down her back, Jill still looked like that child she described. Seagulls took flight, while sandpipers scurried as fast as their spindly legs would let them as she splashed through the swallow water. Finally Jill stopped and stretched her arms over her head toward the sky.

'Feel good to be back?' he asked once he caught up.

'You have no idea. Thank you, Eric. I forgot how much I missed this.' Jill took his hand.

'Should we sprint all the way to the Borellis' or take it nice and slow?'

'Nice and slow sounds good.'

With nothing but dunes on one side and pounding waves on the other, they both remained quiet for a while. Eric had forgotten how peaceful Kiawah Island was.

'I gather you've been inside their house?' she asked, finally breaking the silence. 'How did you manage an invite? I thought the two families have hated each other a long time.'

'They have. But when the Borellis moved in, Salvatore

threw a huge party and invited hundreds of people. He spared no expense. Sal sent us an invitation because he wanted to show his house off. Of course, Dad refused to go, but Nonni and my mother insisted, so I got stuck driving them.' Eric stared out at the horizon.

'Your mother? That couldn't have gone over well with Alfonzo.'

'He didn't talk to her for a week. Truth is she hated the house.'

'Why? What's wrong with it?'

'Judge for yourself. It's the next one but be careful, someone could be out on the deck.'

Jill didn't listen. She ran to the next property, kicking up the soft sand as she went. Dissatisfied with the view, she kept running until she reached a lifeguard platform, mere yards from their pool compound.

'Jill,' he hissed. 'Stay out of sight. The Borellis will recognize you.' Eric caught up to her, but four upright posts and a ladder didn't create a good hiding place for two people.

'Oh my goodness.' Jill covered her mouth with both hands yet couldn't stem her laughter. 'It's *ghastly*. It's like the designer started with a good idea but didn't know when to stop. Are those statues of Roman gods?'

'Yes – Zeus, Neptune, Venus, and Mars.'

'How does their priest feel about that?'

'This was Sal's end of the garden. On Sofia's end, there's a lovely meditation garden with a statue of the Blessed Virgin. The inside of the house has the same over-the-top excessiveness.'

'Uh-oh,' Jill whispered. 'Looks like we've attracted attention. What should we do?'

Eric peeked between the slats. 'Sure enough Renaldo Manfredi was leaning over the deck rail, staring in their direction. Although they both stood very still, Renny headed toward the steps leading to the garden and pool.

'Run!' Eric ordered. And so they ran. They didn't stop running until they were back at the car.

Jill collapsed against his side, breathless and panting. 'I haven't felt like that in a long time. Do you think Renny recognized us?'

Eric unlocked the doors. 'Most likely. You and I make a recognizable pair.'

Jill leaned her head back and closed her eyes. 'So much for *subtle, unobtrusive surveillance*. I sure hope Renny doesn't call Lieutenant Schott.'

'Renaldo would be more likely to call you, thinking you have a crush on him.'

She slouched down in the seat. 'That's even worse. Take me home, Manfredi. I've done enough damage for one day.'

Home. Eric knew it didn't mean anything but nevertheless, coming from Jill, he liked the sound of it.

'Yes, ma'am.'

TWENTY

Jill woke up refreshed after sleeping like a baby. Funny what an enjoyable evening will do for a gal's outlook on life. But after her second cup of coffee, she remembered she wasn't on vacation. And wasn't being paid to date the client paying her expenses. She had work to do and started by calling David Sugarman and Ralph Norris. Although neither of them picked up the phone, Jill learned from the University Medical Center that nothing had changed – neither Emma nor Charlotte could have visitors other than immediate family.

When Jill entered the kitchen, Mrs Donatella Angelica Manfredi was already sitting at the family table, and carpenters were installing the last of the cabinets, appliances, and fixtures. Soon Bella Trattoria would be ready to reopen.

'Nonni, you're up bright and early for a Monday morning.'

'That's because I have big plans today, *mia piccola*. And I was hoping you could join me.'

'Thank you, but I need to go to the courthouse. I'm hot on the tail of my next suspect.' Flashing a smile at the older woman, Jill headed for the door.

'*My* plans might help your case more than yours.'

That stopped Jill dead in her tracks. 'What's up? You've got my attention.'

'I'm having lunch with Francesca Borelli. Care to join us? Just think how many questions you could get answered.' Nonni took a sip from her mug.

It didn't take Jill long to decide. 'I will try. Where are you dining?'

'Husk, on Queen Street,' said Nonni. 'They serve delicious Southern food and we're meeting at twelve o'clock.'

'Is Eric around? Will he be able to drive you? Because I'm not sure how long I'll be at the courthouse.'

With the dignity of a queen, Nonni rose to her feet. 'Not to worry. Eric was up early too. He made some calls and then Alfonzo sent him on a wild-goose chase for the grand reopening. He said he'll see you later. And me? I plan to take an Uber.' The lines in her face deepened. 'Eric was whistling when he went to bed in his cramped office last night. Anything you care to share with your new *Nonni*?'

'No, ma'am. You'll have to wait to read it in the *Post and Courier*, same as everyone else.'

Nonni's laughter startled one carpenter and his supervisor. 'Come to lunch. I have a feeling you'll be able to get plenty out of Francesca.'

'Why?' Jill asked, remaining in place.

'Huh?' The question took Nonni by surprise.

'Why would Francesca Borelli help me? Salvatore was her son.'

Nonni lifted and dropped her shoulders and then met Jill's eye. 'I'm not sure she will. I just know she loved Salvatore. And she doesn't believe for one moment that my Alfonzo murdered him.'

Jill smiled. 'I'll see you at noon.'

On her laptop in the courtyard, Jill learned that liens were filed at the Charleston County Building on Meeting Street. The RMC's Office recorded all land titles and claims by unpaid contractors, called mechanic's liens, and made sure the information was available to the public. Quite impressively, their record books dated back to 1719.

Once Jill arrived on site, she soon discovered a total of ten liens had been filed against Salvatore Borelli's property on Kiawah Island. The unpaid debts involved everything from foundation masonry to roofing materials to imported brass hardware. Five had been removed after Sal submitted proof of payment. Of the five remaining, four were under eight thousand dollars – a sum Jill figured no one would kill somebody over. The fifth was for sixty-four thousand, eight hundred and some odd dollars. *Winner, winner, chicken dinner.*

At the time of his death, Sal Borelli owed Robert Johnson of Johnson Landscaping for work on his quarter-acre Roman garden, including stone retention walls, fountains, fish pond, installation of statuary, and the horticulture around the pool and throughout the backyard. *Sixty-five grand?* Jill imagined that kind of unpaid debt could cause homicidal rage in some small contractors. She jotted down Johnson's address from the lien, thanked the helpful people in the RMC's office, and checked her watch. With just enough time to walk to Husk, she left her car where it was and avoided paying for parking twice.

When Jill arrived at the Victorian mansion converted into a restaurant, Donatella and Francesca were already seated with glasses of lemonade. 'Am I late, ladies?' she asked.

'You are not. Jill, this is Francesca Borelli, my BFF. Francesca, this is Jill Wyatt, Enrique's girlfriend.'

She didn't know what to respond to first. 'How do you do, Mrs Borelli.' Jill extended her hand politely.

'I am well, thank you. But my grandson, Renny, will be sorry to hear that you're spoken for,' said Francesca. The full-figured woman wore an expensive outfit and had bright auburn hair. She would still turn heads at a senior citizen center.

'I didn't know I was, ma'am. And who taught you about BFFs?' Jill directed this question at Nonni.

'Danielle, who else? And of course, you're spoken for. You're dating Enrique, aren't you?'

Jill chose not to explain dating in the current century. Instead she sipped water and listened to Francesca bemoan her daughter-in-law's lack of restraint following Salvatore's death. Apparently, Sofia packed up his clothes for charity the *next day* after the funeral. It didn't take long to realize Francesca didn't care much for the other woman living in the mansion.

Nonni tried to placate her friend. 'Ach, maybe Sofia doesn't like the constant reminder.'

'All she had to do is close Salvatore's closet doors.'

After placing their lunch orders, Jill decided to take the lead. 'Eric said you lived on Kiawah Island with the most beautiful garden in the world.'

Nonni barely batted an eyelash at Jill's fib, while Francesca's face glowed. 'Yes, parts of the yard are quite serene. I will miss reading under the grape arbor if I decide to move.'

'Do all of your grandsons live there?' Jill asked.

'Renaldo has an apartment near our restaurant for workdays, but he does come out to swim and relax on his days off. We eat lunch together. However, John lives in Columbia and Dominic – who knows? Dom comes and goes. Half the time he probably sleeps in his car.' Francesca's mouth twisted into a frown.

'Getting back to your lovely yard, Eric is thinking about redoing the courtyard behind Bella Trattoria. Would you mind sharing the name of your landscaper? That is, if you can still remember.'

Francesca snorted. 'You bet I remember who built Sal's Roman garden – Bob Johnson. He came to see my son a day or two before he died and they had an awful row. I couldn't hear everything said, but apparently Sal still owed him a lot of money.' She dabbed her eyes. 'Sal had been getting so forgetful. I told him to give the checkbook to Renaldo. After all, Renny does a fine job of running Tuscan Gardens. But no, Sal turned their personal account over to Sofia.'

'Why not put the fox in charge of the henhouse?' asked Nonni, no longer the peacemaker at the table.

'Exactly. Well, that landscaper doesn't have much chance of getting paid now. So although Johnson did a wonderful job, I wouldn't drop our name if Eric decides to give him a call. He might run in the opposite direction.'

Nonni crossed her arms, grinning like a Cheshire cat.

'Thanks, Mrs Borelli. I'll be sure to tell Eric.' Jill leaned back as the waitress delivered three identical plates of shrimp and grits. The ladies dug in with pleasure, but soon Nonni and

Francesca put down their forks and started gossiping about mutual acquaintances.

Jill understood why their lunches took two hours, but she had a job to do. Her shrimp and grits was so good, she had no trouble cleaning her plate. Then she pulled a twenty from her wallet and waited for a pause in their conversation. 'Forgive me for eating and rushing off, but I have to work this afternoon.' She laid the bill on the table.

Nonni looked horrified. 'You put that money away, young lady. I invited you so I pay. No arguments!'

'Yes, ma'am, and thank you.'

'A pleasure meeting you, Jill.' Francesca grinned warmly.

'The pleasure was mine.' Jill scooped up her money and shoved it into an SPCA collection bottle near the front door. *One good turn deserves another.*

Setting her GPS for the address on the mechanic's lien, Jill soon arrived at Robert Johnson's home in North Charleston. Fortuitously, Johnson was just getting home from work when she parked at the curb.

Jill shrugged into her blazer for a more professional appearance. 'Mr Johnson,' she called, 'may I have a word with you?'

'Who are you?' Johnson halted with one hand on the door handle.

'I'm Jill Wyatt, an investigator working the Salvatore Borelli homicide.' She hoped Johnson would think she was with the police, despite the fact she hadn't flashed a badge.

'What would I know 'bout that?' he asked.

Jill waited until she reached his side. 'Probably nothing, but I'm talking to everyone who spoke with the deceased before his death.'

'Look, I'm hot and tired and don't think I can be much help.'

'Please, this will only take a few minutes.' Jill offered a charming smile.

'Five minutes and that's it.' Johnson unlocked the door and held it open. Trying not to consider he could be a murderer, Jill followed him inside.

Whereas his yard was full of well-trimmed ornamental trees

and blooming shrubs, the kitchen looked sorely neglected. 'Mind if I sit?' She plopped down at the cluttered table.

Johnson opened a Coke and leaned against the sink.

'According to my report, you went to see Salvatore at his home and argued with him, rather heatedly.' Jill pulled out her notebook.

'You bet I did. That bum still owes me sixty K. Have you seen that monstrosity of a mansion? Look around. Which one of us needs the money more?' Johnson gestured at his modest furnishings.

'That is quite a garden, even for Kiawah. Did Mr Borelli settle his debt with you that day?'

'He did not. Now that Sal is dead, who knows how long I'll have to wait for my money.'

'Considering you filed a lien more than five years ago, why did you pick now to demand payment?'

'Oh, I called him plenty of times, both at his restaurant and at home. But *now* was when I needed the money.' Johnson focused his gaze out the window.

'May I ask why?'

'What would *that* have to do with your investigation?' His tone indicated a waning of patience. 'That ain't none of your business.'

'You're right, it's not. I just want the facts to eliminate you as a suspect.'

'S'pose it don't make no difference.' Johnson finished the Coke and crushed the can in his massive hand. 'I needed the cash for a new chemotherapy drug for my wife. Insurance denied coverage – they said it was still experimental for her type of cancer.'

Jill heard the pain behind his words. 'Forgive me for prying, sir. Sometimes I hate this part of my job.'

'Work's the only thing I have left any more.' He looked up, his eyes bloodshot and heavy-lidded. 'My wife is dead, but then again, so is Sal Borelli. I call that justice.'

Jill rose to her feet, not liking his evil little smile. 'My sympathy for your loss. Thank you for talking to me.'

When Jill tried to step past him, Johnson grabbed her arm with a vise-like grip. 'You wondering who killed that tightwad? I'd take a good look at his wife if I were you. They fought like cats and dogs the entire time that house was being built.'

'I'm sure plenty of hard decisions had to be made. Men and women don't always agree on decorating. Now if you don't mind . . .' Jill glared at the callused fingers still holding her arm.

'What are you – twelve? I ain't talkin' about paint colors or window treatments.' Johnson released her. 'Get out of my house.'

Jill couldn't get away from the nasty man fast enough. She punched in Lieutenant Schott's number before she reached the end of the street. Unfortunately, she got Schott's voicemail instead. 'Lieutenant Schott, Jill Wyatt, the PI working for the Manfredis. I think you should look into Robert Johnson, a landscaper from North Charleston. Mr Borelli owed him sixty-five thousand for work done on his house. Johnson needed the money for his wife's cancer treatment. I'm not sure when she passed, but Borelli never gave him the money. Johnson could have killed him when he refused to pay, or after her death for revenge.' Jill left her number and hung up, feeling stupid for leaving such a long message. After checking her watch, she headed to the University Medical Center of South Carolina. She still hadn't heard a word from either husband, and Jill wanted to see her two favorite patients in person.

When Jill got to the hospital she was ready for some good news. Maybe she would make farm animals from modeling clay with Bobby and little Joan. Or perhaps Ralph would be there with his three, and she'd have a chance to bring his older two out of their quiet shell. Or at least make the Norris baby giggle.

But good news was not to be.

David Sugarman, who Jill found in a chair outside his wife's room, had taken the children to his sister's house. Charlotte was showing signs of rejecting her sister's organ. And if that happened, Charlotte would be transferred to hospice for her next step in life's journey. Jill was not permitted into her room, so she asked question after question of the tall, harsh man. Sugarman's answers were brief and succinct. The husband seemed to be in a state of shock.

'I don't know what to do, Jill. They're going to change the dosage and add another drug to the mix, but they can't tell me if . . . this . . . will . . . work or not.' His voice cracked while his lower lip trembled.

'All I know is you shouldn't be alone.' Jill pulled out her phone. 'Do you have any family I can call?'

'I only have one sister. She would have to bring the kids to the hospital. I don't want them here now. They shouldn't see me like this.'

'You must have friends. Let me call someone.'

'My boss said to call him if I needed anything. I get along well with him.' Sugarman met her gaze with moist eyes, pulled out his phone, and punched in the number.

Jill waited until David talked with his boss and heard the man was on his way. Then Sugarman headed to the men's room, and Jill headed to the fifth floor to see Emma Norris.

Unfortunately, the news from Emma's husband wasn't much better. Ralph stepped from the room when he spotted Jill on the other side of the glass. 'Emma's resting now, Miss Wyatt. The nurses keep giving her medicine so she'll sleep.'

'Well, that's good, right?' she asked. 'A body needs rest in order to heal.'

Norris looked up at the ceiling tiles. 'I guess so. I don't know much 'bout that.' Whereas Mr Sugarman seemed to be already grieving for the inevitable, Emma's husband seemed to be in a stupor.

'What did the doctor say?' she asked.

'He said Emma has an infection. He mentioned where – some sort of lining. I don't remember exactly what kind.'

Jill grabbed his arm. 'They're giving your wife antibiotics, right? Emma agreed to take meds. She told Charlotte.' As Jill's voice lifted in intensity, she started to attract attention from passers-by.

'Yup, they're giving her medicine, Miss Wyatt. The doctor has been here several times, nurses too. I just don't know if it'll be enough.'

When Ralph finally looked up, Jill noticed how blue his eyes were. *As blue as the sea*, her mother used to say. His serenity scared her more than Sugarman's premature grief.

Both women are going to die. And it's my fault.

'What can I do, Mr Norris? Should I go sit with your children?'

'No, they're back at the hotel. A lady from church is staying with them.'

'Do you want me to drive you to the hotel?' Jill heard the desperation in her voice.

'No, I got my truck here. I'm going to kiss Emma and head there now.'

'I . . . am . . . so . . . sorry I got you into this.' Jill burst into tears, rendering the apology barely decipherable.

'Stop that talk. This was Emma's choice. I know I was sore at you at first, but not any more. If she is being called home, home she will go.' His expression held nothing but pity. 'Just pray for her. That's all we can do.' Having run out of things to say, Ralph walked into Emma's room.

Jill couldn't watch him kiss his comatose wife goodbye. She knew she should be comforting Norris, not the other way around. But she couldn't think of a single intelligent thing to say. So she ran to the elevator and pressed the button half a dozen times. On the ride down she felt herself getting nauseated. Once she reached the parking lot, she punched in the first number that came to mind.

'Eric?' Jill concentrated on taking deep breaths to slow her racing heart.

'Yep, I had a feeling you would call. Nonni said she took you to lunch with Francesca Borelli. Get any new leads in exchange for listening to them gossip about fellow bridge players?' He issued a hearty belly laugh.

'Oh, Eric, I do have news on the case, but that's not why I called.' Hiccupping, Jill gasped for air. 'I really messed up.'

'What's wrong? What happened?' His tone changed from jovial to heartfelt concern.

'Don't . . . feel sorry for me. This is my fault. I'm at the hospital. Emma Norris and Charlotte Sugarman have taken turns for the worse. Either or both might die.' Jill dissolved into tears.

'I'm sorry to hear that, but you can't blame yourself, Jill.'

'Oh, really? Maybe I'm not responsible for Charlotte rejecting the transplanted organ. But if not for me, Emma Norris would still be picking tomatoes in her garden or baking cookies in the kitchen. Now she could die of some mysterious superbug.'

'You were doing your job,' Eric said, the consummate voice of reason.

'No, Eric. I was paid to track a woman down, which I did, not stick my nose into another family's business.'

'OK, even if it wasn't your job, you did what you thought was best.'

'I don't remember anyone putting me in charge of the universe.' Jill forced herself to stop crying. 'Want to know what Ralph Norris asked me to do? Pray for Emma. *Me* – a woman who's been to church six or seven times in the last ten years.'

'Anybody can pray. You don't need a formal training.'

'Look, I'm sorry I dumped all this on you, but I didn't know who else to call. I'll see you later tonight or maybe tomorrow.'

'Wait. Don't hang up. You need to talk to someone. I'm just not the right one.'

'This isn't about me. It's about poor David Sugarman and Ralph Norris. They could lose their wives and five kids might lose their mother.'

'I understand, but I'm worried about you right now. It'll take at least forty minutes to get back here. By then I will have found someone who can help.'

'Thanks, Eric, but—'

'No, Jill. I thought we were friends. Let me do this for you.'

The cold, hard lump of fear sitting in her stomach shrunk by half, but it still took all her strength to utter a feeble, 'OK.'

When Jill walked through the back entrance of Bella Trattoria, the room was uncharacteristically silent. Glancing around, she saw that the kitchen and storage area renovations were almost finished. She was headed toward the steps when Eric stopped her.

'I thought I heard a car in the driveway. Don't go upstairs, because I found someone who can help.'

She pivoted on the bottom step. 'Who did you get to talk to me? Nonni?'

'Nope, not my grandmother. I'll tell you on the way, but we've got just enough time to get there.' Eric led her to his car by the hand.

'A psychiatrist? You might not be rich enough to fix what's broken in my head.'

'Not a shrink. What you said gave me an idea. Anybody who thinks they are in charge of the entire universe needs to talk to someone.' Eric pulled on to Bay Street after traffic cleared.

Jill grabbed his arm. 'I was *joking* about that. Did you call your parish priest? I hope you told him I was raised Baptist, not Roman Catholic.'

'Would you relax? Try some of that deep breathing I heard on the phone. My priest is conducting a funeral at the moment, so I went through the phone book. This pastor's name is Greg Berman. For the next sixty minutes you'll be part of his flock. I gave him a brief outline of . . . what's bothering you.'

Jill shrank down in the seat, scared and embarrassed. 'You shouldn't have done that. I call this interference into my personal space. Everyone is entitled to their own neurotic tendencies.'

Unfortunately, Eric pretended not to hear her until he pulled up to the side door of a small brick church. From where they parked, she saw no sign indicating the denomination.

'We're here.' He leaned across her and opened the door. 'Give the guy one hour of your time. He might be able to help you sort through this. What do you have to lose?'

'You are coming in with me, right?'

'Wrong. I need to pick up linens, paper products, and ad materials for the grand reopening. I'll be back in an hour. Reverend Berman is expecting you, so be brave. You can thank me . . . or beat the tar out of me later.'

Fresh out of excuses, Jill climbed out and marched up the

steps. She had to try. Eric in his misguided wisdom thought she needed intervention, even though she'd lived for twenty-five years without spilling her guts to anyone.

Just as she reached for the handle, the door swung wide. 'Miss Wyatt? Hi, I'm Greg Berman, the pastor here. Come in. I've got fresh coffee in my study. Would you like a cup?'

Jill practically had to run to keep up with him. 'Yes, that would be nice. A little milk or cream, please.'

Once they were seated with mugs in hand, Pastor Greg wasted no time with preliminaries. 'Your friend told me about the natural sisters you brought back together and are now sharing a liver. Wow, what a blessing for them to find each other. And how brave those women are.'

'I suppose, as long as they both live through this.' Jill studied the forty-something pastor over the rim of her cup. He wore jeans, a plaid shirt, and loafers – not exactly ministerial garb. 'It won't be a blessing for Emma, the liver donor, if she dies from infection.'

'And you hold yourself responsible?'

'If not for me, Emma would be living with the family she created, blissfully unaware of Charlotte.'

'But she might never get the chance to save someone's life.'

'They might both die, Pastor.'

'Call me Greg. And I understand that, but Emma made the choice. Not you. Only a very self-centered person would think they have such power over another human being . . . or perhaps an atheist. Are you an atheist?'

'No, I don't think so. I guess I believe in God, but He doesn't always answer prayer, does He? Sometimes good people die, and sometimes bad things happen for no good reason.'

'It would seem that way, but that's because you and I can't see the full picture. We look at events through a very small lens, from our own perspective. God sees everything simultaneously and knows what each of us needs to grow during our short time on earth.'

'And Emma Norris needed my interference?' The sarcastic inflection Jill perfected years ago reared its ugly head.

'Absolutely she did. No matter what the outcome, she has

placed all her trust in a God who can heal us, or call us home if our time is finished. It's all part of a master plan. And of course, Charlotte needed you. That goes without saying. Few other PIs would have gone beyond the call of duty. You were truly of service to that family.'

Jill snorted. 'Yep, that's what I was telling myself until both of their conditions deteriorated.'

'You're not in charge of the universe, Jill.'

She dropped her face. 'I know I'm not. Eric shouldn't have told you that.' When she lifted her chin, Reverend Berman was grinning.

'I fail to see what's so funny.'

'Because you're viewing the situation from a limited perspective. Eric is very fond of you, in case you haven't noticed. He knows exactly how important this is.'

'Yes, it's very important that both women live. They have husbands and children.'

'I agree. But it's also important you understand this is part of God's plan, including your role, even if you don't believe in Him. You have been placed exactly where you could be useful.'

'You make life sound like God's giant chess board.' As soon as the words left her mouth, Jill regretted them. She had no reason to be disrespectful to a clergyman.

'Oh, it's far more complex than that. Chess is a game easily understood by those who study the mechanics and play it often.' He set his coffee cup on an end table. 'Spiritual men and women know they don't have to understand. They try to live the best they can, being of service to one another, while recognizing the outcome is beyond their control.'

'Then why bother to pray, if everything is out of our control?'

Berman arched an eyebrow. 'Ahh, you have been giving this some thought. For those with faith, prayer is simply communication – giving thanks, asking for help with a problem, and then listening for some kind of answer. The better people get to know God, the better they become at recognizing those answers. It might not be the answer they want, but it'll be the one they need. That's what Emma is willing to accept.'

'This is way over my head. You make it sound easy.'

'It's not easy, but people have their entire life to practice.'

'Ralph Norris asked me to pray for his wife,' Jill whispered. 'Since I really don't know how, would you do it for me?'

'I would be happy to, Jill. But if you wanted to try you don't have to get fancy. You don't have to wait until bedtime. Just turn off the radio, quiet your thoughts, and speak your mind. It could be while walking or running or driving, as long as you can still be safe. If you're grateful about something, say so. Talk about anything that you regretted doing that day. Ask for help in not doing the same thing tomorrow. Today, you could ask God to spare the lives of Emma and Charlotte. But no matter what happens, someone other than you or me is in complete control.'

Jill stared at the floor as hot tears rushed to her eyes that were impossible to stop. Borne of personal frustration and fear she cried helplessly for several minutes. Then she rose to her feet. 'Thank you making time for me. You are really a nice guy. I'll think about what you said, but if it's OK with you, I'll wait for Eric outside.'

'Of course, call me whenever you want to talk. And please feel free to show up for Sunday services. No strings attached.' The minister waited until Jill reached the door before delivering his final salvo. 'Aren't you curious why *you* were picked to reunite the sisters?'

Jill glanced over her shoulder. 'You said it was because I would go the extra mile.'

'True, but I also think He noticed you've been away for a long time and He wants you back.'

How did this guy possibly know her mom had taken her to Sunday school when she was a little girl? Jill yearned to come up with a snappy comeback, but her well of sarcasm had gone dry. Now she had something else to think about later because just at that moment, Eric pulled up to the curb.

'How did it go?' he asked.

'Fine. Greg disabused me of the crazy notion I'm responsible for what happens to Emma and Charlotte. But other than that,

I don't want to discuss it.' Jill winked as she climbed into his car.

'Whew, I started to worry after my third trip around the block.'

Jill might have elaborated on her conversation with the preacher, but her cell phone rang. 'Uh-oh, it's Lieutenant Schott. I need to take this.'

'Put him on speaker,' Eric demanded.

'Hi, Lieutenant. Eric Manfredi is with me and you're on speaker.'

'Man, Miss Wyatt, you say a mouthful on the phone even when nobody picks up the other end. Not even my wife leaves such long messages.'

As Schott laughed, Jill felt a blush rise up her neck. 'I wanted to share all my information. What did you find out about the landscaper, Bob Johnson?'

'I'll admit, he was worth looking into – sixty grand is a lot of money to be owed. But Johnson was with his dying wife when Borelli was being shot.'

'He could have been lying about that.'

'Hospitals have surveillance cameras that are date and time stamped. Johnson got to the hospital Friday night and didn't leave until Sunday morning. Call me with your next hot tip.'

When Schott hung up, Jill turned toward Eric. 'What did you find out about Colin MacFaren, the seafood purveyor? Sal owed him a bundle too.'

Eric rubbed his jawline. 'I called Colin the next day. He told Sal Borelli that if he didn't pay every cent he owed, he would ask his friends and relatives to start an internet smear campaign. Thanks to cell phones, nasty reviews posted on Yelp or Google hurt restaurants more than complaints to the Better Business Bureau. Colin said Renaldo Manfredi delivered a check to his office the very next day.'

'Another dead-end. On to my next lead.'

Only Jill didn't want to admit MacFaren and Bob Johnson were the best leads she had.

TWENTY-ONE

When they got back to Bella Trattoria the last thing Eric wanted was for Jill to run up to her room. 'Come take a look at the kitchen and employee lounge, Jill. The restoration work is just about done except for a few decorator touches.'

After Jill delivered an appropriate amount of oohs and ahhs, he broached the subject foremost on his mind. 'Give me an update on my father's case. We haven't talked since last night and I know you learned something at lunch.' Eric pulled out the pitcher of iced tea and two glasses. 'I gather from Schott's call, Borelli owed Johnson Landscaping sixty thousand.'

'Sixty-five, to be exact. Thanks to Nonni and Francesca, I learned that Johnson came to see Sal shortly before his death and they argued.' Jill's eyes filled with pain. 'Johnson needed the money for an experimental cancer treatment, but Sal didn't pay. His wife died shortly afterward. So although Johnson had a very good motive, he's not our killer.'

'Neither is MacFaren, so money owed doesn't seem to have been a factor.'

'Maybe not directly as in old liens, but Mr Johnson pointed me in a different direction. At the time I didn't give it much credence since he looked so guilty. So much for my intuition.' Jill rolled her eyes.

'Maybe nasty people like Sal have plenty of people who mean them harm. Who's next on your list?'

'Sofia Borelli, Sal's wife. During construction of that monstrosity, Sofia and Sal fought like cats and dogs – about money, Sofia's extravagances, and something seedy-sounding.'

This was the last thing Eric expected. 'What do you mean by *seedy*?'

'I don't know. That's just how Mr Johnson made it sound.'

'Come on, Jill. *Mrs Borelli*? Even if she lost her temper,

do you really think a woman can shoot the father of her children in the face? Maybe hire a hitman or slip sleeping pills into his nightcap, but not something so up close and personal.'

'If you check the case files for homicides, you'll find that plenty of bad marriages end with a nasty act of violence.'

'I know, but you won't stay on Irena's good side if you start digging into Sofia's and Sal's past history.'

Jill's eyes bugged out. '*Irena*, as in your mom?'

'One and the same.' Eric slouched in the kitchen chair.

'I knew there was no love lost between those two, but you've been keeping things from me.' Jill shook her fist at him.

'Only for a few days. I just found out when I bailed Dad out of jail.'

'OK, I'll calm down. But you need to tell all.' She sat opposite him at the table.

'Irena was already dating Sal Borelli when my father fell in love with her. In fact Sal and Irena had already announced their engagement. Dresses bought, catering lined up, the whole nine yards.'

'Wow, how tacky is that?'

Eric glanced around the room. 'I wouldn't repeat that in my mother's presence.'

Jill straightened her spine. 'Absolutely not. Sorry. Mind telling me how old these people were?'

'I'm guessing nineteen or twenty. Alfonzo and Irena fell madly in love. Irena called off her engagement, and Sal was humiliated.'

'They were all very young, Eric. Plus this must be at least forty years ago.'

'Forty-one, to be exact. My parents married one year later and Bernadette came along within a year or two.'

'My point is this is water long under the bridge. Nobody carries a grudge this long. Sal met and married Sofia and had three sons. Everyone lived happily ever after. Even if Sal still hated your father, it doesn't give Alfonzo a motive for murder.'

'That's what I thought too. So when Nonni got home after your lunch, I made her tell me parts of the story my father left out.'

'Oh, dear, I'm not going to like this.'

'Apparently, my parents lived happily ever after, but the Borellis have never been happy. Francesca told my grandmother that Sal had divorce papers drawn up. The only reason they hadn't divorced before now was they were afraid of getting kicked out of the church. Either the church relaxed its rule, or the Borellis don't care any more.'

'How sad,' Jill said, 'after all these years. What was their major bone of contention – money? According to Nonni, Sofia loved to shop.'

'I'm sure money factored in. Plus Renny was Sal's favorite son, while Sofia doted on Dominic.'

'No wonder poor John left home and changed his name.'

Eric focused on the new ceramic tiles around the sink. 'Nonni also said Sal never got over my mother. He was still in love with her.'

'*What*?' Jill sounded skeptical. 'You're pulling my leg. After forty years, Sal was still in love with Irena?'

Eric shrugged. 'Hey, what do I know about romance? So far, you and I have had exactly one date. I'm just telling you what Nonni said.'

'Your mom *is* very pretty, but it's hard to imagine anyone could carry a torch that long.'

'Sal had a vicious streak. He constantly compared his wife to Irena, and poor Sofia always came up short. He never let Sofia forget she was his second choice. Plus, Nonni believes Sal has had a roving eye for years – something Granny Francesca wouldn't confirm or deny. If that's true, and I doubt my grandmother would make something like that up, it had to be hard on Sofia. Whenever the four of them attended the same civic or charitable event, Sal never missed an opportunity to flirt with Mom, just to rub salt in old wounds.'

'That must be what Bob Johnson referred to as "something seedy,"' Jill murmured more to herself than to him. Then she looked Eric in the eye. 'Not that I have more romantic experience than you, but I always thought by the time people reached forty, let alone sixty, this kind of stuff would be behind them.'

'I certainly can't disagree with that.' Funny how Jill's admission seemed to make Eric feel a tad better.

Jill pulled out her notebook. 'Sofia could have reached breaking point when Sal cut Dominic out of his will, in favor of that blue-eyed Renaldo.'

'But I know Sofia has never dined in our restaurant, nor would my mother ever invite her into their home. No way could she get her hands on my dad's gun. So where does that leave us, Jill?'

'I'll tell you where it leaves me . . . too tired to think straight. Let's pick this conversation up another time. Maybe after a good night's sleep, I can formulate a new battle plan.'

Eric studied her face. Truly, she looked more exhausted than he'd ever seen her. 'You're right. You've had a long day. Get some rest and I'll see you tomorrow.'

But when Jill got to her room, she didn't sleep. She couldn't sleep. Instead she paced the suite from one end to the other, and then began a circuitous route around the perimeter while her mind was anywhere but in Charleston. She thought about all the families she had joined for brief intervals of time and friends that had come and gone from her life. Playground, high school, and college chums that had been so important once upon a time were quickly forgotten when circumstances changed. When had she become a shallow, careless person? When did she start discarding people when no longer useful? Had it been when her parents were killed in a traffic accident? Or when she and her brother were separated by a heartless social worker? Or maybe she had been born genetically predisposed to shun deep attachments in favor of temporary, convenient liaisons.

With her head throbbing, Jill finally pulled off her clothes, slipped on a fresh nightshirt, and crawled between the crisp, clean sheets. But still sleep wouldn't come. She wondered what it was like to be part of a close-knit family like the Manfredis, or the Norrises, or even the Sugarmans. That family was by no means perfect but they had each other's back when the chips were down. Then her thoughts wandered to what it would be like to have Emma's kind of faith. The outside world scoffed at the ultra-religious, but during critical times Emma and her husband had other church members to prop them up.

Her belief system amounted to a generic 'be a good person' and 'try to always tell the truth because getting caught in lies could be downright embarrassing.'

Her dead mother would not be proud of her.

So Jill did something she hadn't done in years. She dropped to her knees next to the bed – despite Greg Berman saying it wasn't necessary – and prayed. But she didn't pray to be delivered from her self-absorbed reclusiveness. That was probably hopeless. She prayed for Emma and Charlotte – that their lives be saved for the sake of their families. And she prayed for the Manfredis – that Alfonzo be absolved of false accusations and that Eric find what he was looking for. Even if it wasn't her.

With her kneecaps aching, she finally crawled into bed and slept without stirring. When she awoke eleven hours later, she felt better than she had in ages. She made coffee, did her floor exercises, and took a long shower. When she eventually got down to the kitchen, she found Eric sitting at the table with his laptop.

'Good morning, Mr Manfredi.'

'Good morning, Jill. How did you sleep?'

'Like a baby. Thank you for setting up my visit with Reverend Berman.'

'You're welcome. Ready for a real breakfast – bacon, eggs, hash browns? Although it's almost time for lunch.'

'You're singing my song.' Jill poured herself more coffee and watched him buzz around the kitchen, doing what he did best. Soon buttered toast, golden hash browns, fried eggs, and crispy bacon arrived at the table, all at the same time. 'You are amazing,' she said.

'You haven't tasted it yet.'

'The show alone is impressive.' Jill picked up her fork and ate more than twice a normal breakfast's worth. 'My description of "amazing" still stands.' She wiped her mouth and tossed down the napkin.

'Thanks, and I know you don't throw compliments around lightly. Are you ready to tell me about your next suspect?' Eric asked.

'Not quite yet; my mind is already thinking about dinner.'

'We've just finished breakfast. You're joking, right?'

'Not by a long shot, my favorite gourmet extraordinaire.' Jill buzzed his cheek with a kiss on her way to the sink with her dishes. 'I'll be gone for a few hours, but tonight I expect one of your Italian specialties in your new kitchen.'

'What do you have a taste for? Your wish is my command. I'll hit the grocery store this afternoon.'

'I'm thinking about your *pappardelle Bolognese.* It's touted to be better than your competitor's, along with a Caesar salad and garlic bread. Can you handle that, Manfredi?'

'With my eyes closed,' he said. However the reference to the competition roused Eric's suspicions. 'What kind of errand do you have? You do realize the Borellis aren't people to mess with. If you have suspicions about Sofia, you need to tell Lieutenant Schott and let him investigate.'

'Don't be silly. I want to drop off goodies at the hotel where the Norrises are staying and then stop by the hospital. But why don't I give you something to remember me while I'm gone?' Jill rose up on tiptoes and kissed him. Not on the cheek or his forehead, but right on the lips. Then she grabbed her purse and ran out the door, leaving Eric speechless.

But Jill didn't head for her car. Instead, she crossed the courtyard, rounded the corner, and knocked at the private entrance to Nonni's suite. 'Good morning, Nonni,' she chimed. 'May I come in?'

The older woman stepped to the side. '*Morning?* It's twelve fifteen. Half the day is gone.'

'But the best part is still ahead of us.' Jill gazed around the girly room with flowered wallpaper, a chintz bedspread, Italian provincial furniture, and a teardrop chandelier. 'This is adorable. Did you do the decorating?'

'Don't make me laugh. Irena created this set for a Victorian melodrama. Me, I would have picked Art Deco or something contemporary.' Nonni sipped tea from a porcelain cup. 'What can I do for you, my favorite secret agent?'

'May I have Francesca Borelli's address? I'd like to write a thank-you note saying how much I enjoyed our lunch.'

Nonni's expression turned doubtful. 'Why? I'm the one who picked up the check.'

'I know. I'm writing you a note too. But Mrs Borelli was so friendly to me. And she didn't have to be.'

'I thought women your age didn't write notes or letters. Everything must be emails or texts or Face Time.' She clucked her tongue.

'Just like you and Francesca dressing to the nines for lunch, I'm trying to preserve a custom. Please, Nonni?'

'Fine with me.' She shuffled to the desk for her address book and a piece of paper. Yet her skeptical expression never faltered. 'What else do you need?'

'Not a thing, see you at supper.' With address in hand, Jill ducked while crossing the courtyard and ran to her car. She didn't like spinning tall tales to Eric and his grandmother, but it was the only way to do her job. Had they known, both would have insisted on coming with her. And Jill needed to do this errand alone.

It was a good thing Beth had left her GPS unit in the Toyota, or Jill never would have found her way to Kiawah Island. She hadn't paid much attention when Eric had been driving – a bad habit she needed to change. But after only three missed turns and one near sideswipe of a delivery van, Jill found her way to their exclusive neighborhood. When the GPS's British accent indicated she had *reached her destination*, Jill turned into the Borelli driveway. There would be no walking the beach or hiding behind lifeguard platforms this time. She pressed the button on the intercom and waited patiently.

'May I help you?' asked a scratchy voice.

'Yes, Miss Jill Wyatt to see Mrs Sofia Borelli.'

'Could you repeat that please?'

Jill did so. After a short pause, the gate swung open and she drove through the main entrance of the Borelli palace. With pillars and porticoes, extensive horticulture and marble fountains, the front was no less extravagant than the pool and garden area. She parked the Toyota, which suddenly looked more rusted than before, and knocked on the massive door.

Much to her shock, Renaldo Borelli, wearing nothing but an incredible tan and a bath towel, opened the door. 'Miss Wyatt, what a lovely surprise.'

Red-faced, Jill pointed with her index finger. 'Did you just get out of the shower?'

'Of course not. I have on swim trunks. I was headed to the pool.' He dropped the towel, revealing baggy trunks that reached his knees.

'Oh, thank goodness,' she murmured, feeling rather foolish.

'Please come in. Since you're unfortunately not here to see me, I'll take you to my grandmother's suite.' He picked up the towel and re-wrapped it around his waist.

'Thanks, Renny, but I'm here to see Miss Sofia not Miss Francesca.'

He tilted his head to one side. 'But my mother said she doesn't know you.'

Jill gazed into those sea-blue eyes. 'She doesn't. But if she could spare a few minutes of her time, I would be so grateful.'

'Absolutely, she's in my father's study. Follow me.'

Renny led her through the largest living room, dining room, and kitchen Jill had ever seen and then turned down a hallway. They passed bedroom after bedroom, each more beautiful than the last. Finally he pushed open the last door on the right. 'Mom, Miss Wyatt is here to see you.' To Jill, he said, 'If you have some extra time this afternoon, join me out at the pool. There are dozens of swimsuits in the cabana. I'm sure we can find something that fits.' He winked, grinned, and sauntered away.

But Jill had no time to think about Casanova. Mrs Borelli was staring daggers at her from behind the massive teak desk. 'I don't believe we've been introduced, Miss Wyatt. Although I do remember you making a spectacle of yourself at my husband's grave.'

'I'm so sorry about that, ma'am. I caught my heel on the green carpet and if not for Renaldo, the end result could have been much worse. May I sit?' Without waiting for a reply, Jill sat.

'Renny, yes . . .' Sofia dragged the word out into several syllables, but at least her expression improved from pure hatred. 'What that boy sees in women with no meat on their bones is beyond me.'

With bigger fish to fry, Jill let the rude comment slide and laid her business card on the desk. 'I've been hired, ma'am, to investigate your husband's death. Would you be so kind as to answer a few questions?'

One or two creases deepened in her forehead. 'Charleston PD is investigating his murder. They already have the killer, as far as I'm concerned – Alfonzo Manfredi. Who is paying *you* to investigate?'

'The Manfredi family. Alfonzo has no motive to kill your husband.'

'Other than the fact they've hated each other for years?'

'I haven't been around for years, but I would say it was more a case of Salvatore hating Alfonzo.'

Sofia folded her hands in front of her, her nails similar to a hawk's talons. 'What difference does it make? Ask your questions, Miss Wyatt, and then get out of here. I have checks to write. Sal left me with a pile of bills.'

'Is it true that you and Salvatore were getting a divorce?' Jill asked, pen poised above her notebook.

Sofia's lips thinned. 'No, it's not true. We had difficulties once, but neither of us followed through.'

Jill leaned forward in the chair and threw out a fishing line. 'Because my theory is if you did threaten him with divorce, Sal might have taken his own life after his fight with Alfonzo. Life simply got too much for him to bear. But Alfonzo had followed him from the restaurant. When he found Sal dead, he picked up the gun and threw it down the sewer because he didn't want to be implicated.'

At first Sofia just smiled and then she laughed with abandon. 'Oh, my. It's a good thing you're pretty, because you're a terrible investigator. Perhaps you can stop at the mall and put in a few applications.'

Jill pretended to have bruised feelings. 'It's possible to shoot yourself in the face. I practiced with a water pistol.'

Sofia shrugged. 'It probably is possible, but I can assure you Sal didn't kill himself. He was already dying.'

Jill didn't have to fake her surprise. 'From what, ma'am? If you don't mind my asking.'

Another shrug. 'He was dying from heart failure. Sal had been taking medication for it for years. Of course, he was told to keep a strict diet – give up red meat, butter, cheese, pastries, and that bottle of red wine he drank every night.' Sofia's voice rose in intensity. 'But did he listen? No, he did not!'

'That's just awful.' Jill wrung her hands in her lap. 'I know you did your best.'

'There's only so much a wife can do when married to a stubborn bull like Salvatore.' One small tear glistened in her eye.

'I'd say Sal taking his own life makes even *more* sense. Consider this just for a moment, Mrs Borelli.' Jill held up one finger. 'Your husband knew his time on earth was limited.' She held up a second finger. 'He feared losing you and just had another fight with an old friend, Alfonzo. Plus if he couldn't enjoy his favorite foods along with his beloved wine, he decided life was no longer worth living. Those three reasons make a lot more sense than Alfonzo killing him.' Jill crossed her legs with a smug grin.

'You certainly are stuck in a rut! I'm telling you, Miss Wyatt, Sal wouldn't have killed himself, because that would have voided his life insurance policy. And no man wants his wife stuck with lots of bills with no money to pay them.' Her hand flourished over the papers.

'I see what you mean,' Jill said.

'Let this be a lesson, young lady. Someday you will marry and have a husband to care for, but a wife must always think about herself too.' Sofia leaned back in the chair, her expression serene.

'There *are* so many things a wife has to consider,' Jill mused. 'Many Catholic couples will put up with unhappy marriages, because they don't want to get kicked out of the church. But I understand the church has relaxed its rules on divorce.'

Sofia's serenity faded a tad.

'That might prompt an unhappy *husband* to file for divorce and then the wife might not get to spend so much money at the mall any more.'

'Where is all this coming from?'

'Then if that wife realizes after forty years her husband was still in love with another woman?' Jill's tone turned sugar-sweet.

'How do you know that?' Sofia demanded.

'Oh, a little bird told me.'

'My charming mother-in-law. That woman never learned the meaning of "mind your own business."'

'Then if that wife discovered Salvatore had an appointment to change his will the *very next day* . . . Tuscan Gardens would have been left to Renaldo, his favorite, and the only son who cared about the restaurant. John, and your personal favorite, Dominic, would have been cut out entirely.' Jill stopped masking her contempt. 'Maybe, just maybe, Francesca didn't want the business she and her husband started to be sold off to strangers. Maybe she knew Renny would run it well and – this is the good part – she didn't want her charming daughter-in-law to get away with murder.'

Color flooded Sofia's face so fast she looked like she might be having a heart attack. 'Get out of my house and don't come back,' she screamed. 'You have no proof of any of that.'

'You're right. I don't. But the police lifted an extra print off Alfonzo's gun that they haven't been able to match. You're not in the system, but I'd bet dollars-to-donuts they'll be able to match that print to you – a person with far more motive to kill than Mr Manfredi.'

Sofia Borelli howled with rage, like the Wicked Witch when Dorothy threw water on her. But it was hard for Jill to enjoy the moment, because Dominic Borelli had crept up behind her and yanked her up out of the chair like a ragdoll.

'You stupid little bimbo,' he snarled. 'You couldn't be satisfied with making a scene at my father's funeral.'

'Wait a darn minute! You're the one who made a scene, not me!' Jill tried to shrug from his grasp but his fingers tightened like a vise.

'That little bimbo said the police pulled another print from the gun. We've got to do something!' Sofia screamed. 'Or she will ruin everything!'

'She's bluffing. There's no other print on that gun.' Dominic dragged Jill toward the doorway as she fought like a tigress.

'We can't take that chance,' Sofia demanded. 'Nobody

knows she's here but your brother and Renny won't say anything. For once in your life, Dom, do the right thing!'

'It would be my pleasure, Ma.' Suddenly both of Dominic's hands closed around her throat.

Jill wanted to explain she wouldn't make any trouble, but she couldn't even draw a breath, let along argue with a mad man and his crazy mother.

'Don't mess this up, Dominic. Make sure she's dead before you dump her in the swamp. And make sure you weigh down the body. We want the crabs to have a good meal.'

'Stop worrying. I know just the spot. No one will ever find her skinny bones.'

Jill, however, wasn't giving up without a fight. She struggled against Dominic, clawing at his hands with her fingernails. *Now is when nails like Sofia's would come in handy.* She tried to stomp on his toe or bump against him with her backside. But Dominic withstood everything she threw at him as he dragged her into the hall. She had no time to think or even utter a prayer as the pressure on her throat increased and blackness crept in on all sides. The last thing Jill remembered was her knees going weak as she fell to the floor.

TWENTY-TWO

Eric whistled while he worked on his shopping list. Although his regular suppliers would stock the pantry, freezer, cooler, and cellar before the grand reopening, he wanted tonight's dinner to be memorable. Nothing but the best ingredients would go into his *pappardelle Bolognese*, since Jill requested it specifically.

Jill. The woman was such an enigma – one that Eric was bound and determined to figure out.

Just as he completed his list, he heard the back door open. His grandmother sauntered into the room as though she had all the time in the world. 'Hi, Nonni. Ready for tonight's party?'

'As ready as I'll ever be. Where's Jill – is she hiding from you?'

'No, we're over that phase. She's rather fond of me now. In fact, I'm on my way to get groceries. Before Jill left, she asked me to cook one of my specialties for dinner.'

Nonni crossed her arms. 'Any idea where she is or how long she'll be?'

'Jill went to the medical center to visit her clients – the two sisters who are sharing one liver. Then she's delivering treats to the Norris children. Is there anything you want before I head to the store?' Eric grabbed his shopping list. 'Jill should be back in a couple of hours.'

'Maybe not, Enrique, because I don't think she went to the hospital.'

Eric pivoted around. 'Then where is she?'

Nonni slumped into a chair. 'Jill came to see me. She wanted Francesca Borelli's address, saying she needed to write a thank you. What kind of young person writes those? I gave her the address, but instead of going upstairs to write the note, Jill jumped in her car and left. I hope she doesn't get mad at me for telling you.'

'Thanks, Nonni, you did the right thing.'

His grandmother grabbed his sleeve. 'What can I do? I want to help.'

Eric handed her his list. 'Call a grocery store that delivers and order everything on this list. Make sure you order ground veal and not beef and don't forget the ground pork. For all we know, this is a wild-goose chase and Jill will be expecting dinner tonight.' He retrieved his gun from the storage room and headed toward the door.

'What if she calls here? Where are you going?'

'Kiawah Island. Please try to get Jill on the phone.'

Punching one of the speed-dial buttons, Nonni followed after him. 'It's going right to voicemail. Why would she go see Francesca?'

'I might be overreacting, but I believe Jill went to question Salvatore's widow. She thinks Sofia might be the murderer. We'll talk more later.' Eric jumped into his SUV, threw it into reverse, and trounced down on the accelerator. Next he punched in the number for Charleston PD and asked for Lieutenant Schott in Homicide.

'I'll see if he's available,' replied a bored dispatcher.

'This is Eric Manfredi. Tell him this is an emergency.'

It took a little while, but Schott finally came on the line. 'What's the big emergency, Manfredi?'

Eric inhaled a breath and explained as succinctly as possible that he should go to the Borelli residence on Kiawah Island because Jill Wyatt was in grave danger. If he was wrong, he would take the heat for making a false report. But at least Jill would be safe.

'I'm on Folly Island,' said the detective. 'But I'll call central dispatch. They'll send someone to the house immediately. I'll get there as soon as I can.' Schott hung up without demanding more details.

Folly Island – not an easy place to get to Kiawah from, even with lights and sirens on. Eric wove around two slow-moving cars as he punched in his grandmother's number. 'Have you gotten a hold of Jill yet?' he asked without preamble.

'No, but I left her three messages. Should I call the police?'

'No, I already did that. Stay by the phone, Nonni.' Eric hung up and concentrated on driving, ticking off miles at an agonizingly slow rate. Finally, when he arrived at their development's security booth, the gate was open and the guard waved him through. *Helpful to have friends on Charleston's PD.*

However when he stopped in front of the Borelli mansion, that gate was closed.

Eric parked his SUV sideways on the tree lawn, studied the fence around the perimeter, and considered his options. He knew he could get over the fence – height had its advantages. But what if Jill wasn't inside? He would willingly pay a fine for trespassing or spend a few nights in jail. Eric climbed up as fast as he could, pulled himself to the top, and dropped to the ground on the other side. Scanning the area, he heard no blaring alarms and no motion-sensed lights illuminated the yard. Eric rang the doorbell twice, waited as patiently as he could, and rang the bell again. No one appeared to allow him inside the home of his family's arch enemies.

With sweat beading on his brow, Eric tromped through the foliage around the house. Were overgrown bushes their idea of another layer of security? When he reached the pool area, Eric crouched behind a huge bougainvillea. From his vantage point, he spotted Renaldo swimming laps from one end to the other. He knew it was Renny, because Dominic could probably drown in a bathtub, let alone a swimming pool.

Eric waited until Renny made a smooth underwater turn and started toward the opposite side. Then he left his hiding spot and approached the French doors to the solarium. As expected when a family member was outdoors, the doors were unlocked. With the stealth of a cat burglar, Eric slipped into the house and hid behind an indoor plant.

Thank goodness the Borellis loved their fauna.

From his new vantage point, he watched Renny effortlessly swim lap after lap and heard . . . nothing. There wasn't a sound from anywhere in the gaudy, over-decorated mansion. Then Eric heard the unmistakable screech of Sofia Borelli

'For once in your life, Dominic, do the right thing.'

He didn't care if Renaldo saw him or not. He bolted through the dining and living rooms in the direction of the voice. When he reached the entrance to a long corridor, Eric stopped to listen.

'It would be my pleasure, Ma,' said a male voice.

With horror, Eric watched as Dominic dragged a woman into the hallway. Then both of his hands closed around the woman's throat.

The woman was Jill. Dom was trying to strangle the woman he loved.

'Don't mess this up,' Sofia called from inside the room. 'Make sure she's dead before you dump her in the swamp. And make sure you weigh down the body. We want the crabs to have a good meal.'

As Jill fought to free herself, Eric crept down the hall, grabbing a metal sculpture from a pedestal along the way.

'Stop worrying,' sneered Dominic. 'I know just the spot. No one will ever find her skinny bones.'

Her skinny bones? Those would be Dominic's last words

for a while. Because before the man knew what hit him, Eric raised the sculpture high in the air and smashed it down on Dominic's head.

'Jill, are you OK?'

A familiar voice broke through the fog, while a pair of strong hands dragged her to her feet. Jill tried opening her eyes but the light intensified the pain. Next she tried to ask what had happened, but not one sound issued from her throat. When she attempted to stand, her legs refused to cooperate.

'Take it easy. You'll be all right,' said her mysterious rescuer. 'The police are on their way.' He swept her up in his arms and carried her down the hall.

From over his shoulder, Jill heard Sofia Borelli sobbing hysterically. 'You killed my son.'

When Jill forced her eyes open a second time she recognized Eric Manfredi. 'What are you doing here?' she croaked in a harsh whisper.

'Saving you, apparently.' Eric deposited her unceremoniously on a silk sofa that must have cost ten grand.

'Did you kill Dom?'

'I don't think so. But I did whack him over the head with an iron sculpture that Sofia called *artwork*.'

Jill rose up on her elbows and gazed around. Francesca Borelli was talking on the phone, Renny stood at the patio door, and in the distance she heard sirens.

'What happened? What are you doing here, Manfredi?' Renaldo spouted questions at a rapid-fire pace.

With her head still throbbing, Jill fixed her focus on Eric. 'How did you find me? I did my best to ditch you.'

'There'll be time for explanations later. Right now, you should rest until the police get here.'

'Maybe you're right. I don't feel so good.' Relaxing against the silk fabric, she concentrated on forcing air in and out of her lungs. As darkness blotted out the world around her, Jill went back to sleep. After all, if she was somewhere on Kiawah Island with Eric Manfredi she had to be dreaming.

* * *

The next thing she heard was the gruff voice of Lieutenant Schott. 'Charleston PD. Everyone stay where they are,' he thundered at the patio door.

Jill bolted upright. This was no dream. A cool wash cloth lay across her forehead, while Eric held her feet in his lap.

'Welcome back,' he said.

'Thanks for not listening to me at the restaurant.'

'It was my pleasure.'

'Oh, Eric. You were right. I should have let Lieutenant Schott interrogate Mrs Borelli.'

He plopped down on the sofa next to her to inspect the welts around her neck. 'I'll kill Dominic for doing that to you, if he's not already dead.'

'It was Sofia's idea. That *nice old lady* wanted to kill me.' Jill glared at Sofia as the police brought her out in handcuffs. 'Dominic wanted to protect his mother. Sofia murdered her husband and framed your dad.' Jill gingerly touched her throat. 'If not for you, I'd be dead. How did you know where I was?'

Eric patted her bare feet tenderly. 'As soon as Nonni told me where you might be headed, I got here as fast as I could. I was afraid it wouldn't be fast enough. I'm just glad Renny left the patio door open.'

Renny, who'd been sitting with his grandmother, stood and crossed the room. 'I'm glad too, and deeply sorry for the pain my family caused you, Miss Wyatt. And I apologize to you, Eric. This stupid feud has gone on long enough.' Tentatively, he extended his hand.

After a moment's hesitation, Eric shook with his former enemy. 'Apology accepted. Now could you get Jill something to drink? She's had quite an ordeal.'

'Would you like water or a cup of coffee?' Renny asked. 'Maybe a glass of wine?'

'Water would be great, thanks.' Jill fell back against the pillows.

As soon as Renny left the room, Eric pulled her into his arms. 'Why did you come to question a potential murderer without a weapon? You could have been killed.'

Gasping, Jill pushed him away. 'Please, I just got my breath back. If you must know, my gun is in my purse, which is still in the study. Dominic took me by surprise.' Then Jill softened her tone. 'Thanks, for calling Lieutenant Schott when you did.'

'You're welcome. Maybe you'll give *me* a foot-rub later?'

'Maybe after your special dinner of *pappardelle Bolognese*? Is that still on for tonight?'

'You bet it is.'

'Miss Wyatt,' said Lieutenant Schott, 'if you're feeling up to it, I'd like to get your statement. If not, you could stop by the station tomorrow morning.'

Jill swung her feet to the floor. 'Now is fine. The sooner I give my statement and Sofia repeats what she confessed, the sooner you'll drop the charges against Mr Manfredi.'

Schott cocked his head. 'Most likely she'll retract any confession she made to you.'

'Maybe not, once the police and DA listen to this.' Jill pulled the mini tape recorder from her pocket and handed it to the detective. 'See,' she said to Eric, 'I remembered *something* from Beth's expert PI training.'

When Renaldo returned with her glass of water, he and Eric walked outside as she headed to the dining room with the detective. By the time Jill gave her statement, she found Eric and Renaldo on the patio with cups of coffee.

'Wow, Renny. Your garden is far prettier up here than from down on the beach.'

Both men scrambled up. 'Thank you, Miss Wyatt. I'll pass the compliment on to my grandmother.'

'Ready to go?' asked Eric.

'Yes, Lieutenant Schott and the Sheriff's Department have finished with me.' She stifled a yawn.

'Then it's time to get you home.' Eric slipped an arm around her waist.

'Give me another minute.' Jill turned toward Renny. 'This must be really tough – your father is dead, while Dominic and your mom are on their way to jail. I'm sorry how things turned out for you.'

Renny stared out toward the ocean. Sunlight sparkled off the pool, turning the water into a sea of gold. 'I'll be all right. I have the restaurant and plenty of friends. Who knows – now that Dad is gone, John might move back to Charleston. He told me at the funeral he hated advertising.'

'I hope he does,' said Eric. 'From this day on I will do everything in my power to support Tuscan Gardens.'

'Likewise, Eric, and I'll recommend Bella Trattoria whenever I can.' Renny shook a second time with Eric and then reached for Jill's hand. 'I wish you well, Miss Wyatt.' His smile stretched all the way to his blue eyes. 'Now go home to your *pappardelle Bolognese*. Just for the record, Eric's runs circles around mine.'

As Francesca Borelli buzzed open the gate, a wave of fatigue washed over Jill. 'Maybe I should ride with you, Eric, and let one of the cops drive my car.' She dug her keys from her purse. 'I'm too tired to focus, let alone get safely back to Bella Trattoria.'

'It would be my pleasure.' Eric grabbed her keys and disappeared into the house. 'I wanted to talk to you in private anyway.'

When he returned a few minutes later with a Sheriff's Department deputy, Jill hadn't moved one single muscle. 'Why don't you lead the way back to Charleston,' Eric said to the officer. 'We can pick up Jill's car tomorrow at the station.'

After the deputy agreed, Eric took her arm and led her to his SUV. 'I parked on the tree lawn and climbed the fence.'

Jill glanced at the ten-foot fence and shook her head. 'You're a better man than me, Manfredi.'

'Not much competition in the man department,' he said, opening the passenger door.

After buckling her seatbelt, she leaned against the headrest and closed her eyes.

'Do you know why I wanted to drive you?' Eric asked.

Jill kept her eyes shut. 'Probably because you're still worried about me.'

'And do you know why *that* is?' Eric stayed right on the Toyota's bumper as the deputy led them through the development.

Jill shifted uncomfortably. 'I'm way too tired for guessing games, Eric. Please just tell me.'

'Because I'm in love with you.'

It took Jill a moment to process the off-the-cuff comment. 'Goodness, I thought for sure you were a serial killer. And I was about to become your next victim.' From the corner of her eye, she watched his hands tighten on the steering wheel.

'No, I'm not. For once, don't make jokes. I want to know where you stand.' Eric slowed down as the deputy stopped at the guard booth.

'I had suspected you were for a while,' she whispered as moisture flooded her eyes.

'You are such an exasperating woman! Are you in love with me or not?'

She shrugged. 'I think I might be, for all the good it'll do me.'

When the guard waved him through, Eric accelerated so fast he almost rammed into her Toyota. 'I can't believe I'm hearing this. You say you're in love, yet you're this lackadaisical?'

All fatigue from the day's events vanished. Jill pivoted on the seat to face him. 'If you remember what I told you in Savannah, I'm the traveling PI for a reason. No way can I fall in love, get married, and learn how to boil pasta like a *normal woman*.'

'Cooking pasta is simply a matter of dropping pasta into a pot of boiling water and waiting until it's tender.'

'Who's making jokes now?' Jill switched on the radio.

Eric switched it off. 'Maybe these will change your life.' He pulled two tattered envelopes from the sun visor.

'What are those?'

'Letters from Santa Rosa Correctional in Florida. They are probably from your brother. Liam sent them to your friend, Vicky Stephens, at the last place you worked. Vicky Stephens tracked you down in Savannah and then Beth mailed them to me. Maybe Nate Price should hire Vicky as an investigator.'

Jill felt her stomach turn over. 'Oh, this is not good.'

'You don't know that. Vicky sent them in a plain envelope without a return address to Beth and that's how Beth sent them to me. Since I didn't know how safe things are at the restaurant, I waited until we were together. And *nobody* is following us, Jill.'

She stared at the envelopes as though coated with anthrax.

'What are you afraid of? They're just letters, not warrants for your arrest.'

Taking the envelopes, Jill extracted the sheets one at the time. When she had read both, she shoved them deep into her purse. 'The letters are basically the same, except the second letter sounds more desperate. Liam wants me to come see him. He has news that can't be put in a letter.'

'Why not go? I know there has been bad blood between you, but he's still your brother.'

Jill let a few moments pass. 'I know who he is, but there's so much at stake. Please let me figure this out on my own.' She dropped her face in her hands, effectively shutting him and the world out.

Neither of them said another word all the way back to Charleston.

Once they arrived at Bella Trattoria, Eric set the table with linens, china, and sparkling crystal. While he cooked the meal, Jill filled Nonni in on what had happened at Francesca's house. During dinner, Eric waited on Nonni and her as though they were distinguished royalty. Jill forced herself to appreciate his specialty, despite having no appetite. As predicted, his *pappardelle Bolognese* and Caesar salad were superb.

Nonni, however, wolfed down her plate of food in record time, which was very unlike her. 'Grandson, I've never tasted better food in my life. If there's any left over, I'll eat it for my lunch.' Nonni wiped her mouth with a napkin and hobbled away from the table.

'Where are you going in such a hurry?' Eric asked.

'I believe you and Jill need to be alone. I recommend the patience of Job for both of you.'

'We'll do our best.' Eric exchanged glances with her as Nonni headed to her room. 'I'm sorry, Jill,' he said as soon as she left. 'I should have waited to give you those letters until tomorrow. I ruined your evening.'

Jill realized she was alone with someone who'd just confessed his love, but she was too overwrought to find the right words. 'No, this isn't your fault. It's time I stopped burying my head in the sand.'

'If the letters aren't why you were so quiet during dinner, tell me what's wrong.' Eric pushed the dirty dishes aside.

She shrugged. 'I'm exhausted. Plus any news from my jailbird brother is never good. He's part of the past I'd rather forget.'

'Then don't reply. Throw the letters in the trash.' Reaching for her, Eric tilted up her chin with one finger.

'I probably will, but I'm upset because I told Liam not to contact me.'

'You know how men seldom pay attention.'

Jill smiled. 'Sometimes that's a good thing. If you had followed directions tonight, I would be dead. And by the way, don't save all the pasta for Nonni. I'll eat some when I have more appetite.'

'You did well today, Miss PI. Sofia and Dominic are in custody. As soon as Lieutenant Schott submits his report to the DA, along with your statement and the audio tape, my father will be off the hook.'

Normally, a client's praise over her job performance warms Jill's heart, but tonight she felt nothing but sadness. 'Thanks, Eric. Tomorrow I need to visit Charlotte and Emma in the hospital since I didn't go today.' She felt a twinge of shame. 'Sorry I lied to you.'

'You're forgiven. Now go get some rest. I'll see you in the morning.'

'Good night.' Jill pushed to her feet, kissed the top of Eric's head like he was a child, and climbed the steps to her room. She refused to look back. She didn't want to see the disappointment on his face.

TWENTY-THREE

In the morning on her way out the door, Jill received a call from Lieutenant Schott. Last night at the station Sofia Borelli had not only confessed to murdering her husband, but her statement implicated her son in a slew of felonies – mugging Alfonzo Manfredi, starting the fire in

Bella Trattoria, and stealing Alfonzo's gun. All of Dominic's aggression, including dumping the trash, had been instigated by Sofia to fan the flames between the two men. Sofia signed the confession in the presence of her attorney so both would be going away for a long time. When Jill hung up with Schott she smiled all the way to the University Medical Center.

Inside the ICU Jill found David Sugarman sitting in a hallway chair practically where she had left him on Monday. However, he was eating a donut, drinking a cup of coffee, and reading the newspaper. *Those had to be good signs.*

'Mr Sugarman, how is Charlotte today?'

David blinked and jumped up. 'Much better, Jill. The new anti-rejection drug is working. All of her counts have improved, and some of the bloat has gone down. The doctor thinks this new drug cocktail will do the trick. She's sleeping now, but Charlotte was awake a little while ago when I brought the kids to the window.'

Jill noticed Charlotte's bed had been pushed up against the glass, unlike the last time she was here. 'She must be better. You're talking up a storm today.' Jill put her hand on his shoulder.

'Thanks, Jill, not only for finding Emma, but for caring so much about my family.' Clumsily David hugged her. 'We'll never forget you.'

'And I'll never forget any of you.'

Suddenly, the nurse on the other side of the window knocked on the glass, trying to catch their attention. Once she had it, she cranked up the head portion of Charlotte's bed. Charlotte was awake and as soon as she could reach the glass, she splayed out her fingers.

'Go on, Jill,' David said. 'That high five is for you. I've already gotten mine and so have the kids.'

Jill stepped closer and matched up her fingers with Charlotte's.

'Thank you, Jill,' Charlotte mouthed.

'You're welcome. Happy to help,' Jill mouthed in return. Then the nurse waved and pushed Charlotte's bed back in place.

Jill looked at David Sugarman, but speech was impossible. The old familiar lump was back in her throat. So she gave David a teary hug and bolted down the hallway.

On Emma's floor, Jill found more good news. Ralph Norris met her at his wife's doorway. 'The medicines are working just fine. The nurse said she never saw azithromycin work so fast. It's probably because Emma never took antibiotics before.' He shook Jill's hand like a pump handle. 'You still can't go into Emma's room, but two of my children have something to say.'

Turning around, Jill spotted the older Norris kids on a bench. They ran to her like lightning once Ralph waved at them.

'My name is Jason. Thank you, Miss Wyatt.' He shook hands like a gentleman.

'My name is April.' Then the little girl motioned for Jill to bend down. When she complied, April kissed her on the cheek. 'Thank you, Miss Wyatt.'

'You're both welcome. If it's OK with your dad, I have candy in my car for you.' All three looked at Ralph.

'It'll be fine, but first we want to take you to Burger King for lunch. That is, if you like hamburgers.'

'I love them, but isn't it a tad early for lunch?'

'If you don't mind, can we check out of the hotel first? No sense running up David's bill any higher. Emma will soon be coming home, and the Sugarmans will need their money with two kids to put through college.'

'I don't mind at all.' Jill waved goodbye to Emma, while the Norris kids blew kisses. When they got to her car, Jill passed out candy and then followed Ralph to the hotel. After helping him pack up and check out, they drove to the nearest Burger King for sandwiches and fries. Throughout the meal, April and Jason chattered like magpies, while baby Andrew slept in his carrier as though everything was right with the world.

Because at least for now, everything was. Thanks to prayers – including hers – two families would have more time together. Jill felt nothing but gratefulness. With Ralph and his children on their way to the farm, she headed to the historic section of Charleston.

It was time to make things right in her little world. Eric

had gone out of his way to make a special dinner that she barely touched. Why would she allow some cryptic letters from the past to ruin the best thing ever to happen to her?

Tonight, she would take Eric out to *his* favorite restaurant. They would dine under the stars and laugh at how paranoid she was acting. If he refused, she would follow him around, begging for his forgiveness until she was old and gray like Nonni.

The ring of her cell phone jolted Jill from her wool-gathering. But when she spotted 'restricted' in caller ID, she knew it wasn't the man of her dreams.

'Hello?' She switched to the car's bluetooth.

'Hello, Kathryn or Kate . . . or is it *Jill* now?' The mysterious male voice sounded hauntingly familiar. 'You sure do live above a sweet little restaurant. I can't wait for them to reopen and taste some *Italiano* haute cuisine – my favorite!'

'How did you get this number?' she barked into the phone.

'You shouldn't have been using a phone under the agency's corporate plan. It wasn't hard to deduce which employee had this number, no matter what name you're calling yourself now.'

'OK, you found me. What do you want? I'm minding my own business here and not bothering you. Why can't you do the same?'

'I would love to, except that your big brother started making trouble for us again.'

'*Liam*?' Jill feigned shock at the news. 'I haven't seen my brother in years. What trouble could Liam make in prison? He still has decades left on his sentence.'

'That's what we thought too. But your brother might be making plans to cut his sentence short. I suggest you talk him out of that silly notion and just tell him to serve his time.'

Jill mustered a little courage. 'Why would I do that? I told you I haven't seen Liam in years.'

'Because, sweet Kate, if you don't, your brother is a dead man. We have plenty of friends in Santa Rosa Correctional too. And your tall, handsome boyfriend might also suffer an unfortunate accident.'

'Eric has nothing to do with this!' she shouted. 'If you want to hurt me, go ahead. But stay away from the Manfredi family.'

'How would killing you manipulate Liam into keeping his mouth shut?' The voice asked calmly. 'And to prove I'm not blowing smoke, your favorite chef is inside an Office Max right now. He appears to be having banners and flyers made at the customer service desk. If you're even remotely fond of him, tell him not to climb into his Ford Expedition and turn the key. Mr Manfredi would be in for a *huge* surprise. Oh, and Kate? Don't ever speak to me in that tone of voice again.' The caller hung up.

For a few seconds, Jill sat paralyzed. Then she punched in Eric's number.

He picked up on the third ring. 'Hi there, beautiful. Are you ready for leftover *pappardelle Bolognese*? Of course, by now the salad will have wilted and turned brown.'

'Eric, which Office Max are you at?'

'How on earth did you know—'

'Never mind that, please tell me your exact location!'

'Let me look at the address on the receipt.' After a pause, Eric read off a street name and building number. 'I'm finished shopping. So if you're close by, I'll pick you up and we can go—'

'No! You must listen carefully. I'm punching that address into my GPS. In the meantime, stay inside the store and don't go near your car. If you see anyone pushing a shopping cart toward it, wave them off. I'll get there as fast as I can.'

'What's going on, Jill?' Eric demanded.

'I'll explain when I get there.'

'Should I call the police while I wait?'

'No, Eric. If you love me, you'll trust me and do *exactly* what I said. I know this isn't the time or the place, but I love you too.' Jill hung up, knowing if she didn't he would pepper her with questions. Instead she plugged in the address and drove as fast as she could, weaving in and out of traffic like a madwoman.

Despite her promise not to bother God with another desperate request, Jill prayed all the way there.

Eric didn't know what to think. So he followed Jill's instructions to the letter. Explanations – and he expected plenty – would have to come later. He stood outside under the overhang staring at his one-year-old SUV. At the moment, no one was parked close to him. He'd decided a long time ago to maximize his number of steps by parking far from buildings and never use elevators unless absolutely necessary. So Eric simply watched his car, scanned the parking lot, and waited.

Jill was in love with him? At this point, he was too confused to believe a word the woman said.

When Jill arrived at Office Max fifteen minutes later, she parked across the striped yellow lines and jumped from her car.

'I . . . am . . . so . . . glad . . . to . . . see . . . you,' she stuttered and wrapped her arms around his waist.

Eric hugged her tightly and then held her at arm's length. 'What's going on, Jill? It's time for the truth.'

'After visiting Emma Norris and Charlotte Sugarman at the hospital, I was on my way back downtown – to make up for last night – when I got a phone call.'

'From whom?' he asked.

'I don't know. A voice just said you shouldn't start your car. Something bad might happen.'

'I'm calling the police.' Eric pulled his cell phone from his pocket.

'Wait! This could just be a hoax – someone's sick idea of a joke. Where is your car? Is it that black one sitting all by itself?' Jill sounded close to hysteria.

'Yes, you've ridden in it several times. Who on earth would call with that kind of hoax?'

Jill ignored his question. 'Do you have remote start on your key fob?'

Nodding, Eric dug his keys from his pocket.

Without another word, Jill grabbed the keys from his hand. She quickly scanned the parking lot from left to right and pressed the 'start engine' button.

Eric's beloved SUV, the one with every available option because he had planned to keep it a long time, exploded into a ball of fire and smoke. The percussion of the blast rattled the windows behind them and set off several alarms in nearby vehicles. Debris rained down over them like hail, quickly coating the other cars with ash and shards of metal. Instinctively, Eric pulled Jill against his chest and dropped to the ground, covering her with his body. A plume of flames shot skyward from the fireball, while the intense heat made his lightweight jacket unbearable.

Employees and customers poured from the store, pointing fingers and staring at the spectacle. Eric waited until he heard the approach of sirens and then rose to his feet, dragging Jill up with him. With her face buried against his chest, she gripped his jacket with both fists. Within seconds store employees crowded around them, asking a litany of questions.

'Do you know whose car that is?'

'Are either of you hurt?'

'Did you see anybody near the car before it blew up?'

Someone wearing a tie pushed his way through the crowd. 'I'm Randy Williams, the store manager. Police, fire, and EMTs are on their way. Sir, I saw you outside before the blast. Did you see what caused it?'

'No, I was waiting for my . . . friend who was meeting me here. The burning vehicle is mine, but I have no idea why it blew up. This is Miss Wyatt. She might know more, but she's pretty shook up. Let's wait until the police get here to answer any questions.'

Eric's ambiguity didn't please the store manager. But when Williams spotted several teenagers videoing the blaze, he ran off to corral them. Soon other employees moved closer to the fire too, leaving them alone.

Eric gently extracted Jill from his chest. 'You just blew up my car. Before the police get here, tell me what's going on.'

'I am so sorry. I thought they were bluffing, trying to scare me.'

'*Who?* Do you think Dominic Borelli did this? I doubt anyone has posted bail this soon, but he might have hired someone.'

Jill shook her head. 'No, this has nothing to do with Dominic or any Borelli. The voice on the phone said I needed to stop my brother or they would kill him – and then they would kill you.'

Eric stared at her like she was a stranger. 'Stop him from doing what?'

'I don't know.' Jill wouldn't meet his eyes.

'You must have some idea who made the call.'

'Yes, they're the men Liam hooked up with in the county jail. Liam was the only one who went to prison, because he refused to turn on his friends. Please believe me, Eric. I don't know their names.' Jill was sobbing so hard it was difficult to understand her.

Eric stroked the back of her head. 'I do believe you. This must be why your brother wanted to see you.'

'Most likely. These men are the reason I keep moving and changing my name.'

'Your name really isn't Jill?'

Again, she shook her head but remained silent.

'It doesn't matter. After you tell the police what you know, they'll track down those men in Florida and bring them to justice.' Eric glanced up as two police cars arrived along with the fire department.

Jill grabbed his arm. 'Let me take the lead, Eric. Those men aren't in Florida, they're *here*. They were watching while you ordered banners for the restaurant. This was a warning. If I tell what I know to the police, someone will kill Liam in prison long before law enforcement arrests his former cronies. I won't let him die, and I won't let them hurt you.'

'Fine, Jill.' He shrugged off her hand. 'You tell the police whatever you like. And I'll tell them what I know – which is *absolutely nothing*.'

TWENTY-FOUR

Although Jill and Eric each made statements to the police officers while his Expedition smoldered, it was clear that law enforcement wasn't satisfied. They couldn't believe she had pushed the ignition button after being warned not to. They doubted that she didn't recognize the voice. And they must have asked six times why she didn't call 911 immediately following the threat. Jill stuck to the same weak explanation, no matter how many times they repeated themselves. *I didn't call 911 because I thought it was a hoax. I pushed the button to prove it was. And I have no idea who made the threat.* Finally the officer told Eric to call his insurance agent and told Jill to come to the station tomorrow for a follow-up with a police detective.

When they were allowed to leave, it was a quiet ride back to Bella Trattoria in her Toyota. Jill's apology of *I'm sorry I blew up your car* sounded incredibly lame. Yet she had no clue how to make things right. Once back at the restaurant, Eric had to explain to Nonni why he no longer had his Expedition. Needless to say, that conversation didn't go well. So after they ate leftover *pappardelle Bolognese*, wilted salad, and dried-out garlic bread, Jill said goodnight to the man she, just today, realized she was in love with. But obviously her being in his life was not a good thing. Since she moved in, his father had been framed for murder, his restaurant caught fire, and his car exploded.

This time, Eric didn't beg her to stay downstairs and chit-chat.

In the morning she arrived at the station as instructed and went through her story with a detective. *No, she didn't know who was sending her a message. Yes, she pushed the start-engine button because she assumed the call was a sick gag. Yes, she was as shocked when the car blew up as Mr Manfredi was.* Luckily, Lieutenant Schott hadn't caught the case since he worked homicides. Jill's answers remained the same no matter how many times the detective rephrased the question. Eventually, she was permitted to sign her statement and leave, feeling exactly like what she was – a big liar.

Since the Florida thugs had her cell number, Jill stopped at a discount store to buy several burner phones. She returned to the restaurant and luckily when she crept into the kitchen no one was around. Nonni was probably napping, and Eric was out preparing for Saturday's grand reopening. So Jill headed upstairs to call Beth and Nate.

Neither of those conversations went well. Beth insisted on driving to Charleston, but Jill insisted she stay away just as vehemently. Beth told her to smash her phone, throw it in the trash, and start packing her bags – all of which Jill had done the moment she got upstairs last night. Next Beth asked her to come to Savannah. Jill accepted the invitation because with what she had in mind, she needed to talk to her friends in person.

Jill began the phone conversation with her boss by telling Nate the good news about Charlotte and Emma. Nate declared that case officially closed. Next, she brought him up to speed on the Salvatore Borelli murder investigation, including how she'd taped Sofia's confession along with an explanation of her motives. Jill chose not to mention Dominic throttling her until Eric bashed him over the head with a metal sculpture.

'Doesn't it just figure?' asked Nate. 'How many times does the spouse turn out to be the killer? Makes you wonder why people aren't afraid to get married.'

'Hopefully, your lovely wife isn't in earshot,' Jill teased.

He laughed heartily. 'No, I'm still at the office. Tell me how Mrs Borelli got her hands on Alfonzo's gun.'

'I'll get there in a minute. Sofia's favorite son, Dominic, was truly a bad egg. He and a friend were the ones who mugged Alfonzo on his way to the bank with the night deposit. They could have killed him with that pipe. Dominic was also the one who started the kitchen fire in Bella Trattoria the night I had to climb out on the roof.' Jill shivered with the memory. 'Before Dominic started the fire in the kitchen, he rifled through Alfonzo's desk until he found the gun and clip.'

'Dominic knew that you and the grandmother would be there alone?' Nate asked.

'Yes, apparently Sofia Borelli overheard her mother-in-law talking with Nonni Manfredi about it. I believe that's also how Sofia found out about Alfonzo's gun. All of Dominic's handiwork – overturning the dumpster, mugging Alfonzo, starting the fire – was part of Sofia's plan to fan the flames between her husband and Alfonzo. She knew if Salvatore was found dead, the police would immediately suspect his long-time enemy. Alfonzo played right into her hands when he lost his temper inside Tuscan Gardens in front of witnesses. All Sofia had to do was follow them down the street and bide her time. Once Alfonzo got tired of arguing with an equally stubborn man and left, Sofia came out of hiding and shot Salvatore. Then Sofia threw the gun into the storm drain and waited for it to be found. Apparently, she's watched more than one police drama on TV.'

'That is cold-blooded, not to mention premeditated murder.'

'Yes, but in Sofia's sick mind, she thought she was doing this for her family. If Renaldo inherited the restaurant by himself, John Borelli would never move back from Columbia. And Dominic would never straighten out his street life. She thought sharing Tuscan Gardens would finally bring the three brothers together. Plus Salvatore had made Sofia miserable for forty-odd years. I'm sure the jury will take that into consideration.'

Nate snorted. 'Like I said, it's a wonder people aren't more fearful of marriage. Now Sofia and her favorite son will sit in jail for a very long time, if not for the rest of their lives. How did Dominic know the restaurant's security code?'

'I have a good suspicion, boss, but I need to ask a few more questions before finishing my report. And I know just who to ask.' Jill smiled to herself.

'Speaking of which, since you're wrapping things up in Charleston, are you ready to work in Natchez for a while? I've got a few cases I could use help with.'

'Actually, I can't. That's the other reason for my call. I plan to leave here first thing in the morning. Tomorrow is the grand reopening of Bella Trattoria, and I'm not sure I'm up for a party. I will go to Savannah for a couple days to talk to Beth and Michael. Then I'll head to Pensacola, Florida, to the town where I grew up. There's an urgent family matter that no one can take care of but me.'

For a few moments, Nate was silent. 'Not a problem, Jill. How much time off do you need? I can hold the fort until you get here.'

Jill winced as her beloved career vanished before her eyes. 'I wish I could give you an answer, but I can't. What I'm saying is I need to *move* back home. I can't keep running from my past. It caught up with me with a vengeance.' Briefly she considered telling Nate about blowing up Eric's SUV, but she knew how he would react. 'I know this leaves you short-handed, so I understand if you must replace me. What are the chances of you landing a case in Pensacola?'

'I'm not worried about being short-handed. I'm worried about you needing your friends at the agency and being too proud to ask.'

Nate's answer made the pain of leaving hurt that much more. 'Right now I don't know what I'll find in Florida until I talk to my brother. Beth will tell you I'm not too proud to ask for help.'

'All right, I'll put you on a family leave of absence with an open return date. Make sure you keep in touch with Beth and Michael and me too. You've still got pay coming from these two cases, plus expense money. How should I get it to you?'

'Wire it to Beth if you don't mind. She can give me the cash when I see her.' *The less paper trail the better.*

'Will do, and regarding a Pensacola case? You never know what things will pop up.'

When Jill hung up with her boss, she already felt homesick. Funny how the people at work had started to feel like family.

For a few hours, Jill caught up on emails, completed the two case reports the best she could, and cleaned out the mini refrigerator. She also finished packing, except for her pajamas and the outfit she would wear tomorrow. All she had left to do was talk to Eric, which she knew would be the hardest task of her life.

Eric. Right from the start, she'd known any kind of relationship was a mistake. Yet sometimes the heart refuses to listen to reason. So now she would pay a very dear price.

Jill inhaled a deep breath, opened the door, and ran headlong into a brick wall. 'Eric, how long have you been standing there?'

'Apparently not long enough. I still haven't figured out how to say I'm sorry.' Eric seemed to fill the entire doorway.

'What are *you* sorry about? I blew up your car, not the other way around.'

His features softened. 'Insurance will replace the vehicle.

I had no business getting mad as though this was all part of your sinister plot. I'm sorry, Jill.'

She held up her palms. 'Anyone would overreact in that situation. I probably would have done far worse, so don't apologize.'

'And there's a second reason I'm here. I came to ask you to stay and see where this goes between us. Your rent is cheap and Charleston has several PI agencies.' Eric craned his neck to look around her. 'But I see you've already packed. Were you going to slip out without saying goodbye?'

If a hole opened in the floor, Jill gladly would have jumped in. 'Of course, not. I was just coming downstairs.'

'Let's talk here. Lots of people in the kitchen and courtyard.' Eric crossed his arms over his chest.

'I meant what I said on the phone, but it makes no difference. You and I won't work. I'm going back to Pensacola to help my brother any way I can. I'm tired of running from my past. Your home is here in Charleston – you have a restaurant to run.'

'Those men in Florida are dangerous. You should—'

'Stop, Eric. What kind of PI would I be if I ran from danger? If I need to involve law enforcement, I will. If I need Beth or Michael, I'll call them.'

'What you don't need is an Italian chef who loves you.'

It was a statement, not a question, but Jill needed to make a clean break, no matter how much it hurt. 'No, Eric, at this point in my life, I don't.'

Her words seemed to hang in the air for a few moments. Then he spoke. 'I appreciate your honesty, Jill, but there's a third reason I'm here. We're having a little family get-together before we open to the public – my dad, mom, Bernadette, Danielle, Nonni. Could you tolerate a little more Manfredi cooking so everyone can say goodbye?'

Jill grinned. 'Of course I can. I have a few questions to ask your grandmother, like how Sofia found out the security code and where the gun was hidden.'

'We'll ask Nonni together, far away from my parents. We don't want any bloodshed on your last night in town.'

Together Jill and Eric joined the *little* party happening in all three dining rooms, plus spilling into the courtyard. Jill talked and laughed and ate way too much food. As Jill had expected, Nonni had told Francesca *everything*, including that Alfonzo bought a gun for protection, where he kept it, and what their security code was. *After all, what if Francesca had to rescue her when everyone else was out of town?* Unfortunately, Nonni had dropped these tidbits while dining in the Borelli home – a place where Sofia was always lurking.

Jill accepted fond farewells, hugs, and kisses from everyone, including Irena Manfredi. She promised Dani she would be back for a visit – a promise she doubted she could keep. Nonni packed up a bag of food to take, while Alfonzo slipped her extra traveling cash. She would miss all of them.

Then Jill waited until Eric went down to the wine cellar to run up for her bags and leave through the kitchen. It was the coward's way out, but for the best. Because if she looked at his handsome face again she might change her mind. And there would be no happy ending for Jill Wyatt. Not until the real Kate Weller faced her past once and for all.

ACKNOWLEDGMENTS

The first time I read Margaret Mitchell's southern classic, *Gone with the Wind*, I loved the part when Rhett said to Scarlett, 'I'm going to Charleston to see . . . if there isn't something left in life of charm and grace' and off he went. Right then I knew I wanted some of that for myself. I have returned to that gracious city many times for research and pleasure. Since dinner is taken seriously in Charleston's historic section, what better place to set a mystery involving two rival Italian restaurants? People who know me know I am no gourmet, so I'm grateful to every chef I've peppered with questions for the past two years. I especially want to thank Pat Marconi, who makes fabulous gravy, and wouldn't be caught dead using pasta sauce from a jar, and a big thank you to her sister, Joanne Thomas for letting me use her Charleston condo. Because a writer is nothing without brainstorming buddies, I'm grateful to Peggy Svoboda and author, Casey Daniels. And finally, I'd like to thank my agent, Nicole Resciniti, and my husband, Ken, who's always ready to pack a bag and head south in the name of research.